CHRISTMAS EVE AT
CRANBERRY CROSS

CHRISTMAS EVE AT CRANBERRY CROSS

Kate Forster

An Aria Book

First published in the UK in 2022 by Head of Zeus Ltd,
part of Bloomsbury Publishing Plc

9 7 5 3 1 2 4 6 8

A catalogue record for this book is available from the British Library.

ISBN (PB): 9781803281476
ISBN (E): 9781803281452

Cover design: illustration: Ray Shuell / Advocate Art

Typeset by Siliconchips Services Ltd UK

Printed and bound in Great Britain by
CPI Group (UK) Ltd, Croydon CRO 4YY

Head of Zeus Ltd
First Floor East
5–8 Hardwick Street
London EC1R 4RG

WWW.HEADOFZEUS.COM

This book is dedicated to my dear friend and fellow creative, Taurus soul sister Narissa. I don't know if you will still be here when this is published but if you have already headed on without us, I want you to know that I love you. You are the most beautiful light in a sometimes dark and unfair world. It has been my honour to laugh and cry with you through these years.

'B ut it's Christmas,' Eve Pilkins cried.

'There are plenty of others wanting this job, Eve,' her boss Serena Whitelaw said, staring at Eve with such disdain that she wondered for the one hundredth time that day if Serena regretted hiring her and was looking for an excuse to fire her.

'But it's also my birthday on Christmas Eve.'

Serena shrugged her white-silk-covered shoulders and pushed her tortoiseshell-rimmed glasses on top of her blonde head.

'Nobody cares about that anymore.'

Eve wasn't sure if Serena meant her birthday or Christmas but was too afraid to ask.

'If you don't get Edward Priest to deliver this book then it's on you. You can explain it at the redundancy party when we let you and many others go.'

Today was one of those work days where Eve wondered if she should just run away and open a café or a bakery like they do in the romance novels her company published, but then she remembered she couldn't bake or work a coffee machine. All she was good at was reading books, playing electric guitar and wrapping presents.

What could Eve had said in reply to that? Two hundred jobs relied on this book. Was that even true? She knew Edward Priest's books were the money-spinner for the company. His books sold faster than any adult book on record and even though they weren't to Eve's taste, she admired his dedication to research and to the dogged process of writing such enormous tomes.

But Edward Priest didn't do interviews and he didn't deal with anyone at the company but Serena Whitelaw – and that was only by phone.

All she knew about Edward Priest was that he had made all the other editorial assistants cry and that's why Serena personally managed him.

'Why can't you go?' Eve had tentatively asked and Serena had shot her a look that would have turned anyone else into a gelatinous mess, but Eve had survived them before and was sure she would survive this one.

'Because I'm going to New York for Christmas,' she stated proudly. 'Edward has a lovely country estate in Northumberland – quite posh I believe – but then you would have something grand with those royalties. Apparently, the wife bought it, wanted to play the lady of the manor from what I heard. I've also heard she grew tired of that pretty quickly.'

When Eve had read *The Devil Wears Prada*, she had thought it read like a non-fiction book. Just change the names and change fashion to publishing and that was Eve's working life at Henshaw and Carlson.

One day everything would be fine – meaning Serena was ignoring Eve. Then the next day Serena would scream at Eve for not remembering that Serena's white Carolina Herrera shirt was waiting to be picked up from the dry-cleaner. Even though Eve had no memory of being told that the blouse was at the cleaners and would need to be picked up. She had checked her texts, emails and phone messages and there was nothing about the blouse. In the end, Eve apologised and worked late to finish the edits on a book that Serena would then claim as her own work.

Eve tuned out from Serena's gossip. Her boss was always indiscreet about her authors but there wasn't much she could say about Edward, other than what anyone could read on the internet.

Edward was married to a former supermodel from America, and they had a daughter, who was about seven or so, according to one of the magazine articles Serena sent her later when she was back at her desk.

Eve had wanted to cry and then resign, or she wanted to resign and then cry, but instead she took her phone and went into the bathroom.

She put down the lid of the toilet, closed the door and dialled her mum's number.

The phone rang out and Eve sat staring at the screen when her mum's face popped up with an incoming call.

'Hello, pet,' she said. 'I was outside feeding the dogs before I head off to work. Everything all right?'

Donna Pilkins had four rescue dogs and counting. She found them all on the streets, watching them beg or dodge the cars and buses as she drove the number 23 bus through Leeds. She would go back after her shift and gain their trust with her gentle nature and treats. They seemed to be very fond of her rissoles, which was understandable; she had inherited the recipe from her grandmother, who had always said it was the Worcestershire sauce that made them so moreish.

Clearly the dogs agreed, as she had rescued twelve in all and kept four.

Eve felt the tears release. 'I can't come home for Christmas,' she sobbed.

'What? Why?'

'Serena is making me work, go to an author's house and edit as he writes. It's awful. She's awful.'

Donna sighed. 'Oh, dear me, that's a nasty thing to do to someone and on their birthday too. Did you tell her it was your birthday on Christmas Eve?'

'Mum, she doesn't care. She doesn't care about anyone but herself. And she's bloody well going to New York. I want to resign.'

'You can't come back for the day?' Donna asked.

'Serena said he will be working through Christmas Day. He's a workaholic at the best of times but he's really behind on this book for some reason. I don't know. I'll be shoved into the maid's room and he'll send me pages, which I have to copy-edit, and then I'll send them over to her to check my work and so she can look at the structure – which is the reverse of the way we usually do things. Then I have to send them to the proofer, who will send them to the typesetter. The turnaround is so tight I don't even think it can be done, but Serena said there are two hundred people relying on me not to join the unemployment line.'

'Then we will pause Christmas until after you've finished your work and you can come home.'

Eve could hear the disappointment in her mother's voice

but also her resilience. Donna Pilkins was the strongest woman she knew and her biggest cheerleader.

'No, Mum, the boys would be devastated.' Eve's younger brothers, Gabe and Nick, were fifteen and gorgeous boys who defied the teenage clichés and were chatty, funny and engaged in everything in the family.

'Dad is going to be furious,' she said.

'I'll talk to him. We will work it out, pet; we always do,' Donna said cheerfully and Eve knew she meant every word.

The last time Serena Whitelaw had pulled something similar was when she said Eve couldn't have a day off to head to Leeds to see her grandmother before she died. Eve's father, Sam, was ready to call in the transport workers' union and go on strike from driving buses until Eve was allowed to return home.

Donna had talked him down but Sam never forgave Serena, especially when her grandmother died without seeing Eve.

'It will be okay, Mum,' said Eve, trying to take some of her mother's strength.

'Of course it will, Eve. It's Christmas. Things are always okay at Christmas. Just wait and see.'

Eve hung up from the call and stared at her phone when she saw a text come through from Serena.

Where the hell are you? I need coffee and a tampon immediately. In that order.

Eve pretended to hit her forehead with her phone and she closed her eyes and thought a silent wish.

All I want for Christmas is a new job and to see my family. I promise I won't kill Serena and I will stop drinking wine on weeknights and getting takeaways. And I will be a better person and stop smoking when I drink wine and I will take my makeup off every night.

She opened her eyes as a text message sounded.

Hello? Have you fallen in? I'm under-caffeinated and bleeding.

This is a dire combination.

Eve sighed. Christmas couldn't come fast enough, especially if it delivered her wish.

Zara was waiting for Eve with a large glass of wine at the door of their shared flat.

Eve took the wine as she shrugged off her coat and dropped it onto the chair in the hallway and did a double take at the size of the glass and the measure of rosé.

'Does it come with a goldfish?' she asked and then took a gulp.

'After your day, I figured you needed it,' said Zara. 'Everyone was talking about it around the office – Serena is truly the worst.'

Zara worked with Eve at Henshaw and Carlson, but Zara was in the publicity department and seemed to know everything before anyone else in the company. Zara had moved up from intern to junior publicity coordinator within a year and now was a publicity manager who looked after commercial books. Edward Priest's next book would be on her list to promote, not that it would be hard to sell into the stores or to his avid reader base, but Eve had no doubt that Zara would push harder than anyone else on selling the book.

Eve kicked off her shoes and shoved her feet into her favourite Christmas slippers, which were stuffed reindeers complete with two light-up noses if she pressed a little button on the side of each slipper. She lifted her feet and switched on the nose lights. She needed all the cheer she could tonight.

'Anita is getting us a curry and we can sit and bitch about Serena all night if you like.'

Eve smiled at her best friend. They had met at work but Zara was loyal and kind and always gave quality fashion advice. Anita, their other housemate, was Zara's friend from school who was a junior architect at a large firm and who had just been put onto a huge project team for a new skyscraper.

It seemed everyone around Eve was on their way up and she was stuck being Serena's slave.

Anita arrived with their dinner and they ate the fragrant food while sitting around the coffee table, sharing naan bread and the rest of the wine.

'And what happens if you don't go?' asked Anita.

'I get fired,' Eve answered.

'Did she say that?' asked Zara.

'"Plenty of others wanting this job, Eve," she told me. And she also said I could explain it to everyone at the redundancy party if I failed.'

'Honestly, she's such a cow,' Zara told Anita. 'She told me

once when I was wearing a skirt from H&M that she had the real one from Gucci. As though this was supposed to make me feel shite about myself or something.'

'She is the queen of the put-down,' said Eve.

Zara looked furious. 'And now you have to babysit her biggest author because she wants to go to New York and continue her affair with Paul from Non-Fiction, whose wife is pregnant.'

'Paul Wallis? He's awful. He gets spit in the corner of his mouth when he's pitching.'

Anita laughed. 'Oh my God, your work sounds insane.'

Eve put down her fork. 'I really need to find another job.'

'Publishing is tough at the moment,' said Zara. 'Why don't you wait until Christmas is done, and then you can look. The job market always opens after new year. All those people drunk and deciding they hate their boss and need a new direction.'

'I don't need it to be new year or to be more drunk than I am to know I need a new direction.' Eve started to clean up.

'Stop, we're on duty tonight,' said Zara and she turned on the television. 'Look it's *I'm a Celebrity, Get Me Out of Here*. They're going to eat spiders.'

Eve lay on the sofa. 'Sounds better than what I have coming for me,' she muttered.

2

The train rocked in a soothing rhythm as though trying to calm Eve's nerves and anger.

It was the third of December and she hadn't even thought about her Christmas cards. Eve mentally made a list of who she needed to send cards to. Serena Whitelaw wouldn't be getting one – of that she was certain.

God, this was going to be torturous, she thought as she watched the country landscape pass her by.

She was to meet the housekeeper – someone called Hilditch – at the station, who would drive her up to the house, and then she would be straight into work. Hilditch? Was it a man or a woman or a man or a they?

Edward Priest must be very rich to have his housekeeper meet her. Or lazy, or busy? Her mind was whirling at the same speed as the train.

The email from Edward Priest to Serena had come through the night before she left. Serena had taken pleasure in schooling Eve on what to do and not do on the manuscript.

'Just do the copy edit and I will look at the structure when you're done with it. I don't want your mucky paws on it – you're not experienced enough, but I can't start straight away so we'll have to do things back to front.'

Eve wanted to punch Serena with her mucky paws but said nothing. There were plenty of times Eve had edited works and Serena had taken credit for her work.

Breathe, she reminded herself, *and just get through Christmas and then look for a new job.*

Eve had taken a copy of Edward Priest's previous book from the shelf at work to look at on the train. It was a best-seller but not as high in the charts as his previous books.

It was a historical thriller about World War Two and Nazi hunters who also collected art or something, but she lost interest a quarter of the way into the book. It was overwritten and hadn't been edited the way it should have been, but Eve found this to be true with any successful author. Once they reached a certain level of success, some authors refused to be edited or pushed back on the changes.

Eve could think of at least five authors who were on the rich list and who needed a machete taken to their books. *Cut, cut, cut,* she would mentally say when she was reading one of their books. *You don't need this much backstory.* The corridor of backstory she called it when she read some works. *We don't need to know all about why little Johnny didn't get a red truck one Christmas and how that led to him become a detective with one arm and a lisp.*

But this book of Edward's was lazy, and it rushed through some of the more promising themes.

Serena had done the edit, but she was as afraid of Edward and his reputation as Eve was of Serena and her constant threats about unemployment.

She put her head against the window of the train. The cool glass calmed her a little. The countryside flew past, little stone houses and walls, then busy stations and towns and so many people coming and going.

Cows watched the train, and fat sheep huddled against each other from the cold as the wind blew over them.

There was snow on the forecast and ice on the roads. The cold weather didn't bother Eve; at least in London it didn't. She ran from her office to the tube to home and repeat. She hardly ever went out as Serena was always making her work late.

Why did she put up with Serena's bullying? 'No job is worth that,' her dad had said and told her to call the book readers' and writers' union. Eve had explained that wasn't a union and then her dad told her to start one.

Why was everything so exhausting at this job? Eve had assumed she would do her job and not have to worry about anything else when she had left university. Serena had made sure that was not the case. All she did was worry and organise Serena's life, and then became frustrated when Serena would throw her an editing job to assuage her frustration.

Books had always been her escape at school, hiding in the library where the librarian had taken pity on her and had let her eat her cheese and gherkin sandwich in the Encyclopaedia section while reading The Hunger Games trilogy.

As the years went on, the lunchtimes and the sandwich stayed the same but the books changed as fast as Eve could devour them and the faster-paced and more exciting the book, the better. Other people claimed it was Jane Austen who propelled them into publishing or the collected works of Proust, but for Eve it was the paperback books on the spinning stands at the Leeds library that thrilled her. Agatha Christie was always her first love but she read everything she could. James Patterson, Patricia Cornwell, Minette Walters, even that silly git Jeffrey Archer. She had read many of the classics but she had a soft spot for the best-sellers of their day. Charlotte Brontë, Mary Shelley, Scott, Dickens.

It had never occurred to her she could be a part of the process of getting books onto the spinning stands at libraries and in the bookshops on the high street and in airports, but it was a goal that felt like her calling.

Instead, it seemed travelling to the centre of nowhere to babysit a spoiled author was now her calling.

She found some older images of his wife and daughter on an American website from when they attended the opening of a movie in Los Angeles. His wife, Amber, was very beautiful, like a thinner Jennifer Aniston, if that was even possible.

The child looked like her father. She was about four or five, Eve thought. Pleasant-looking but with a strong bone structure and wide-set eyes. She imagined the girl as a teenager, wondering why she didn't get her mother's high cheekbones. Eve still couldn't forgive her twin brothers for getting their dad's long eyelashes while she got her mother's, which resembled iron filings.

It wasn't easy being in a relationship with a writer, and Eve wondered how Mrs Priest was handling being in the country with a child and with Edward Priest, whose research was extensive and often first-hand. As she clicked on more links with his name she went down a rabbit hole on the web, reading about Edward and his writing routine and research process. Apparently he had travelled the route of the missionaries from Spain to Santo Domingo on the same sort of boat used in the 1800s so he could write about the experiences on the boat of the Augustinian friar who was the hero of one of his books.

Eve had rolled her eyes at that story. Pretty sure there weren't travel vaccinations and mobile phones when the friar was afloat back in the day. Why did Edward Priest and other writers like him, usually men, decide they needed to experience it before they could write about it? Didn't they have fully working imaginations? Why couldn't they research and read and discover instead of throwing themselves into an 'experience'? It was just such a pretentious and entitled male thing to do.

The train slowed down and Eve closed her laptop and packed it away. She stood as the train stopped and got her balance before making her way to the end of the carriage to get her cases. She had one large and one small, but she hoped she wouldn't need anything else. The plan was she would stay until before new year, so at least she could get back and see her family for the last weekend before she had to face Serena again.

Eve exited the train with no grace whatsoever as she struggled to get her large pink suitcase off easily.

'Christ on a bike,' she said to herself as people pushed past her to get off the train. 'Some people have no Christmas spirit at all.'

She stopped and adjusted her coat to try and get some control over her situation.

'Eve Pilkins?' She heard her name spoken in a deep baritone and looked up and saw a handsome woman, who must be close to six feet tall, of an indeterminate age between forty and sixty, Eve guessed. She was dressed in purple jeans, topped off by a jumper with a Union Jack knitted into it and a brown corduroy trilby hat. She wore a quilted vest in pink and was the most astonishing woman Eve had ever seen.

'Yes?' Eve was aware she was staring at the woman, whose hands were on her hips. As she surveyed Eve her eyes narrowed.

'I'm Hilditch, housekeeper to Mr Priest. I've come to pick you up.'

'Thanks, Hilditch, that's very kind of you,' said Eve, feeling like she had failed whatever test Hilditch had set for a first viewing.

Eve tried to drag one of the suitcases and heard a terrible screeching sound.

'Oh, I've lost a wheel,' she exclaimed and tried to lift the case but failed. Too many coats and scarves preparing for the arctic blast that her mother had warned her would be coming.

Hilditch picked up the case and the overnight bag and walked ahead of Eve while she struggled to keep up with the woman's long stride.

'This is us,' said Hilditch, nodding at a red Mini Cooper. She wasn't sure how Hilditch would fit in the car but she managed to fold up, like human origami.

Eve nodded, trying to act like she wasn't a complete dunce.

'How old are you?' asked Hilditch as they got into the car.

'Twenty-seven,' answered Eve.

Hilditch sniffed as she started the car. 'And you work with that Serena Whitelaw?'

'Yes, she's my boss.'

Simply thinking of Serena made her angry. She was off flying to New York, and Eve was stuck in outer nowhere to edit an overpaid, self-important writer whose next book was probably overwritten and lazy like his last one.

'She came up here a bit,' said Hilditch with a sniff.

'Did she?' Eve was surprised. Serena had behaved as though coming up to Edward Priest's house was a foreign mission about which she knew nothing.

'Yes, after Mrs Priest – Amber – left, she was hanging around quite a bit.' A censorious tone was evident in Hilditch's voice, but Eve wasn't sure if it was directed at Serena, the boss from hell, or Amber Priest, Edward's wife.

'Is Mrs Priest returning for Christmas?' Eve asked, wanting to check whether Serena's gossip about the Priest marriage was true.

Hilditch snorted, as the Mini Cooper picked up speed, and they passed through a large village that was being decorated for Christmas with pretty red wreaths and green and silver ribbons along the main street.

'Mrs Priest is in America, unsure when she will return. Let's just say no one is holding their breath.' She cleared her throat and changed her tone. 'This is Crossbourne, a lovely community. Everything you need is here. It's more of a town but we still like to think of it as a village.'

Eve noticed the people walking about, and the shops and decorations, and thought how much she would like to have a good wander about. It did indeed look like the basics were covered, plus there were some nice little independent stores that looked to be selling arts and crafts.

'There's a lovely market the week before Christmas and some fun activities,' said Hilditch. 'If you like that sort of thing.'

If only Hilditch knew how much Eve loved that sort of thing – but she was here to work, not mess about at markets and buy presents.

'I think Mr Priest will keep me busy working on his book,' she said.

Hilditch snorted again and gave a laugh of no faith at all.

'He is writing isn't he?' asked Eve. She had promised Serena she would do a first edit of the book, but she hoped she didn't have to parent a grown man into delivering on time.

Hilditch pretended to lock her mouth and throw the invisible key out the closed window.

Eve sighed and looked outside. She had little to nothing to do with the authors on Serena's list unless Serena told her to do the work that she didn't want to do herself – the slog of the edit, word by word. But this sounded like she was being forced to babysit Henshaw and Carlson's biggest author.

'He has a commitment, a deadline,' she said to Hilditch.

'Nothing to do with me. I'm not his mother.'

'Neither am I,' mumbled Eve.

God how she wished she was at home, talking rubbish with Zara.

As they reached the countryside, Eve wished she could enjoy the views of the fields of green and then a large forest and some hills in the distance.

'That's where we're off to.' Hilditch nodded to the forest ahead.

'Wow, it looks very JRR Tolkien,' said Eve.

'Well, it is called the Tower Forest,' said Hilditch proudly. 'Cranberry Cross is at the top of the hill. You can see the whole region from the tower.'

'The tower?'

'You haven't seen Cranberry Cross before?' asked Hilditch, clearly surprised.

'No.' Eve shook her head.

'It was on *Gardeners' World* last year,' Hilditch prompted.

'I don't watch *Gardeners' World*. Sorry.' Eve felt she needed to apologise because it was evident from the sound of Hilditch's tutting under her breath that she was disappointed.

'We've won the coldest winter in England three years in a row,' Hilditch said. 'I hope you brought your thermals.'

Eve shivered. She hadn't brought any thermals. Instead she had brought a new camel coat at Mango that in hindsight looked smart but wasn't world-record-winter ready. Why were people always so proud of living in the freezer section of the country? First off they didn't control the weather and secondly, they chose to live there. It didn't make them better than anyone else, just sillier.

She checked her phone and saw emails from Serena and then put it away. They could wait; she needed to keep Hilditch talking because the woman revealed more in what she didn't say than she realised. Hilditch was one of those people who thought they were being discreet but their body language gave away volumes about what they thought.

So far she had learned Serena had been to Northumberland

more times than zero, which was more than what Serena had claimed, and that Edward Priest's wife had left him. Gosh, this was turning into a mystery and Eve loved a mystery story.

'How long have you worked for Mr Priest?' she asked.

'Seven years – since they first bought the house. Flora was only a baby when they came.'

Eve nodded. Flora was the child, she thought, making a mental note. She was trying to think of something else to ask but she was struggling to focus because it was so cold in the car and she didn't want to ask this rugged woman to turn up the heating.

Hilditch turned off the main road through the forest and drove up a gravel driveway before stopping at a set of iron gates. Hilditch leaned out of her window and typed a series of numbers onto an electronic screen that looked out of place next to the old gates and stone fence. It was the security system of a man who did not want to be bothered.

'Is Mr Priest well known in the village?' she asked. 'Does he, you know, visit the library or the school or anything? Make himself a part of the community?'

'People know of him but he doesn't head out much. I do all the running around since Mrs Priest has gone,' Hilditch answered but there was a pinch in her voice, as though Eve had touched a nerve.

If Eve was a famous author, she would share her success with everyone, she thought as Hilditch started driving along the road that stretched ahead, sloping upwards.

Edward Priest was probably one of those people who wanted to be mysterious and enigmatic but was actually just plain rude.

Large trees lined the way on either side and large brown rocks were dotted about the landscape, popping out of nowhere. It was a dramatic landscape, very Brontë-esque.

Eve knew well enough to be silent as Hilditch's car went into the next gear and the hill became steeper as they began their ascent. Soon the trees began to clear and then the car rounded a corner and there stood an imposing Jacobean manor, complete with fog surrounding it and a single light on in the top tower.

There was a steeply pitched roof, with a perfectly symmetrical display of chimneys, gables, dormer windows and ornately carved arches around the windows. The house was grand but bleak in its outlook, its smoky shade of grey stone and the wind that was making the trees wave in protest.

There were two large urns on either side of the magnificent front door, with a conifer tree in each, and one had a sad-looking piece of red tinsel hanging on for dear life in the wind.

There was nothing welcoming about the house, Eve thought. It looked like a place where children were sent for punishment in Victorian times.

There were yew trees topiarised into cone and cylinder shapes dotted about the lawn, and paths leading to ornate gardens that spread beyond the house. A large fountain seemed to be an afterthought, perhaps installed by a previous mistress of the house to try and make it look less gloomy. The car stopped next to the fountain and Eve could see it was dry.

'Geesh, that's something out of a Gothic novel. It's what I imagined Lowood School to look like in *Jane Eyre*.'

Hilditch stopped the car and looked ahead. 'Welcome to Cranberry Cross.'

Her voice had lost its warmth and was there a chill in the car or was she imagining it?

Eve felt the hairs on her arms rise and she shivered.

'Someone walk over your grave?' asked Hilditch as she opened the car door.

Probably Serena if she messed up this assignment, Eve thought, and hoped to the gods of writing that Edward Priest was ready to get to work.

3

Edward often told people that being an author was like having homework for the rest of your life. If truth be told, Edward was very behind on his homework on the day Eve Pilkins was travelling to Cranberry Cross.

'Hilditch,' Edward yelled from the doorway of his study.

Silence answered and he slammed the door shut and went back to his desk.

This book was proving to be impossible. He had started it four times and now it was a cobbled-together mishmash of ideas and chaos.

Of course, Serena Whitelaw had sent one of her lackeys up to spy on him under the guise of editing his work. Eve Pilkins. What a terrible name, he thought, as he poured himself a whiskey for lunch since Hilditch had gone missing.

Eve Pilchards, he would have called her if they were at school together.

But that was the name of an older woman, with a sour expression and who carried brown bread sandwiches in her handbag.

He sat at his desk and tapped at the keyboard of his computer.

I am a terrible writer, and nobody knows. The end.

Sighing he spun around in his chair and looked out the window over the parklands with the woods in the distance.

He didn't have to write another book ever again. He was more than a best-seller; he was an extraordinary seller with a film franchise starring Ewan McGregor as his signature character.

But he liked the challenge of writing a book, or at least he used to.

Having an idea and then pulling all the threads together, weaving them into a story that made people want to turn the page was like a jigsaw puzzle.

It wasn't easy to write the way he did and while literary snobs mocked him and envied his money, they failed to realise that it was his books that made enough profits for the literary ones to be published. They might sell a few thousand and win important awards but he sold hundreds of thousands on the first day of release and kept selling, reaching six figures within a year.

A figure in the doorway caught his eye.

'I'm writing,' he lied.

'I'm hungry.'

'Hello, hungry. I'm Dad,' he answered and looked up to see his seven-year-old daughter Flora, loitering and scuffing her shoes against the oak panels of the hallway.

She rolled her eyes. 'Dad,' she half growled and he laughed. Flora could always lift his mood, albeit temporarily.

'I have no idea where Hilditch is,' he said, closing his laptop and standing up.

'She's gone into town to get Christmas Eve pilchards,' Flora said.

'You mean Eve Pilkins,' corrected Edward, trying not to laugh. 'She's coming to help me with my book.'

Flora rolled her eyes. 'You just need to put your bum on the seat and do the work.'

Now Edward laughed, hearing his own words to Flora about her homework when she complained.

'The student becomes the master.' Edward gave a mock bow and then kissed the top of her head.

'Have you been to the tower?' asked Flora, worry crossing her little face.

'Yes and everything is fine,' Edward replied kissing her head. 'Come on then, hungry, let's feed you.'

Edward chatted to Flora cheerfully as he made her a cheese and pickle sandwich cut into triangles with the crusts trimmed. Some days she was easier to distract than others. Today she was easily led because she was hungry and there was a visitor coming to the house. After he poured her a glass of milk, he sat with her at the large kitchen bench, both father and daughter perched on the old oak stools he loved.

When he bought the house, he imagined his family surrounding him, while he cooked something hearty and slow, and music would be playing and there would be laughter.

Now it was just him and Flora, sitting in the kitchen silence, eating a cheese sandwich.

'What's your plan for the afternoon?' he asked. 'Solving world hunger and climate change?'

Flora ignored his comment. 'I have some babies lost in the garden so I need to find and rescue them later.'

Edward nodded. 'Good idea – they will be very cold.'

Flora chewed her sandwich slowly. 'I plan on washing them in the sink with hot water. That would warm up a baby, wouldn't it?'

Flora's game of rescuing baby dolls from the perils of the weather had been a common theme since her mother had left them last year. Edward had tried to explain that her mother would be back and there was no need to leave dolls around the estate, but nothing would dissuade her from her search and rescue mission.

'I think that's a great idea, and maybe ask Hilditch to pop the baby clothes in the dryer to really warm them up for when you dress them.'

Flora seemed to appreciate this idea and she nodded; her little fair brow furrowed. 'If I was lost in the wood, would you find and rescue me?'

'Indeed, and I would put you in a warm bath and then put your flannel pyjamas on that I'd warmed by the fire.'

'You're a good daddy,' Flora announced as she finished her sandwich and pushed her plate towards him. 'I have to go now; I'll be back.'

'Good luck. I hope you find them. And wear your coat,' he reminded her.

Flora gave a small eye-roll. 'Daddy, I know where they are. I put them there.'

'Coat and mittens please,' he called out to her disappearing figure.

He wished he could explain to Flora that her mother left her because she was lost – lost as the dolls in the woods

– and no matter how hard Edward had tried to keep her mother alive in Flora's mind and heart, and reassured her that Amber would never leave her daughter out in the snow, it didn't seem to register.

Edward cleaned up the lunch items, knowing Hilditch would reclean everything because that's who she was and because Edward wasn't very masterful in the kitchen. The only thing he seemed to be able to master was words, but nothing clear and crisp enough to get through to his daughter.

Amber Priest was never meant to be a mother. She liked children when they were babies and young toddlers but the minute a child decided they weren't their mother's accessory and had their own opinions on what they wanted to wear or eat, or who they wanted to be with, then Amber struggled.

The clashes between mother and daughter when Flora began to explore her independence were apocalyptic and it was Edward who would have to explain to Amber that it didn't matter if Flora wanted to wear the sparkly pinafore with a summer top underneath it and her gumboots. Flora would wear what she wanted. She had her own mind and opinions; shouldn't she be encouraged to be herself?

But Amber wanted a little doll, a mini me who would allow others to compliment her beauty by praising her daughter.

Poor Amber. He felt sad for her. She was the little girl lost in the snow, except no one ever came to rescue her until she met Edward. That's why he'd persevered with her for so long. Encouraging her to come back to their home, their lives, the world they had created. Paying for therapy, rehabilitation centres, coping with the affairs and then forgiving her over and over again until a part of him had died from lack of nurture. He used to think that self-help and all that jazz was nonsense until a fellow author and psychotherapist told him that he had given everything to Amber and had nothing left to give himself. It wasn't even love he felt for his wife now; it was pity. He was simply trying to keep her alive.

And that's when he told her enough. She had to show she had changed and work for it if she wanted to be back in their lives. He wanted a divorce and he would be seeking full custody.

Amber hadn't fought him, which was perhaps the saddest part of all. The weekend after he took custody he saw a picture of her dancing at a rooftop bar in Los Angeles, all bangles and a new tattoo on her collarbone of a Celtic knot and a belly button ring.

She was in a manic phase. Meanwhile he was trying to get his daughter to understand that her mother loved her but was trying to find herself, trying to get well. Things he shouldn't have to explain to a seven-year-old.

A year later and there was nothing from Amber except a request for more spousal support and a postcard from a cat café in Tokyo for Flora, with a drawing of a mother cat and baby cat on the back in Amber's signature aqua-inked scrawl.

Flora carried it everywhere for months until it had been left in the pocket of a dress and Hilditch had inadvertently washed it, but Edward had never quite believed it was a mistake. Hilditch was meticulous in her housekeeping until that moment.

He heard the sound of the front door opening and Hilditch

stepped inside first. He braced himself for the battle-axe who would be Eve Pilkins. He had prepared himself for her to come and be officious and demanding and to smell of mints and with chin hairs, just like his fourth-class schoolteacher who told him he had a vivid imagination and perhaps he should direct his tall tales into writing stories instead of terrifying his classmates with the tale that his father was an international detective who specialised in serial killers masquerading as schoolteachers.

But this wasn't the Eve Pilkins he imagined. A small, dark-haired young woman walked inside, her hair in a black bob that framed her heart-shaped face and dark eyes. She was wearing a green coat that suited her better than the model the designer had probably envisaged when they had sketched the idea. She had on sturdy boots and jeans and a large pink suitcase was by her side, sitting at a peculiar angle as it looked like a wheel was missing.

'Mr Priest, this is Eve Pilkins,' said Hilditch with a raised eyebrow.

He ignored the eyebrow and looked Eve in the eye, leaning forward to try and understand her. She looked about twenty-five at most, and probably only read poetry and literary fiction. She would be filled with dreams of one day editing a Booker-Prize-winning novel and no doubt she colour-coded her bookshelves.

She smiled at him and he sighed. Another little fan girl who would be less help than useless. He was used to them coming up to him at festivals, hanging around and flicking their hair and asking him where he found his ideas.

'You better be ready to work,' he snapped.

He saw her brow furrow and then she stepped forward.

'Ready when you are, Mr Priest. Let me put my case away and I will be down to edit immediately. I'm looking forward to reading what you have... so far.'

The challenge was there in her tone. The way she stepped forward and the way she paused and then said 'so far' was a call to arms.

Perhaps Ms Pilkins was not to be dismissed after all. He couldn't smell mints nor see any sign of a moustache but he wondered if she was his fourth-class teacher in a much prettier form.

4

Eve's first impression of Edward Priest was how handsome he was and then he became infinitely less attractive when he tried to intimidate her and sighed at her presence. But after working with Serena, she was used to standing people down and reminding him that she might be five foot two but she was fierce, smart and above all, not to be underestimated.

She had only ever seen him in the dust jacket photos taken when he was twenty-five. Now he was over forty and my God, he was handsome. Tall, well built. His dark hair was receding, but it suited him, messy as though in need of a haircut. He ran his hand through it and scratched the back of his neck.

He wore a grey knitted jumper and jeans and a frown. He had the look of someone who understood how to live well. His clothes suggested quality without having a single label on display. The jumper was cashmere, and good cashmere, she thought. No pilling, no pulls in the thread, beautifully fitted with the sleeves casually pushed up on his forearms.

She tried not to think about his forearms, which were always a weakness for Eve. She had once dated a man a few times who worked a jackhammer for a living and she spent most of the dates looking at his arms like some deranged idiot.

Edward had good forearms – not like he worked a jackhammer day and night but it was clear he did some sort of physical exercise.

But what she noticed the most was his elegance, the casual run of his hand through his hair. His posture wasn't like that of other writers. His had been taught as a child. It came from someone close, probably his mother, poking him between his shoulder blades whenever he slouched.

He looked like he could sit and eat oysters at Bentley's in London with a glass of Laurent-Perrier with Serena any day of the week, unlike her the time Serena had taken her and told Eve not to make silly faces when she swallowed her first oyster. Eve couldn't have said to Serena the only oysters in her house came in a can and had the word 'smoked' on the wrapper, and her dad liked to eat them on toast while she and her mum complained about the smell. Instead, she swallowed them whole, like her pride when working with Serena.

He seemed surprised by her presence, as though he was expecting someone else and had received a lesser version. And he was so rude it nearly took her breath away. The entitlement and privilege dripped from him and the assumption that she wasn't ready to work goaded her. As though she was there for some sort of holiday. The audacity of this man was astonishing. She had fumed as she followed Hilditch to her bedroom. She would probably be put in the maid's room at the top of the house, with a single bed and a washbasin, knowing Edward Priest for the short moment she had.

Hilditch guided her through the house, which seemed to go on forever. There was a maze of corridors and separate staircases and a lot of portraits of stern-looking people in various costumes through the ages.

Her room was a long way from the entrance, she noted as Hilditch finally stopped at a large oak door.

'This is you,' she said and opened it to reveal Eve's quarters. She stepped inside with Eve following her.

The room was romantic, beautiful, dreamy and extremely cold.

Wood-panelled walls greeted her with a large, canopied bed draped in raspberry damask with gold tassels tied at end corners. The bed was made of a dark wood with barley twist posts and small carved pinecones on each. The top of the canopy was lined with white pleated silk and the bed itself was made up with thick covers and a matching raspberry and silk quilt. Persian rugs in red and lapis blue covered the dark floorboards around the room, but in front of the enormous fireplace was a thick rug of sheepskins sewn together.

Eve peered into the empty fireplace. It was big enough to roast a boar, she thought as she noticed how worn the bricks were from the heat over the centuries.

'I will get Peter – the outside man who helps in the garden – to come up and light the fire,' said Hilditch as she threw Eve's suitcases on the four-poster bed.

'Oh, I have asthma – fires make me wheezy,' Eve said, hating every word that came out of her mouth.

People like Hilditch probably didn't even believe in asthma.

True to form, Hilditch rolled her eyes. 'It's either wheezing or freezing – take your pick.'

Eve bit her lip as she wondered if she could get to the village to get an extra nebuliser and preventative. God she just wanted to go home and eat a bacon sandwich in the bath.

'Are you ready?' asked Hilditch. 'He doesn't like to wait.'

Eve grabbed her tote bag with her notebook, computer and pens. At the last minute she decided against taking off her coat, choosing warmth over fashion, even though she had a very smart red cable-knit jumper underneath her coat that looked fabulous with her dark hair. But she wasn't here to impress Edward Priest with her fashion, only her exceptional editing skills.

Scuttling behind Hilditch, she tried to memorise the way back using the faces in the paintings.

Head down towards the Jacobean Harry Styles.

Turn left at Elizabethan Emily Blunt.

Straight on until Victorian Judi Dench or was it Queen Victoria? She wasn't sure.

And then right at Victorian Emma Watson.

They came to ornate wooden doors and Hilditch knocked and then entered.

'She's here,' she said. 'I'm off to check the fences at the top of the paddock then off home.'

Eve looked around for Edward Priest but it was hard for her eyes to settle in such a crowded room. There were several desks of various sizes, and sofas and a large fireplace with a fire burning at one end. The walls were covered in bookshelves and there was a slim iron balcony that ran around the shelves, and a circular staircase that allowed the reader to ascend to find the book of choice.

With red carpet and the scent of leather and second-hand books, Eve wondered if she was in a library or heaven.

'Choose a desk and let's get started.'

Eve looked around at the desks on offer. 'Which one is yours?' she asked.

'I don't have a favourite. I move about depending on my book. However, I do find the small chevrette good for editing.'

Eve had no idea what a chevrette was but instead chose the one nearest to her and put her bag down and pulled out her laptop.

Edward looked at her laptop.

'You won't need that yet.'

Eve wanted to roll her eyes but had learned to keep a straight face after working with Serena.

'Great,' she said. 'I have my trusty blue pen at the ready.' She lifted up her pencil case, which was covered in pink sequins and embroidered with WORD NERD on the front.

She saw Edward raise an eyebrow and she made a face behind his back.

There was nothing worse than a snob, she thought as she waited for him to settle at the huge desk but instead put the pen he was holding down onto the desk where it rolled off and landed at Eve's feet.

She bent over and picked it up.

Edward G Priest was inscribed into the side of the stunning fountain pen in gold and natural lacquer.

'This is a lovely pen,' she said turning it over. 'Dupont?'

He looked up at her. 'You know pens?'

'I used to work in a pen shop when I was at university. A dangerous place for a person who loves stationery and pens. But a pen like this was too expensive for a lowly student like me.'

She walked to his desk and placed it carefully on the leather surface and went back to her place and sat down, waiting for instruction.

Edward sat at his desk now and tapped on the keyboard and stared at the screen. Eve looked out the window, trying to remain as still as possible.

What felt like hours was only minutes when Eve glanced at her phone. Two emails from Serena were waiting for her and some texts from Zara and Anita, checking to see how she was and if she had arrived.

She desperately wanted to answer them but she imagined Edward Priest would have a fit if she started texting as he was summoning the muse for his book.

As though hearing her thoughts, he stood up and went to the window.

'It's not happening. We will try again tomorrow,' he stated, his hands in his pockets.

Eve cleared her throat. 'I think Serena will ask where we're up to,' she ventured. 'Perhaps I can read what's been written so far?'

Edward turned, his expression thunderous.

'I don't have anything; do you not understand that? Nothing.'

Eve stared him down. This was ridiculous. She had given up her life to help this man finish his job and he was acting as though he had to summon up a magic spell and his powers had deserted him.

'Will you be long? Or should I get the train back to London? Maybe you can let me know when it will be ready?' She tried to keep the sarcasm down but she was tired, hungry and reminded herself that she had given up her Christmas for this man who had writer's block.

Edward scowled at her. 'It's your job to encourage me, isn't it?'

She tried not to laugh. 'I'm not a cheerleader. I'm a publishing assistant. I'm here to try and coax the invisible words into shape.'

'Then you should go back to London. Because this book is simply not coming to me.'

She imagined heading back to London and Serena finding out she didn't even try to encourage him. She would be out the door with her desk packed and she'd be kicked up the bottom for her trouble.

Eve looked around the room and then stood up. 'What about if we move your desk around?'

'What?' Edward looked at her as though she had just suggested he cut his own nose off.

'Sometimes changing the room can change the energy.'

'Good God, you're into the woo-woo business – fang what's it called?'

'Feng shui, and my beliefs have nothing to do with anything other than, I know that when I get stuck, I like a change of scenery. Being in a new spot can bring new perspective.'

'I have always had my desk like this,' he said gesturing to the large piece of furniture.

'It was an idea, not a commandment.'

She sat down again and picked up her phone. 'I have emails from Serena I need to respond to,' she said.

If he wasn't going to write then she wasn't going to stop doing her work.

'Where would I put it?' he asked.

Eve looked around the room.

'Right now, the desk is facing the room, which is fine, but it could face out the window. Turn it around. Staring into the garden might bring some inspiration.'

Edward muttered something under his breath and then she saw him pull his chair away and moving the items to another desk.

'Do you want me to help?'

He looked up at her. 'You don't look like you could carry anything heavier than a laptop.'

It was Eve's turn to scowl at him because he was right in the fact she wasn't very strong but he didn't need to mock her.

She returned to her emails. Serena wanted to know if Eve could organise a Christmas tree to be delivered to her hotel room at the Four Seasons in New York, fully decorated – and if Edward was writing.

She decided to ignore the email because she didn't want to deal with either of those things. She texted Zara back.

He's a complete tosser as we assumed. Rude. Entitled.
He's perfect for Serena. I wish I was anywhere but here.

The sound of grunting made her look up as Edward was

trying to move the desk with no success. He looked at her and she made a sad face at him.

'I'd help but I lifted a croissant this morning and now I'm plumb tuckered out.'

She wanted for him to lose it at her but instead he laughed loudly.

'Touché, Ms Pilkins.' He stood back at the desk and shook his head. 'I'll get two of the property hands to help later.'

Eve nodded, as though this was a good decision but not really caring who moved the desk, as long as he wrote something.

But Edward had other ideas.

'Well, that's enough for me for the day. Shall we try again tomorrow?'

He walked to the door of the study and gestured for her to follow and leave the room.

She collected her things and went to the door and then looked at him and took her chance.

'Serena said there are two hundred jobs that are relying on this book being published.'

'Despite my surname, I've never responded well to guilt.' He glared at her until she felt her face flush.

'They're her words, not mine,' Eve said, hearing the wobble in her voice as she walked into the hallway.

'Then use your words, not hers,' he said and he shut the door behind her, locked it and walked away, leaving Eve alone swallowing all the words she wanted to say to this arrogant, entitled, stupidly handsome man.

5

There is a particular sort of uncomfortable feeling that comes with being an unwanted guest. The sense that perhaps there are words being spoken about you in hushed tones, aspersions being cast in your direction, and with the headache that was coming on, Eve wondered if pins weren't being put into a poppet in her likeness somewhere.

The house was certainly gloomy enough to warrant a belief in otherworldliness but it also felt like a museum. The tapestries on the wall did nothing to stop the chill in the air, she thought as she shivered in her room. Perhaps she could possibly leg it back to London. She would resign to Serena's face, tell her exactly what she thought of her as a person and a boss, and then move to her parents' house and hide until further notice.

As though summoned from the dark side, her phone buzzed and Serena's name flashed on her screen.

Eve groaned and then answered the phone.

'Any progress with Edward?' Serena was always straight to the point, like an assassin.

'Not yet, but I told him to move his desk around,' Eve said, then wished she hadn't spoken about such a pedestrian topic to Serena.

'Move his desk around? You're editing, coaching, coaxing, not interior designing.'

Eve thought of explaining about a new perspective and outlook but knew Serena didn't care about anything but the final word count.

'I'm at the lounge, about to fly to New York. Tell Edward I need that book or else. And make sure my Christmas tree is set up in my suite. I'm having guests for drinks from Trident Media.'

'Or else what?' asked Eve without thinking. She didn't answer Serena back very often but this situation was truly becoming unreasonable. Besides, she needed some sort of carrot and stick to get him to sit down and write.

'Or else you lose your job,' Serena stated and then the line went dead.

Eve lay back on the bed and stared at the light fitting, which was in the shape of a lantern and looked like it cost more than her entire wage for the year.

If Edward didn't deliver the book, she'd lose her job. Serena had restated her ultimatum without any consultation between them. Of course, she had, because she was truly the evil queen in this story.

What did that make Eve? The helpless heroine? The naïve ingenue? The bookish beauty? All of them made her feel pathetic.

She was a good editor but was stuck being Serena's assistant. But she could tell what a great story was and right now, she didn't want to be a part of whatever drama Edward and Serena were co-writing.

This was ridiculous, she thought, and got up from the bed. She would find Edward and tell him that she needed him to work and focus. That he had to be professional and that his readers deserved a new book from him. Writers loved their readers didn't they? She would remind him that his readers were waiting. They needed to escape, to have Edward help them explore the worlds he created just for them.

Eve took off her coat and instantly regretted the decision, but she couldn't walk around the house in hat and coat without drawing unwanted attention.

She went through the house, desperate for a snoop of the rooms but mindful she wasn't a guest, she was an employee of Henshaw and Carlson.

She followed the scent of roasting meat and found her way to the kitchen where Hilditch was chopping turnips with a ferocity that made Eve step backwards.

'You can chop very quickly,' Eve noted.

'I was a chef in the armed forces,' Hilditch said.

'Oh? Amazing. Was it the army?'

Hilditch looked her in the eye and kept chopping but didn't look at her hands as she worked.

'No, it was a classified organisation.'

Eve wasn't sure what to say in reply. Was this woman for real or some sort of British Walter Mitty?

She decided not to pursue that line of questioning any further.

'Is Mr Priest around?' she asked.

'He's with friends. They're here for dinner.'

'Friends? He's supposed to be writing,' Eve exclaimed.

Hilditch shrugged, as though shaking any responsibility from her shoulders.

A cupboard behind Hilditch opened and a small face peered out at Eve.

'Who are you?' The child was obviously Flora, but she was tiny. Her face had an elfin quality about it and her voice was high-pitched.

'I'm Eve,' she answered.

'Why are you cross?'

'I'm not cross,' said Eve but then she checked herself and realised she was cross. Very cross.

'You sound cross.' The cupboard closed again.

'That's Flora in the potato cupboard. If she stays there much longer she might sprout,' Hilditch said in a loud voice.

The door opened again. 'I'm not staying in here, just until Daddy's horrid friends go away. Why doesn't he ask me to play with him instead of them?'

'Hush, Flora.'

'Myles hates them also. He hates everyone though, especially Daddy.' The cupboard door slammed again.

'Who's Myles?' asked Eve looking around.

'No one, just her invisible friend,' said Hilditch quickly.

Flora opened up the door again. 'He's not my friend – he's awful and mean to me.'

Hilditch closed the door with her foot. 'Mr Priest has friends here for the evening and then tomorrow he will be resting.'

'Resting? Does he have consumption? This is ridiculous,' exclaimed Eve. 'I'm missing Christmas with my family because of this book and he can't even respect me enough to write. I don't think I've met a less professional author, and I've met a few.'

Hilditch shrugged.

'But were they as successful as me?' She heard Edward's deep voice behind her and a shiver ran up her spine to the top of her head. She was sure her hair was standing on end.

Squaring her shoulders, she turned to him.

'No, but they at least met their deadlines so people didn't give up personal time with their important loved ones.'

Edward raised his eyebrows at her. 'You could have said no if you didn't want to be here.'

Eve crossed her arms and shook her head. 'I didn't have a choice, not if I wanted to keep my job. Not that you would understand the concept of a job, working for a living and having to navigate corporate rubbish and keep your personal integrity and live on a shitty wage and not hobnobbing it like you're in some sort of Elizabethan cosplay or amateur drama performance.'

'Very witty,' he said to Eve. 'You should be a writer.' He walked behind the counter and opened the cupboard.

'Hello, sweetie, don't eat the raw potatoes. You'll get a tummy ache. Your ancestors did it eons ago and we've had starch allergies ever since.'

He wandered about the kitchen, opening cupboards at random intervals.

'Hil, I'm looking for the case of Vosne-Romanée that was delivered. Is it up here or in the cellar?' he asked Hilditch.

'Butler's pantry.' She tossed her head at the door behind her.

Edward went in and then came out holding three bottles of wine. He looked at Eve. 'Can you bring some glasses to the library?'

Hilditch didn't stop chopping and Eve looked around.

He was staring at her expectantly.

'Me? You want me to serve your guests?' Oh, this man was something else and not in a good way.

Edward part scoffed and snorted at her. 'No, Miss Pilkins, I was wondering if you wanted to come and drink wine with myself and my friends. Who knows? It might loosen the muse inside me.' He made a silly face at her and then he was gone.

Eve sighed and Hilditch looked up at her, while still chopping without missing a beat or losing a finger. How many turnips did this woman need?

'Wine glasses in the sideboard; library is down the hall, turn left, double doors.'

'You aren't saying I should go?' Eve was incredulous at how much this woman allowed Edward to get away with. He was just awful. She had no idea why Serena was usually so positively gushing about him.

Hil had finally finished her task and wiped her hands on a tea towel.

'He does write more when he's had some wine. Take six glasses.'

Great, Eve thought as she went to the sideboard and found the glasses. An alcoholic with writer's block. How did she get to be so lucky?

'Where is the library again?' she asked.

Hil escorted her to the library and then turned and left Eve alone outside the door.

The library doors were closed. She tried to knock but then they swung open and Edward bellowed her name.

'I'm here. You don't need to yell,' she sniped at him.

'We were about to swig from the bottle.' He laughed and

took three glasses from her and waited for her to pass him into the room.

'Everyone, this is Eve. She's come from Henshaw and Carlson as a spy. Apparently if I don't write my book she and hundreds of others will lose their jobs, so let's get drunk and help Eve rework her résumé so she can find a wonderful job when she returns to London off the back of my talent and hospitality.'

Eve gasped and turned to see four pairs of eyes looking shocked and embarrassed.

'Edward,' said one of the guests in a sharp tone.

'Yes, Caro?'

'That's rude.'

Edward laughed. It was a mean sort of laugh. Almost bitter.

'All these people at the company sucking from the teat of my talent and they send a child here to try and coax me on. Have you edited many books, Eve?'

Eve was silent. She had edited some parts of books at Henshaw and Carlson. Structural edits on the flow of a story and recommendations, but she had also worked her way from being freelance reader of the slush pile to where she was now. And she had recommended some books that became best-sellers. She had an eye and Serena knew it, even if she never said as much to Eve.

For a moment she felt a hot flush of shame and insecurity on her face and then she remembered that she actually had a choice.

Perhaps it was too much of Serena over too long a time – the constant snide remarks and unrealistic work expectations. There was a snap of realisation that she could go. No one could treat people like this, even a relative stranger.

Eve placed the glasses down on the wine table and then clasped her hands and took a breath. 'Not everyone has the privilege to come and go from their talent and calling. You might not care about my life. You don't even know me – I get that. But I deserve more than this display of arrogance and rudeness.'

The strangers in the room were silent but it wasn't a hostile silence. She took strength from it and went on.

'I don't know if you're already drunk or deliberately mean but do not belittle me. You don't know anything about me. And don't bother calling Serena to tell me I'm fired. I'll be leaving as soon as I can get the next train back to London, because I would rather eat raw potatoes with your daughter – who, by the way, is in a cupboard because she hates you spending time with your friends rather than her – than stay here another moment. And for the record, your last book didn't sell as well as the company hoped. You were outsold by Lee Child and Dan Brown, who I know you believe to be inferior to you. And I think Serena is currently in New York wooing Dan Brown instead of being here but what do I know? I'm nothing as far as you're concerned.'

At least Eve could take some pleasure in the shock on his face at her outburst. And as she ran up to her room, she wondered if she should use Calibri or Times New Roman for her résumé after Serena fired her.

6

Eve lay in her bed, again wearing her coat and her hat, trying to not let the tears fall. Serena's phone was off, so her planned texts telling her that Edward was a complete prick and she would resign, effective immediately, were not being delivered.

Her career in publishing hadn't been anything like she had expected when she finished university and interned at a small niche publisher who specialised in literary fiction and poetry. She had lucked out and read a volume of poems by a young writer who had a unique turn of phrase that resonated with Eve. The writer also had a huge Instagram following and Eve had convinced the company to publish the work.

Fifty reprints and still going, the book had made the author a millionaire and a much-wanted public speaker. It had given Eve a reputation for being prescient about what women her age wanted to read and she was offered a job she couldn't refuse at Henshaw and Carlson on twice the money, propped up with all the promises in the world.

Since taking the role a year ago, she was still no more than a glorified assistant to Serena and none of the promises about championing young authors into the fold of Henshaw and Carlson had come to fruition. And now she was being abused by Edward Priest.

There was a knock at the door and then it opened. She sat up, expecting Edward, but it wasn't him. It was Flora with her long flaxen hair and pale face looking like her namesake in *Turn of the Screw*. She was wearing a dark navy woollen coat and what appeared to be black Mary Jane shoes and no stockings, the colour of her skinny legs nearly matching the coat with the cold.

'Hello,' the little girl said.

'Hello,' Eve replied and flopped back onto the bed.

'Are you sick?'

'Sick and tired,' said Eve.

She could hear Flora walking around on the wooden floorboards, her feet making a very loud noise.

'Why are you so loud?'

'I'm wearing tap shoes.' Flora gave a quick step ball change and Eve rolled over to look at the child.

'Why are you wearing tap shoes?'

'Hilditch found them at the charity shop and I like them. I've been teaching myself how to tap-dance. I watch videos on YouTube.'

'Hilditch mustn't like your dad very much, if she got you those shoes. They must be noisy when he writes.'

Eve looked down at her feet. 'Daddy doesn't write much now. Not since Mummy went away. He has no words left.'

Eve gave a small sigh. This poor child with such selfish arses as parents. She thought about her own parents – warm, present, always willing to lend a hand or an ear.

'I bury babies out in the snow,' announced Flora.

Christ on a bike, thought Eve.

'That's very Gothic of you,' she muttered.

'What's Gothic?'

Eve sat up and adjusted her woollen hat. 'It means mysterious, a bit gloomy.'

Flora shrugged. 'I don't think it's Gothic then. I think I just like to find them out there and come and save them.'

Eve didn't think she had to be a psychologist to work out what the child was seeking. Someone to come and rescue her from this cold house inhabited by her angry father.

'Are you staying here? Hil said if you leave you'll have to take the train tomorrow as it's going to snow and she won't drive in this bleeding weather.'

Eve stood up and started to do some star jumps to get warm. 'I'm not staying,' she said. 'Your dad needs to do more work and I am not going to waste my time if he's not prepared to sit down and do it.' Eve looked out the window.

'Do you want to come and look for dolls with me?'

'It's night-time. Do you go out at night?' Eve was shocked.

'Sometimes, when Hil has gone home and Daddy is in his study. He doesn't know where I am. You can come if you want?'

'No thank you but that's kind of you to include me,' said Eve shaking her head. This man was a terrible father, a lazy writer and a prick.

'Another time then,' said Flora as she tapped her way to the door.

'Another time, then?' Eve mumbled after the door closed. The kid was from another time.

Clearly Cranberry Cross was not a lucky place for her. She knew it gave her the creeps for a reason. Now she had to wait out the night until she could leave tomorrow. She wondered who else would hire her now, but she also knew that Serena would poison her name in publishing. She would have to go and work at a bookshop but knowing Serena's reach they might not have her either.

She would just have to hide in her room until the morning and then escape Cranberry Cross as fast as she could.

7

'That was so rude, Edward, even for you.' His oldest friend Sasha spoke and stood up adjusting the Hermès scarf around her neck. 'You need to apologise to her immediately.'

Edward rolled his eyes at her and looked to her husband Sanjeev for support. Sanjeev and he usually agreed on everything, except the look on Sanjeev's face told him that perhaps there was one thing they disagreed on.

'Brutal, mate. Might want to sort that out,' Sanjeev said and he looked at Sasha who nodded.

'We're going to head back home. We had enough stress before we came without more family drama,' said his other friend Caro.

'Too right, if we'd wanted to watch people fight we would have stayed at home with Caro's parents while they minded our kids,' agreed Phillip, Caro's husband.

Edward glanced about at their faces. He wasn't used to this, but then again he hadn't had anyone to Cranberry Cross for the weekend since Amber left.

Perhaps he was antisocial; perhaps he was avoiding writing by having them here. Perhaps he was a rude bastard.

He sat down on an armchair. 'I was awful, wasn't I?'

'Yes,' came the chorus of replies and he slumped backwards.

'What's going on, Ed?' asked Sanjeev. 'Do you want me to put my psychiatrist hat on for a minute?'

Edward shook his head. 'I know what's going on,' he said. 'I'm stuck. I have been since Amber left and because I have this bloody contract, I have to finish the book but I don't have it in me.'

He paused.

'And she's been sent by the publisher to whip the book into shape while I write.'

'So, you projected your anger and frustration onto her? That doesn't seem fair does it?'

'Shut up, Sanj. I know, I know.'

Edward closed his eyes. Sanjeev had recommended some tablets to help him manage his moods since Amber had left, but he hadn't taken them for long. Preferring to feel it all – except he was becoming angrier and mean. He hated that side of himself. He knew he could be cruel. It wasn't something he was proud of and now, as he faced his close friends, he felt truly accountable. That girl had done nothing to him and he had lashed out because he didn't want to admit he was out of ideas.

He was stuck, in both his writing and his life.

'I need to apologise,' he said.

Phillip shook his head. 'You absolutely do or else we're leaving.'

Caro leaned over to Sasha. 'Phillip must be furious to be prepared to go home to my parents. They call him Phil, which you know he loathes.'

'Okay, I'm going,' Edward said.

As he climbed the stairs, Flora passed him on the way down.

'Where are you off to?' he asked.

'I'm off to find some Gothic babies in the snow.'

'I have no words,' he said.

'I know. I told Eve you didn't have any more words left inside you. If you want some words, you can come and borrow some from my books.'

'Thank you, darling but you can't go outside now. Back to bed,' Edward called out to her as she disappeared down the dark hall.

Flora came back to him and sighed dramatically. 'If the Gothic babies die overnight then it's your fault.'

Gothic babies? Where had she learned that word?

'The Gothic babies will be fine. They're used to these sort of conditions; that's why they're Gothic,' he said. 'Go on, into bed and I'll tuck you in once I've spoken to Eve.'

He waited for Flora to head towards her room and then knocked on the door to Eve's room and waited.

'I'm not up for looking for babies right now, Flora.'

Edward opened the door a little. 'It's not Flora, it's her silly father.'

Eve was sitting on the side of her bed in her coat and a woollen hat.

'You're leaving already?' he asked.

Eve crossed her arms.

'No, I can't leave until tomorrow because of the snow and Hilditch doesn't want to drive that far.'

'Are you going somewhere in between?' He gestured to her coat and hat.

'No, it's just so cold in here and I can't have a fire because I get asthma.'

'We can arrange a heater for you. I'm getting heating installed in some of these rooms but it takes time and money, or I can get Hilditch to move you to a room with heating. Stupid to have you in here.'

He looked around at the room. It was very gloomy, he thought. He wondered why Hilditch put her all the way on this side of the property and then he remembered.

'I'll get you a heater, immediately.'

Eve shook her head. 'Please don't – I'm not staying. You're clearly not in the right space to work. I think it would be best if you let Serena know you're not going to deliver.'

Edward put his hands in his pockets and paced, something he found soothing but used to drive Amber mad.

'I need to apologise to you,' he said not stopping his pacing. 'I was so rude – completely awful. It was unacceptable and uncalled for.'

He looked at Eve who was staring down at her hands.

'I am very sorry, Eve Pilkins, for being such an utter prick.'

She was silent.

Silence made him uncomfortable, which was ironic since he moved to a house in the country where it felt, at times, that this is where silence originated.

Amber had always filled the space with her constant talking, and later, arguments. Maybe that's why he married her, so he could avoid the silence unless he was writing. And even then, his book filled up the silence. All the characters talking and arguing about their paths forward in the novel.

But Eve wasn't doing the work for him in this conversation and part of him respected her for her silence.

He stopped pacing. 'Can I sit?' He gestured to one of the armchairs in her room.

She shrugged, seemingly nonchalant.

'I'm stuck.'

'Okay?' she said. 'In the book?'

He sighed and leaned back, almost slumped in the chair.

'Yes, completely in the book, and in many other ways also, but to mention those is unprofessional and not why you're here.'

'But you did mention them,' Eve said. She adjusted her hat slightly as though she was about to take off at any minute and he didn't blame her.

'The writing is hard. I'm bored. The book is boring to write so I assume it will be boring to read.'

Eve nodded. 'It would be. Readers can tell when authors phone it in.'

'Exactly, and I have been writing something different and it's fun and new and exciting but it's not what I'm contracted for and not what my readers are used to.'

He felt a chill and looked around the room. 'It's cold in here. I have to see about that heater.' He paused. 'If you would stay.'

Eve said nothing.

'Perhaps you can read what I have written so far in both books and tell me if either one is worth pursuing?'

Eve took off her hat, which he took as a good sign, and she smoothed down her hair.

'Why haven't you shown Serena these?'

He sighed and clasped his hands. 'Serena is a good operator and does tremendous deals but I'm not sure her editing eye has been a focus for a few years now. She seems to be interested in the business side more than the words.'

He looked for Eve to give him a clue about her opinion, but she didn't flicker an eyelid.

'Serena has a big job,' she countered, and he wasn't sure what she meant by the comment.

'Would you read them? Please, Eve Pilkins? And then tell me if the words are worth staying for?'

Eve stood up and smoothed down her jacket. 'Okay, but if you ever speak to me like that again, I will go. Even if I have to sleep in the streets of Cranberry Cross till the next bus comes.'

Edward wasn't sure what it was about her in that moment that intrigued him but he found himself wanting her approval. Was it her disdain for him? Her self-respect? Her careful response about Serena? The way her hair fell forward even after she had tucked it behind her ear?

Was she twenty-five? Twenty-six? He was nearly forty, far too old for her, he thought and then he corrected himself. Why was he thinking about her in that way? She was a member of his publishing company; it was unprofessional and unethical to even consider her as something other than a conduit to him writing a great book.

He made a mental note to remind himself of this fact whenever his mind wandered to Eve. Professional standards always.

'Come downstairs and meet my friends properly. I promise I'm not awful all the time. And they're angry with me so they'll be super nice to you and tell you embarrassing stories about me. It could be fun for you and hell for me? Come and have dinner with me.'

She was silent for a moment and then she looked at him. He could hear her stomach rumbling and she had to eat, didn't she?

'Okay, that could be good. Let me freshen up,' she said. 'I'll be down in a minute.'

8

Edward left her alone and she went to the bathroom. She reapplied her eye makeup and put a little highlighter on her cheeks and added a slick of pink lip gloss.

She took off her jumper and changed into a pretty black knitted top with a bow at the neck and a high collar. It was both chic and professional and she knew it showed off her skin and hair.

A quick spray of perfume and she headed downstairs and into the library.

'Eve, please, come and sit with me,' said a woman with long dark hair. 'I'm Sasha and I think you're fabulous.'

Eve walked into the room and went and sat next to Sasha on the sofa.

'This is my husband Sanjeev. He's a psychiatrist and if you're lucky he will tell you all about your childhood wounds after dessert – it's his party trick.'

Eve laughed. 'I can't wait. That's like the modern equivalent of the parlour séance from Victorian times.'

'I like her,' said Sanjeev to Edward. 'Still not a fan of you though.'

Edward rolled his eyes and handed Eve a glass of wine.

'I would have suggested this is for courage but it seems you don't need any.'

Eve took the wine and gave him a wry smile. 'I just don't have a lot of patience for self-indulgence.'

'Ouch,' said the other woman who was standing by the fire. 'Nice shooting, Eve.'

'So you're here to sort out Edward and his writer's block?' asked another man.

'Phillip, don't hound her,' Edward said.

'I'm not hounding, I'm sleuthing – it's different. Besides, I want to understand writer's block. What's your take on it, Eve? Sanjeev was giving us his psychiatric perspective but I think I would like to hear what you think from an editor's perspective.'

Eve was about to correct him and explain she wasn't a real editor but then decided she couldn't be bothered to explain Serena and the whole mess as to why she was here.

'Writer's block? You want to know what I think it is?' she asked and looked at the faces around her who all nodded and encouraged her in different ways.

She took a breath and then let it out slowly and looked at the fire jumping in the grate.

'I think writers get blocked when they don't know enough about who or what they are writing about. They need to do more character work and explore the motivation of the characters and the backstory as to why they are making the decisions they are, or I think some writers...' she paused and looked at Edward '...are bored of their own work. They are formulaic and can probably write the book in their sleep. They know what the reader wants and they give it to them, but it's a compromise because they used to deliver something exceptional and the reader would be in shock if they did anything differently. Now the reader knows the twist is coming and they spend all the time waiting for it. That's why some writers can't finish. They are stuck in their own shit.'

Sanjeev clapped his hands. 'You are utterly brilliant. I love that – I'm going to steal it and use it as my own but tell people it came from my friend Eve, the editor. I'll boast about you for years to come.'

'You used to boast about me.' Edward pretended to sulk.

'You're old news, my friend. We have all moved on with the young people now. Eve is the leader and we are her followers.'

Eve laughed and so did Edward as Hil came to tell them dinner was ready.

Edward grabbed the wine and ushered the guests from the library, urging them to follow Hil to be seated for dinner.

'Thank you for coming downstairs,' said Edward to Eve as she stood up.

'That's okay – your friends are funny.'

'They're good to me. They know the real me,' he said looking around.

Eve looked at him; his face was anxious. He seemed worried.

'I didn't mean you were bored of your own shit,' she said. 'When I was talking about writer's block.'

Edward gave a small laugh. 'Yes you did, but it was deserved and it was also correct. I am bored but that's a conversation for tomorrow. Now we will drink wine and talk about other things with some of the smartest people I know, and you can pretend I wasn't a complete idiot earlier and hopefully forgive me.'

Eve took her wine glass and followed him up to the dining room. Everything was an act with this man and she wondered if she would ever see the real Edward Priest.

As they came to the dining room, Edward turned to Eve.

'They knew Amber, all of them. They stayed with me because they saw what it was like. Sanjeev has been my anchor. They're all my chosen logical family – more than my biological family.'

Eve nodded. 'Okay. I get it.'

'Do you like your family, Eve?'

What a strange question, she thought, but he seemed to really want to know the answer.

'I do, I love them,' she said.

'Then you're very lucky, Eve Pilkins,' he said and he walked in and lifted the wine bottles up above his head. 'Now let's eat.'

When the evening finished, Eve was slightly drunk and very full of food and smart conversation and hilarious laughter. When Eve was ready to make her way to bed, Hilditch told her she had moved her things to a new room.

'Come on, I'll show you before I head home,' she said.

Eve's new bedroom was much warmer and larger. Another huge four-poster bed carved with oak leaves stood in the centre of the room, draped with green silk brocade curtains tied back with large purple-tasselled ropes. There was a tapestry on one wall of four women in a garden of orange trees and some quail or peacocks scattered about. It was as old as the house, she thought as she unwrapped her scarf and touched her neck. It was all a bit too Anne Boleyn for her liking.

Hilditch walked in behind her and looked around.

'If you hear strange noises at night, be aware that it's just the wind. It runs through the dormer windows on the tower.'

Before Eve could ask any more, Hilditch had gone and Eve took off her coat and hung it in the large and empty walk-in wardrobe.

The fireplace in the room was empty, thankfully, Eve thought, as she unpacked her clothes and then sat on one of the small sofas in front of the fireplace and surveyed the room.

There was a small ladies' writing desk with a chair, looking over the grounds. Eve imagined a woman in a voluminous skirt dipping her pen into an inkwell and writing a letter to a cousin or sister.

A painting of a large still life of fruit hung above the mantel and two small coffer stools sat on either side of the fireplace. It was very austere and grand, yet despite the threat of beheading in the air, the room felt better because of the warmth from the heater.

Eve changed into comfortable clothes and then set up her laptop on the desk and opened her email.

Edward's manuscripts came through and she paused before she clicked on the first file.

She had agreed she would read them, make notes and then they would start again in the morning.

But she was tired, it had been a long day and she had drunk more wine than she was used to.

She thought about his apology before dinner. It had been sincere, if not a little disconcerting, as he seemed so intense when he spoke and invited her to dinner. But it was better than him expecting her to wait on him or look after his child like some sort of old-fashioned governess. Not that Edward had explicitly asked for her to care for Flora but Eve knew it would be encouraged by a man like Edward Priest. He probably hadn't even made his child a sandwich in her life. No wonder she hid in a cupboard.

The files flashed on her screen. She knew she had to read them so she changed into her nightgown and wrapped herself in a large quilt that was on the end of the bed.

She dragged one of the wooden coffer stools over to the desk and settled into her chair, with feet up on the ancient wood to read Edward's writing.

She was in for a long night but Eve had promised him she would read the pages he had written so far and she never broke a promise.

It was three in the morning when Eve finished her first pass of the manuscripts and she went through her notes. Her eyes were sore, and words were swimming in her head but she had a clear picture of where Edward's work was at, so she would sleep and then speak to him in the morning.

After showering and cleaning her teeth, she turned down the bed and then she heard a noise. It was not a quick sound, a fleeting creak in the night, but a long wail. It certainly wasn't the wind that Hilditch had suggested she might hear in the night.

She stood still, straining to hear it again. There was nothing. She got into bed and pulled the heavy covers up to her chin and listened.

Silence.

Her eyes closed and she felt herself drifting into sleep and then the wail came again.

It was a scream of sorts but was it human?

Was it Flora?

She jumped from the bed and went to the bedroom door and opened it, half standing in the hallway, when the door nearest to her opened and Edward walked out, his phone light shining on his face. He was wearing the clothes he had worn all day and it didn't look as though he had slept.

'You look like a Victorian ghost,' he joked, gesturing to her nightgown.

'I thought I just heard a Victorian ghost,' she replied. 'What the hell was that noise? Is Flora okay?'

Edward smiled at her, perhaps too quickly. 'Flora is fine. It's the wind circling the tower and around the old weathervane.'

Eve laughed at his explanation. 'If by weathervane you mean a madwoman standing on the roof wailing while bending some notes with an electric guitar?'

'What do you mean?' The smile on Edward's face had disappeared.

Eve lifted her chin and stared at him.

'I'm saying the noise sounded human and I definitely heard a guitar being played, loudly.'

Edward shone his phone light in her face.

'Don't be ridiculous. You've read too much Brontë. If you don't think you can bear the noise, you can head back to the other room where it is quiet, albeit colder.'

'I don't remember the Brontë sisters playing Hendrix,' she quipped but Edward ignored her. 'I'll stay in this room, where at least I won't get consumption, but thanks for the offer.' This man was moodier than her younger brothers when her mum turned off the Wi-Fi until they did their jobs around the house. She turned back to her room and she heard Edward's door close behind her.

Weathervane my arse, she thought and she got back into bed. She expected better from him considering he made up stories for a living. He could have told her they had a resident ghost – that she would have believed more than his rubbish weathervane story.

Cranberry Cross was proving to be more than she had bargained for in every way.

A morose child who buried dolls in the snow.

Her father who ran hot and cold.

Unexplained noises in the old house that sounded suspiciously like an electric guitar.

A mother who had abandoned her own child.

This really was a modern-day Brontë novel. So, who did that make her? Jane Eyre?

God she hoped not, and she rolled over and fell asleep, dreaming of the snow and being buried until Flora found her and warmed her in the kitchen in a cupboard while feeding her baked potatoes.

9

Eve's internal alarm clock woke her at half past six in the morning, even though she had set her phone alarm for seven thirty. The room was dark but she could see a chink of light between the moss-green velvet curtains.

She had slept well, better than well actually. There wasn't a sound in the house, unlike the sound she heard last night. Edward had looked at her as though she was drunk when she said it sounded human.

Her hand stroked the linen sheets and she pulled the heavy covers up to her chin. Could she edit the book from this divine bed?

'Time to get up,' she told herself, but a whistle of wind rattled the window and she closed her eyes. A little sleep-in wouldn't hurt.

It was after nine thirty in the morning when a knock at the door woke her.

Hilditch's voice came through the heavy wood, sounding muffled and somewhat peeved.

'It's after nine thirty. If you want breakfast you're on

your own. I'm off to Crossbourne with Flora. Mr Priest is waiting for you, has been for the past hour.'

'Christ on a cracker,' Eve muttered as she threw back the heavy covers. 'Coming,' she called, trying to sound awake but her voice came out strangled and high-pitched.

After brushing her hair and cleaning her teeth at the same time, she pulled on some clothes and ran downstairs.

'How are we this morning?' he asked as she walked into his study. He looked up and smiled at her politely, as though nothing had happened the night before and she wasn't an hour late on her first day.

She felt like she had been dragged backwards through a bush but Edward looked fresh, and she could smell the scent of soap and something leathery, a cologne but very subtle.

'Fine thank you,' said Eve, following his lead. If he wanted to pretend everything was normal then she was well practised. Used to Serena's outbursts one minute and then complete denial the next.

Edward gestured to his desk. 'I turned it around as you suggested.'

'Excellent.' She smiled.

'Did you get any reading done?' he asked. Was he being sarcastic? Was he setting her up to fail? Plying her with wine so she couldn't do the job and then he would tell Serena she had failed from the outset? Perhaps her imagination was being a little overactive. She was so used to being set up to fail by Serena that she was immediately defensive until she realised it was a natural question to ask her.

'I did,' she said. 'I have read both sets of pages and I have notes on them.'

Edward seemed surprised but also pleased.

'Well done you, even after the wine. I thought you would just go to sleep. I wasn't expecting you to have done both of them.'

Eve wasn't sure if he was being sincere but she went with it anyway.

'Are you ready to hear my thoughts?'

Edward sighed and sat in his chair. 'Okay but be kind. I am a sensitive artist.'

Eve tried not to roll her eyes and looked at her notes.

'You have two works; one is your standard Edward Priest epic historical thriller about the stolen artworks from an Armenian Apostolic monastery and the chase to find them as there is a supposed curse on the art if they are removed from the Tatev Monastery.'

Edward let out a long groan. 'God it's terrible isn't it? What a cliché.'

Eve shrugged. 'It's not terrible. It's what people expect from you. It's what they know and like. I did think you went a bit too in depth on the struggles of monastic life. I mean it sounded like they all needed rescuing along with finding the artwork. Also, a lot of chapters on that monk bringing gingerbread to the west... I became a little lost.'

Edward started to laugh. 'Can you tell I'm struggling? I'm filling up pages about gingerbread as I have lost the thread of the story.'

Eve nodded. 'Like Hansel and Gretel, we just needed less gingerbread and instead a few crumbs to lead the reader along.'

Edward gave a small round of applause. 'Well done. Tell me about the other one.'

Eve paused, trying to find the words.

'You hated it. I knew I shouldn't try anything different. I can tell a story but I can't write – is that it?'

'No!' Eve exclaimed. 'Not at all. I thought it was wonderful but it's so different from what you have written previously, I wondered if it was the same writer.'

Edward raised an eyebrow at her.

'I'm not accusing you of plagiarism but it's dynamic, clean, crisp writing. It's a proper page-turner. I mean who knew Edward Priest could have a little Ian Rankin inside him.'

He looked confused. 'How so?'

'What you have so far is a terrific crime novel. Really good. It's simpler in some ways but more complex in others, and I love that you have written a female detective. And she's not described as anything other than the smartest woman in the room. Kudos for that.'

He nodded but she noticed the look of self-doubt.

'Should a man write a female detective character? Can I work this crime out properly with no plot holes? I mean, I'm no Ann Cleeves. Good crime fiction should have a wonderful central character. I'm worried my Detective Anna isn't strong enough.'

Eve scrolled through the pages. 'Not at all. She's great. I will find the plot holes if there are any, so keep writing. I read a lot of crime for my own pleasure.'

He looked surprised. 'I thought you would be a Sally Rooney type of a reader.'

She frowned at him. 'Is that meant to be an insult?'

'No, I'm just surprised to hear you read crime in your personal time.'

'You would be surprised how many women love crime, especially true crime. There's something so calming about a well-planned murder.' She looked at him and smiled sweetly.

To his credit he laughed. 'Point taken, there are no wrong books to read, just books.'

'Exactly.'

Edward ran his hand through his hair. 'What about the other book?' he asked. 'Is there any value in it?'

'That's the book you're contracted to, but the other book you're writing – the crime novel – that has something special. I want to keep reading it.'

Edward stood up and walked to the window. He seemed restless in his uncertainty.

'I need to write something different. Those reviews for the last one, I read them all.'

Eve was silent. The reviews ranged from calling the book uninspired to terrible. It still sold but not as many as Serena had hoped.

'They were right. I was bored and it showed. This detective I am writing, Anna Tilson, she feels so real when I write that it's as though I'm transcribing her life, thoughts, what she sees and feels.'

He turned to face Eve.

'When was the last time you were in the flow?' she asked.

'The what?'

'The flow, when the words come easily, when it's not a slog. That's what you're describing. Artists get it, songwriters, novelists, anyone who creates.'

'I know what you mean but you don't think I was in the flow when I wrote the other books?'

'I didn't say that,' she said. 'But there is something

different in this writing. It's cleaner, crisper. You get straight to the point. It makes me want to read more.'

A knock at the door interrupted them and Hilditch walked in with a tray of coffee and what looked to be freshly made crumpets with a small glass bowl of jam and another of butter.

'I thought you were heading to Crossbourne?' she asked Hilditch.

'I am but I'm bringing breakfast to Mr Priest first.' It was pointedly obvious that it was only for Edward with one cup and one plate on the tray.

'Thank you, Hil,' said Edward barely glancing at the tray. 'Can you bring back a cup and plate for Miss Pilkins? You must be starving after such a late night, reading my ramblings.' He looked at Hilditch. 'The wind interrupted her. We must try and keep the doors shut at night.'

'I will be sure to check that each night, sir,' said Hilditch.

There was something in his tone when he spoke to Hilditch that bothered her. A shared look, her giving a small nod as though she understood something unsaid. Hilditch disappeared and came back quickly with a plate and cup and saucer.

'We're off to Crossbourne. If you think of anything you need, text me.'

Edward nodded as Hilditch left the room.

Eve's stomach grumbled as Hilditch left but Edward made no attempts to serve himself anything.

Was it rude to jump straight in? He seemed to have been up late, like her. She needed the coffee to get through the morning.

Edward started talking about the books but she could only smell the crumpets and the coffee.

She couldn't wait any longer. She wanted the butter to melt and drip, and if Edward kept talking they would be as cold as Flora's babies.

'I'm eating. I can't concentrate unless I have some food in me,' she announced and started helping herself.

Edward stared at her. 'I never eat when I'm writing.'

Eve wanted to laugh at his pomposity but managed to control her disdain.

'No wonder you're behind in your book then – you're hungry. Try eating and writing; one helps the other.'

Edward took a sharp breath and she wondered if this would result in another outburst but instead he laughed.

'I meant to say, I forget to eat when I write. I just zone out.'

Eve poured them each a coffee into lovely coffee cups on saucers.

It was a change from drinking instant from her 'Fuck off I'm Reading' mug that she used at home. It was a present from her brother Nick and it made her laugh more often than not.

She could not imagine warming her hands on that mug in this setting.

The coffee woke her up and the crumpets stopped her stomach from protesting and she settled into her chair.

'Why haven't you shown Serena this novel?' she asked.

'Manuscript, not a novel yet,' he reminded her.

She shrugged. 'Whatever. Why haven't you shown Serena?'

Edward took his coffee to his desk and stirred it slowly. He was so deliberate in his movements, Eve felt herself almost hypnotised.

'Serena likes what she likes,' he said. 'She doesn't think crime is interesting anymore, said it's overdone.'

'That's not true,' Eve said. 'At all. Thrillers still sell in huge numbers. Crime is the same. People want to be the armchair detective – it's a huge market.'

Edward shook his head and walked to the window. 'Is it true Serena is looking to bring Dan Brown over to Henshaw and Carlson?'

She sighed. 'No, not that I know of. I'm sorry – I shouldn't have said that.'

Edward turned to her. 'You should have actually. It's good to remind me I'm not as invincible as I think, as evidenced by my latest work.'

Eve thought for a moment. 'You could publish it under another name?'

'Too complicated. And it's disingenuous.'

'Plenty of successful authors do it, JK Rowling, Stephen King, Nora Roberts. Even Agatha Christie did it.'

'No, I'm not convinced. If Serena Whitelaw, who is the smartest woman in publishing, said crime doesn't pay then I believe her.'

Eve laughed at both his pun and at the idea that Serena was the smartest woman in publishing. She was clever but she wasn't the smartest. She surrounded herself with brilliant readers, editors, marketers and publicists. They were her smartest decisions, and she was clever to hire them, but she also did the worst thing and took other people's work for her own. She claimed the ideas, the hours and the outcomes, and Eve could never respect her for that.

'What does your agent say?' she asked. She knew some agents loathed Serena but she seemed to remember industry gossip that Edward's agent used to date Serena, so there was history, and since Serena was a demon, she would always have a hold on him.

'He thinks Serena is always right as long as the advances and royalties keep coming in.'

Sometimes Eve wondered what the authors would think if they knew how awful Serena was to her staff, how she gossiped about other authors and publishers and agents, and how she would play them all off against one another.

But then again, so many people were so desperate to be published, they said nothing even when they saw Serena being awful at work.

'What do you think I should do, Eve? Should I stick to the Armenian monk heist or write the crime work?'

His question surprised her.

'I thought you had made up your mind already?'

'I haven't yet but I want your opinion. If you were Serena, what would you tell me?'

Eve laughed despite herself. 'I can't be Serena. I would only have to be myself. If I were the publishing director at Henshaw and Carlson, I would ask you what gives you the most pleasure to write? Then write it. Your readers are going to buy it anyway and you will get new crime readers. It will be easier to market as we can push the new genre and discuss the character that you are developing in the manuscript. Your detective's good but don't be afraid to write a strong woman. She could be amazing if you trusted yourself to write her the way I think you want to. And I think we should try and sell it with a film option also. Get someone attached.' She paused and could feel Edward staring at her intently.

'What I have read would make a great TV series. You could turn it into a *Vera*. If I had to imagine someone playing the lead character, I'd suggest Kristin Scott Thomas.'

Edward jumped up from his chair. 'That's exactly who I was thinking of when I was writing.'

Eve smiled at him. 'Great, so we're on the same page.'

'How can I tell Serena she won't be getting the book she's expecting though?'

'That's what your agent is for,' Eve replied. 'Tell them the news and let them deal with Serena. They're not going to let you go, so don't worry about that.' She thought about Serena's response and knew it would involve a lot of swearing and threats and then she would move on and tell everyone that it was her idea that Edward turn to writing crime.

'Do you think? I must have something to give her by the end of January. I'm only ten thousand words in.'

Eve opened her calendar. 'It's the fourth of December today. To reach your goal you would have to write minimum fifteen hundred words a day while I edit and sculpt as we go along. How long has it taken you to write the ten thousand words?' Eve knew she was under strict instructions to copy-edit only, but if Edward made revisions along the way according to her feedback, how would Serena even know?

Edward looked sheepish and he rubbed his head and then grimaced. 'Six months.'

Eve let out a deep breath. 'Then maybe you need to tell Serena you can't deliver next year?'

'I can't. I need the money – this place is a sponge for cash.'

Eve looked around the room. 'It's a lot of house, isn't it?'

Edward gave a small laugh, 'My ex-wife wanted it and then left me holding the baby, so to speak.' Then he clapped his hands. 'So fifteen hundred words a day minimum, and you edit as we go. I write every day?'

'Yes.' Eve laughed. 'Every day. Maeve Binchy wrote every day, even Christmas Day. She probably wrote the day of her own funeral.'

'Bully for Maeve.' Edward stuck his tongue out at the ceiling and then looked at Eve. 'I usually write on Christmas Day also. I'm as dedicated as anyone; I'm just in a bit of a lull at the moment.'

'Then you need someone to shake you out of the lull,' she said.

'I would need a schedule. You would need to boss me around. Order me to sit and write, challenge me, push me.'

The way he spoke, Eve wasn't sure if she was turned on or surprised.

'I can do all of those things,' she heard herself saying. 'I can be very dominating if I need to be.'

'Good to know,' he said and their eyes met for a moment and Eve felt the flicker of something inside her.

Don't you even think about it, Eve Pilkins, she told herself. *He's too old, he's too wealthy, he's too arrogant and he's far too successful. Stick to your own kind. Those dreadful boys you met at the pub last week, the one who asked for your number and who said his favourite writer was the Guinness Book of Records.*

'I can do this, Eve, I can. I mean I want to but I will need your help,' he said and he stood up and walked towards her. 'Will you help me?'

She found herself nodding, trying to remain professional but instead thought briefly of her mouth on his.

'Yes, Edward, I will. I'm here.' She paused. 'Now sit your bum down and write for your life.'

10

The rules of the day were laid out for Edward.

- 7am – wake, breakfast, shower, etc.
- 8am – sit with Flora and play, read, etc.
- 9–12pm – writing
- 12pm – give pages to Eve to edit
- 1–4 – writing
- 6–7 – dinner with Flora
- 8–10 – go through edits with Eve
- Wash. Rinse. Repeat.

Part of Edward was horrified at the structure and prescriptive routine but Eve reminded him that it existed to get his book finished.

'Routines support creativity,' she informed him when she presented the idea to him.

He had grumbled and huffed but he had agreed with some caveats that if he wrote extra on some days he could have a lesser word target the next day.

Eve had agreed because he needed to have some control of his day.

She sat at the small desk and opened her laptop.

'What are you doing?' he asked.

'Answering emails,' she said.

'I can't write with you tapping away in the corner – you'll make me feel inferior and it will annoy me.'

'I'll go and work in my room then,' she said with a laugh.

'Don't go too far away – I might need to check the spelling of a word,' he said and she couldn't tell if he was serious or not but it made her stomach flip a little, but then she felt silly for thinking this was flirting.

She packed up her things and put them in her tote bag and then moved to pack up the tray.

'Leave that. Hil will get it. She's back – I saw her return a little while ago. Now go away. I'm on deadline and if I don't get these pages done, my editor Ms Pilkins will have my guts for garters tomorrow.'

Eve laughed and left him to work, praying to the god of writers that Edward would stay on track. There were so many rooms she could work in. The large dining room looked like the plans for the Battle of Hastings had been drawn up at the large oak table – not a great place for someone to answer emails about nonsense from their micromanaging boss.

The kitchen was clearly Hilditch's domain and despite its warmth, there was something about Hilditch's manner towards Eve that was cold.

She could head up to her room again but that was a long way from Edward, although he could text if he wanted; but the thought of being cooped up in her room day and night was claustrophobic.

Walking the halls of Cranberry Cross, Eve wondered why Edward's ex-wife had wanted to live in such a huge, cold, spooky house. Perhaps Serena was right and she had seen herself as the lady of the manor, only to see the heating bill and run to the warmth of the California sunshine.

It was a huge house to fund even for someone as successful as Edward. She had seen cleaners moving about that morning, and there was a handful of gardeners pottering about in the cold.

Hilditch was there more than she wasn't, and Eve wondered what else she did besides cook and odd jobs.

Eve walked through the house, looking for Flora, but found Hilditch coming out of a wooden door that was part of the wall panelling. She glanced at a staircase behind her.

'A secret passage? How wonderful. Where does it go?' she asked Hilditch.

Hilditch snapped, 'None of your business. And you're not to go up there. It's not yet been assessed by the builders.'

Eve looked at the plate of a half-eaten tomato sandwich and near-empty glass of milk in Hilditch's hand.

She nearly made a glib comment about Hilditch taking her lunch upstairs to sit in an unsafe environment but decided against it. Hilditch was intimidating on most days, let alone now.

'I'm looking for a spot to work. I don't feel like staying in my room all day and Mr Priest wants me to be nearby in case he needs some editing done.'

Hilditch started to walk away and Eve was unsure if she should follow.

'Come on then,' said Hilditch. 'You can have the snug.'

She stopped outside a small door that Eve hadn't noticed before. It wasn't anywhere near as grand as the other doors and there wasn't a door handle but a small knot in the wood that Hilditch pushed and the door sprung open.

Hilditch gestured for Eve to enter and she saw three flagstone steps that led into a sunken room.

The stone walls were painted white and there was a large rug on the floor that looked heavy and very old, in muted colours of blue and pink. The pattern was fading but Eve felt the quality when she stepped onto it and looked about the room.

A comfortable sofa with a small table that looked to be Moroccan or Turkish was inlaid with pearl and covered with intricate carving.

The bay window looked out over some bare branches and the expanse of lawn showed on the horizon.

There was a small gas fire in the hearth and empty bookshelves on either side of the fireplace. Two cosy armchairs faced the sofa and against the wall was a desk with a round convex mirror above it, showing the view over the branches to the lawn.

Hilditch went to the fire and pressed a button and the fire sprung to life. 'Mrs Priest didn't like wood fires either.'

The room was so obviously different from the rest of the manor that Eve wondered if she had entered another house by accident.

'This is the snug,' explained Hilditch. 'It was decorated for Mrs Priest but she never used it. Mr Priest did it up the way he thought she might like it but she didn't enjoy it at all. Then she left and it's been sitting here ever since.' Hilditch looked around. 'It's a nice little room, and in the summer those bare branches are covered in white hydrangeas.'

Eve touched the back of the sofa and looked at the lovely

William Morris cushions. It was a thoughtful, gentle room and she wondered if Mrs Priest had appreciated it the way Eve would.

'This is perfect, thank you, Hilditch.'

Hilditch went to the door and then turned to Eve.

'Best not to go exploring much around here. Some parts of the house can be confusing and some parts are still undergoing work.'

Eve smiled at her. 'Of course. I'm here to do a job, not to be nosy.'

Relief seemed to wash over Hilditch. 'Thank you. Sit tight and I will bring you some tea and you can get on with your work.'

After Hilditch delivered the peace offering in the form of an excellent mug of tea, Eve sat at the desk and looked at the emails from work.

Onwards, she told herself and she settled into the day, wondering how Edward was going with his writing. It was ten and he was due to get his work to her at midday.

She opened the door just in case he called her as she sipped her tea.

'This is my mummy's room,' she heard Flora say.

Eve turned to the child who was standing in the doorway.

'Do you think she would mind if I used it for a while? Just to help your dad with his book?'

Flora shrugged. She carried a backpack and wore a woollen hat and a nightgown.

'I don't think she wants to live here anymore so it doesn't matter.'

Eve tried not show a reaction to the child's honesty and obvious sadness.

'You can come and play in here if you like,' she offered. 'I have a nice warm fire for you to defrost any babies in front of and the bookshelves would make excellent baby bunk beds.'

Flora peered around the corner and looked at what was on offer.

'You won't let Myles in will you?' Flora asked.

'No, not if you don't want him here,' Eve answered solemnly. She remembered the twins had each had an invisible friend, although they seemed friendlier than Flora's imaginary playmate.

The child looked relieved at this news. 'I might come then,' she said and left Eve staring at an empty doorway.

Eve picked up her phone and dialled and waited. 'Mum? Hi,' she said as she looked at the dormant branches.

Flora deserved a mother like Eve's mum Donna. Actually, everyone deserved Donna as a mum, she thought. Always ready to listen, not quick to judge, encouraging, creative, funny and kind to her friends, family and strangers.

Eve sat back and listened to her mum's chatter and then saw a little figure in the convex mirror enter the room and sit by the gas fire, which was warming the room up.

She heard the sound of a zip and then a tumble of dolls falling onto the carpet.

Eve slowly turned to watch the little girl playing on the floor as she listened to her mum's news from home and she wondered why on earth Amber Priest would leave this house and this child.

'Did you ask your author if you can come home for Christmas?' asked her mother. 'We aren't far from you now. It's about an hour's drive. I looked it up on the map.'

'I didn't ask, Mum, but he will be writing on the day, so I will have to stay here and edit. I set him a really strict schedule.'

'Is he nice to you?' asked her mum.

'He's okay,' she said carefully. If she hinted at Edward being awful to her the first night she arrived her mum and dad would be up on the next train and bus to tell him off and drag Eve away.

'How are the boys?' she asked.

'They're grand – they've started a band. It's called Baked Beans.'

'The band is called Baked Beans?' Eve laughed.

'They said it's their favourite food and they are one bean turned into two.'

Eve expected nothing less of her kooky younger brothers.

'I don't hate it as a name. It certainly sets them apart,' she said.

'Nick is on vocals and piano, and Gabe is on drums. They're looking for a guitarist now. You played guitar at school – you could come back and join them. Then it would be three baked beans.'

'Those days are over.' She laughed. Hilditch walked past and peered in the doorway. She looked at Flora sitting on the floor and frowned.

'I have to go, Mum, I'll call you later,' she said.

'If Flora is bothering you, tell her to go to her room,' said Hilditch.

'She's not bothering me at all. It's nice to have company.'

Hilditch snorted and left Eve alone with Flora, who seemed to be her only friend at Cranberry Cross.

I I

Eve was ready to eat beans on toast in the kitchen for dinner when Edward told her that that wouldn't do, as though she was bringing down the family's reputation within the area.

He insisted on eating in the dining room with Eve, which she thought was ridiculous, but he was the eccentric author and since he had actually delivered sixteen hundred words for the day, she wasn't about to argue with him.

Hilditch had left a chicken pie and salad and Flora had already eaten and was in bed by the time Eve had finished reviewing his pages.

She was surprised to learn Edward had organised Flora's dinner and had got her to have a bath and had read her a book. She assumed that Hilditch did it all and felt guilty for the assumption; but then again, Edward didn't come across as a naturally paternal figure.

Flora had spent most of the afternoon in Eve's small snug, bringing in baby doll bedding and clothes and some small cots. There was soon an orphanage set up, and Flora had asked Eve to write a sign to hang over the mantel that read, *Flora's Baby House.*

Flora was used to being quiet, Eve realised as she worked. The perils of being the child of an author, she thought.

Flora was a good child, a little strange at times, a little morbid but she was sweet.

When Eve was still working, Edward had come and taken Flora to get ready for dinner.

And then when Flora came down from her bath and was all shiny with damp hair and new nightgown and red bathroom slippers, she told Eve that her dad was reading her *Danny the Champion of the World* and Eve again wondered why Amber Priest would want to miss out on any part of this little girl growing up.

And now she was eating a very good chicken pie, opposite Edward Priest in a dining room that was lined with oak panels and a chandelier hanging over the table.

'Tell me your sad story as to why you ended up in publishing, Miss Pilkins,' he said.

'I don't have a sad story,' said Eve. 'I played guitar throughout school but wasn't committed enough to do anything with it, and besides playing music, I liked reading so I found a job that allowed me to read all day.'

'And do you read all day?' he asked.

Eve sighed. 'I used to when I started as a hired reader for the slush pile but then I was promoted to work as an assistant to Serena and now it seems the only things I read are emails and texts from her.' She shrugged. 'I know she's busy. It's fine, I will eventually get a proper editor role. I know I can do it.'

Edward put down his fork. 'You're not an editor already?'

'No, I'm Serena's assistant but I do edit work. I just don't have the title yet.'

'And the wage? Are you paid as an editor or as an assistant?'

Eve laughed. 'There isn't much difference to be honest but it would be nice for my résumé if I were called an editor. Otherwise, I'll be stuck in admin forever.'

Edward ate slowly, as though considering every mouthful. 'Do you edit much of Serena's list?'

Eve knew to be careful how she answered. 'A bit,' she said vaguely.

She could feel Edward's eyes on her and she looked down at her plate.

'What about you? What's your sad story as to why you became an author?'

'None,' he said but she saw a shadow cross his face.

'You know, they say that a writer is someone who managed to escape their unhappy childhood with imagination and then turned it into a career.'

He laughed but it was hollow. 'Perhaps they were right,' he said. 'Whoever they are.'

The sound of a high-pitched scream in the distance chilled Eve's bones.

'There's that noise again. It can't be the wind. It sounds human. Or electric or something I can't place.'

Edward sipped his wine. 'It's the wind. I used to think it was something else also but it's not. Now what did you think of my words? Did I put them in the correct order?'

Eve put down her fork, taking his lead to ignore the noise, but it had unsettled her.

'The words were mostly in the right order but that's a very subjective take.'

Edward leaned forward. 'So be impartial.'

Eve took a sip of her wine. 'You wrote quickly today. I can tell because the ideas were all there but the lines were rushed. This is a crime book; it should be a slow leak. You hit your word target plus another one hundred but you also panicked. I could tell by the way you structured some of the sentences.'

Edward laughed loudly and clapped his hands.

'God, you are absolutely right. I haven't written that fast since I wrote my vows as Amber walked up the aisle.'

A prickle of jealousy spiked Eve's mood. It was unsettling and unfamiliar. Eve had never really been the jealous type. She'd had boyfriends but no one she had said she loved with her whole heart. She loved parts of them but loving someone wholly and completely hadn't happened so far in her life. But then again, she hadn't found anyone who loved silence and books as much as she had.

Her dad had teased her that she needed to fall in love with a librarian and Eve had agreed. A librarian would be her soul mate she had told her father, who had rolled his eyes at her.

'Are you going to tell Serena that I'm writing a crime book?' asked Edward.

Eve thought for a moment. Maybe she could work on the structural edit herself and put Serena off for just long enough that she wouldn't have a choice in the matter. Serena wouldn't like that Eve had taken on the structural edit for a crime book but when the deadline was looming to start the marketing and promotion for the presale, then she would have to accept Edward's book. Besides, it was going to be great – Eve could tell by what she had already read.

Edward was a naturally gifted storyteller and with some good editing this book could relaunch his career.

'I'm going to wait,' Eve said with a smile. 'She will read it in one go and be blown away, I'm sure.' She crossed her fingers as she spoke.

Edward nodded. 'Probably best.'

They both knew what the other was thinking. They couldn't give Serena a choice, otherwise she would scream blue murder over the crime book.

'Serena doesn't like change very much.' Eve was careful how she used her words but she knew Edward understood when he nodded in agreement.

'She likes things to be the same, the staff to stay the same and the books to be predictable?' he asked and then laughed because she knew he knew the answer.

Eve finished her wine.

Edward was right. The nagging feeling that Eve had of late – telling her if she didn't get out of Henshaw and Carlson soon, then she'd be stuck as Serena's assistant forever – now felt like a punch to the gut.

She had to leave, but jobs in publishing in London were highly contested. Even though she had done so much of Serena's editing and work, she couldn't claim any of it because Serena took credit for it all.

'We have to review today's work,' Eve said, trying to keep the yawn from her voice.

'Go to bed – we can do it tomorrow. You're exhausted, I can tell.'

'No, if you can keep to the schedule then I can also.'

'It's not a competition, Eve,' Edward said. 'You're tired; I'm tired. We can go through these notes over breakfast tomorrow.'

'Are you sure?' The more he spoke about tiredness, the more tired she felt. As though he was brainwashing her into bed but for her benefit, not his.

'I might then,' said Eve reluctantly. Eve felt bad about abandoning the schedule on the first day, but she was sure they could get things back on track tomorrow.

She stood up and picked up her plate and glass, but Edward waved his hands at her.

'Put those down, you're a guest.'

'I can do the dishes at least,' she objected.

'No, you can't, you are here to help me save my writing career and put my words in the right order. That's it.'

Eve wasn't sure why but she felt disappointed in his answer. What did she want to be? More than that? The next Mrs Priest? His next editor? *How ridiculous*, she told herself. *Grow up, Eve.*

She put down the plate and glass.

'Okay, well goodnight, Edward. See you in the morning.'

He stood and smiled at her. 'Goodnight, Eve.' And he gave a little sort of a bow, becoming a chivalrous lord in the wood-panelled dining room and making her wonder if she'd been momentarily transported back in time.

The wind howled around the house, waking Eve up with a fright.

There was more snow predicted for the week and even

under the covers and with the heater on, Eve could feel the cold air cupping her face.

She turned her pillow over and snuggled down into the bed, closing her eyes tightly when a scream came echoing down the fireplace.

'Jesus,' she said and sat straight up.

She didn't care what sort of gaslighting Edward was trying on her, that was not the wind.

She stepped out of bed, and pulled on a large, dark orange knitted jumper that once belonged to her father and that her mum had knitted. It was shapeless but so warm and cosy, it felt like being home. She slipped her feet into her sneakers and grabbed her phone.

Edward and Hilditch could say all they wanted about the wind, but she knew the difference between a human scream and a howling gale.

She opened her bedroom door and saw Edward's door was closed. There was no chink of light from under the door and the rest of the house was silent.

There was a tower above this part of the house but she hadn't seen a staircase leading up to it anywhere.

And then she remembered Hilditch and the wooden panel.

If the opening was the same as the snug then she could find out where that noise was coming from.

As she crept through the hallways, she silently prayed to the ghost of Charlotte Brontë. *Please don't let me find Mrs Priest in the attic, mad and ready for arson and my blood.*

She turned the torch on from her phone and spotted the panel, running her hands over the wood until she found the knot, and then she pushed.

No going back now, she told herself and she pushed open the door.

Stone stairs, worn in the centre from the many years of feet traipsing to the tower.

The air smelled clean. She was surprised, expecting it to be musty and old, but there were new lights that ran along the stairs, showing the way upwards.

Finally, she came to the top of the stairs and a small oak door. Her hand touched the brass handle and she twisted it slowly and, to her surprise and fear, it opened easily.

The light was bright and it took her eyes a moment to adjust, and then she heard a voice.

'Who the fuck are you and why the hell are you in my room?'

12

A boy of about fourteen or fifteen stood facing Eve. He was wearing a beanie pulled down low on his head, and a scowl on his young face.

'I'm Eve,' she answered.

She glanced around the tower room. A microphone and guitars of varying types were leaning on stands or against the walls. Amplifiers were littered about the room, along with a collection of plates and cutlery and glasses. Poor Hilditch was obviously not welcome up here as often as she would have liked.

'And you are?' she prompted.

'Shitty,' he answered.

She didn't miss a beat. 'Hi, Shitty, nice to meet you.'

'I told Edward I don't want anyone up here.'

The boy had a strong Californian accent and the pallor of someone who didn't spend any time outside.

'The thing is…' Eve said, '…you're playing or screaming, not sure which it is, is waking me up.'

'So?' The boy shrugged. 'Not my problem.'

Eve nodded. 'No, it's not your problem but you could be more aware and perhaps more considerate of the others in the house.'

'Get some earplugs,' he said, and to prove his point he picked up his guitar and played loudly.

She laughed, not meanly but like when you laugh with a child who is attempting to learn how to do a cartwheel.

'If you want to learn how to shred that Fender Stratocaster like Jimi Hendrix, you need to slow down and practise with a metronome until you get it right. And I suggest practising picking so you can go faster – it will make the transitions smoother.'

He stared at her; his mouth opened in shock.

It wasn't the first time Eve had elicited this response when she spoke about her knowledge of guitar.

When she told people she had once been in a punk band and had shaved her head, they were even more shocked. Little Eve Pilkins could shred and scream up the stage as well as Siouxsie Sioux when she was in her final year of school, but those days were over.

Except for when she played her guitar at home and used her headphones so her flatmates couldn't hear her. She still rocked out and then went to bed and read a book. It was a nice balance.

'Here,' she instructed. 'Let me show you.' She put her hand out for the guitar.

The boy handed her the guitar, mostly out of shock, she thought, and she adjusted the straps and got the feel for the instrument. It was an expensive model, good enough for any professional musician. She started to play a riff and felt her head nod as she fell into the groove as she played.

'Hey, that's Daft Punk,' he said.

'Played by the incredible Nile Rodgers, the Master of

Funk, who also played with Bowie and Madonna, Lady Gaga, so many people. You know his work?'

He shook his head.

'You should.'

She played some Eddie Van Halen riffs and watched his eyes bulge.

'You can really play.'

'I can,' she said, finishing on a slide that sounded impressive but was easy.

She unstrapped the guitar and handed it back to him.

'What's your name?'

'Myles,' he said scraping his foot on the rug.

Flora's imaginary friend was real, she thought, and he looked tired and sullen.

'That's a much better name than Shitty.'

He didn't smile.

'Myles.' She paused. 'It's nice to meet you and thanks for letting me play your guitar; it's a good instrument, but I'm begging you to please use headphones so I can sleep. You need sleep. We all need sleep. Also, it scares the crap out of me when it wakes me up.'

He snarled at her. 'Why should I?'

She peered closely at him. 'Because you're a human being who needs to have empathy and respect for other people, otherwise the world is going to make your life very hard.'

'It's already crap,' he said. 'Can't be any worse.'

He meant what he'd said, she realised. This wasn't the self-indulgent moaning of a teen.

She thought of her brothers. They could be moody but not like this. Something else was at play and it was more than teenage moodiness.

'I'm really sorry to hear that, Myles,' she said. 'Life can be tough sometimes, but there's always someone to talk to, and I think there's a solution for every problem. You just have to ask for help.'

He looked up at her. He didn't look anything like Edward, or Flora, who had her father's strong features. Or even like Hilditch. So how did he fit in?

'That's total bullshit,' he said with a sneer.

'No, it's not,' she answered calmly.

'Maybe in your life your problems are easily fixed but not here.'

'Why don't you tell me one and I can try and help? Sometimes a problem shared is a problem halved.'

As she said the words, she wondered when she'd turned into her mother. Donna always had a saying for moments like this.

'You're weird,' he said.

'I'm not weird, I just remember being your age and people my age not wanting to listen.'

'Seriously, I'm not talking to you or anyone,' he said and walked away from her to the other side of the room in the tower.

And then she got it. He was Amber's son. She could see the fine shape of his nose and the honey-coloured hair.

No wonder he was angry with life. He was locked up in the tower. His mother had run away and everyone in the house spoke of him as though he was imaginary. Poor kid, she thought.

'Listen, I'm helping Edward with his next book. I'm here from the publishing house. I don't want to be here any more than you want me to be here, but I have a job to do. So, if you can meet me halfway and at least stop playing after midnight, that would be great.'

Myles strummed a few bars of 'After Midnight' by Eric Clapton and Eve laughed in spite of her tired frustration.

'Very clever,' she said and she went to the door to go back down to her room.

'If you ever want to talk, I'm downstairs. I'm going to use the snug as my office while I'm here. Although Flora has set up a doll hospital in it.' She smiled.

He stared at her. His face expressionless.

'That's my mom's room,' he said.

'I know but she's not here and I'm sure she'd be happy to share it with me while I help your dad with the book.'

'He's not my dad,' Myles said.

'Okay.'

They were both silent for a moment.

'I'm off to bed,' she said and she opened the door.

'Night,' she said.

'Fuck off,' he answered and Eve was thankful he didn't see her mouth open in shock at his rudeness.

He might not be Edward's son but he sure had the same temper, she thought, and she went to bed, with 'After Midnight' playing in her head.

13

E ve couldn't sleep after she met Myles.

The first thing she wanted to ask Edward was if he realised, when naming Flora, that the children would have the same names as the children in *The Turn of the Screw*.

The second was, why the hell was a child being held in a tower?

Why wasn't he with the family? It put the funk in dysfunctional, she thought as she tried to get the child's face out of her head.

There was no way her mum would let one of the boys stay up all night and not be a part of the family; but then again, she wasn't sure that Amber Priest and Donna Pilkins had the same sort of approach to parenting.

She checked her phone and saw it was nearly two o'clock. She had to sleep, she told herself, and she closed her eyes and tried to clear her mind until the image of Myles had faded. Since she didn't hear anything coming from the tower, she felt her body relax until she fell asleep.

The first thing Eve did when she woke at six was call her

mum. She knew she would be up; she would be already on her way to work.

'The thing is, my love, we don't always know what's happening in other people's families. That boy might not want to be a part of the family, so having him stay in the tower is better than having him run away and end up on the streets.'

Eve knew her mother was right, but it was still upsetting to think of him alone up there.

'It's not like he's been held against his will is it? What was the book where the young prince was in the tower?'

'*The Man in the Iron Mask*,' Eve said.

'He wasn't wearing a mask was he?' asked her mum.

'No, Mum,' she said. 'Don't pretend this isn't serious.'

'And don't you jump to conclusions, Eve,' Donna said. 'Why don't you ask your author and his family if he wants to come for Christmas?'

'What?' Eve was confused.

'You said you couldn't come but if I invite the lot of you, then he has to come.' Donna sounded pleased with her plan.

'I'm not sure it works like that,' she said. 'And they don't even have any Christmas decorations up.'

'Maybe he's Jewish,' Donna reasoned.

'With a name like Priest? I doubt it,' Eve murmured.

'O-o-h it's Edward Priest is it?' Donna wasn't usually invested in any of Eve's writers but she knew Edward Priest. Everyone did.

'Tell him his last one was a bit soggy in the middle. I lost interest and skipped about ten chapters.'

'No, Mum, I won't be telling him that.' Eve laughed although she silently agreed with her mum. Edward's writing had been getting lazy until this new book he was writing.

'I have to go, love, but let me know how it works out,' Donna said. Eve could hear the buses at the depot in the background and the sound of people talking.

'Okay, Mum, bye,' she said and looked at the phone and then quickly did a search on Amber and Myles. No mention of him anywhere online, which wasn't so unusual, but there were a few pictures of Flora and Amber, and Flora as a baby and Edward.

Myles really was the boy in the invisible mask, she thought as she showered and dressed.

Downstairs, Hilditch was in the kitchen, making breakfast for Flora, who was sitting with a collection of dolls around the table.

'Morning,' said Hilditch cheerfully. She was dipping thick white bread into beaten eggs, soon to be French toast.

'Morning,' said Eve wondering if she should ask Hilditch about Myles or if she should ask Edward. She didn't want to be seen as gossiping below stairs but she also wanted to know Hilditch's opinion on the situation. She suspected it would be more balanced than Edward's.

She was about to ask when Edward walked into the kitchen, smelling of cologne and soap and looking handsome in a cream knitted fisherman's jumper and jeans.

'Hello, petal.' He leaned down and kissed Flora's head. 'How are the changelings?' He gestured to the dolls.

'They're okay,' she said. 'They will be cold later so I need to warm them up with breakfast now.'

'Good idea,' Edward said and wandered over to Hilditch. 'Oh fantastic, you do make great French toast, Hilditch.'

'Thank you, Mr Priest,' she said and Edward beamed at Eve.

'And how are you, Miss Pilkins? Planning on tucking into some French toast with us?'

His breezy attitude annoyed her and whatever thoughts she had of him last night being handsome and desirable popped like a balloon. He was carrying on about French toast when a child was hiding from life in the tower of the house? He was outrageous.

'I would like some, but do you know who I think would like some more?' She crossed her arms.

All three faces stared at her, waiting for an answer.

'Myles, I think Myles would love some French toast. Should we call him down and ask him or will we keep him up in his little tower and feed him scraps?'

The look on Edward's face was pure fury but Eve held her ground.

'You have no right to snoop about this house.' Hilditch's voice was strained.

'And you have no right keeping a child away from the world for whatever reason you think might make sense to you and to him.'

Edward's eyes narrowed at her as he stared.

'You know nothing about what has happened in this house, Eve. Please don't interfere in my family again, or I will send you to a hotel to work for the remainder of the book.'

She shook her head. 'No, I'm not going anywhere. That child needs a friend, an advocate. He's clearly unwell. If you're not going to do something then I will call someone who can help.'

'Like who?' Edward scoffed.

'Social services.'

'You wouldn't dare,' said Hilditch. 'The boy's not being abused, he's depressed. He's sad and upset. You think we haven't tried to bring him down to be with us?'

'That's enough, Hilditch,' said Edward and he looked at Eve.

'Come into my study, Eve. I need to speak to you.'

14

Fired for a second time, she thought as she sat on the sofa near Edward's desk.

Edward sat in an armchair and crossed his legs.

He seemed to be thinking for a while and she said nothing. She wasn't going to make this easy for him but she was also tired of the drama in this house. It was a collection of every crazy Gothic story rolled under one roof.

'I can understand why you would think that Myles is being abused or kept away from the family on purpose,' he said finally. 'But that is the furthest thing from the truth.'

Eve looked at him.

'It's not normal to let a child live alone in a tower and keep the hours he obviously does,' she said, crossing her arms.

'I know.'

'And he looks unwell.'

'He is. He's tired, depressed, he eats poorly, doesn't get enough Vitamin D and he's lonely.'

'Yes, so he needs his family, his sister, his stepfather, his mother.'

'I'm aware of that, Eve.' He sounded impatient.

'So why aren't you doing something about it?'

Edward put his head back and let out a huge groan of frustration.

'Don't you think I've tried everything? I have tried to get him to doctors, had phone calls with therapists, tried to coax him to school, to find some friends. He will not engage with anything I've offered. I'm surprised he even spoke to you. Usually he would scream at you until he woke the house up and then have some sort of stress-induced fit.'

'Like Colin Craven,' she said aloud.

He frowned at her. 'This isn't a book, Eve; this is a real boy with real issues.'

'So was Colin,' Eve said. 'In the end it was Mary and Dickon who gave him friendship and company to bring him back to himself.'

Edward rolled his eyes. 'You think I need an angry little girl and a Yorkshire moor boy to befriend him and create a garden and everyone will live happily ever after? Get your head out of books for a minute and see what's happening in real life.'

'These stories, the books, they tell us what people need. And I think he needs friends.'

'We all need friends,' said Edward looking out the window.

Eve's mind was whirring.

'Besides, Colin had the love of his dead mother to guide him through in that story. Myles has a selfish, addiction-addled mother, with narcissistic tendencies who prefers to party in LA than be here with her husband and children, and even though he hates what she does, he loves her, he misses her, or perhaps he misses and loves the idea of her. It's easy to do around beautiful women like Amber. You forget yourself for a while.'

Eve looked at her hands. She was quick to judge and did exactly as her mum had told her not to but she couldn't help herself.

'Listen. I played some guitar with him,' she said.

'You did?' Edward was shocked.

'Yes, I still play, just for me, for fun. I still practise. But I could tell this is more than just an interest. He seems to be really into it.'

Edward sighed. 'It's the only thing that makes him want to be alive, he told me.'

The threat hung over the room.

'I'm sorry, it's awful,' she said.

'It's awful but I am grateful you care enough to confront me.' He leaned forward, resting his knees on his elbows. 'It's more than his own mother does.'

Eve shrugged. 'It sounds like she's in a bad place also.'

He nodded. 'She is. I worry I won't have either of them one day.'

She didn't know why, but she reached out for his hand. 'You can't fix her – she's an adult. But Myles is still a child. An angry child, but he's still here and he has an interest and you care about him. That's enough to start with.'

Edward took her hand and squeezed it. 'I love him. He's my son. I've known him since he was seven.' His eyes were glistening and she saw the fear of losing Myles in his face. 'I couldn't bear to not have him in my life. Or Flora's life. And he can be so smart and kind but he's so damaged and I didn't protect him the way I should have.'

'How should you have protected him?' she asked.

'I should have adopted him, so then I would have some say in what happens to him. To show him I cared, I loved him. But I always put it off, saying I was writing or travelling or whatever. I hate myself for it now. Now Amber has left him with me with no concern for him whatsoever. I'm not even his legal guardian, not that she cares it seems.'

He let go of her hand.

'I'm a selfish prick,' he said. 'And Myles knows it, which is why he won't come downstairs.'

Eve wondered if some of this was true. The Edward she had seen when she arrived was selfish and rude and arrogant. While she knew there were things going on in his life, it didn't excuse his behaviour; but he didn't need to hear that from her. He had to learn this for himself.

Instead she gave him a sympathetic smile. 'It will work out, Edward, I promise.'

'Thank you, Eve,' he said as Hilditch knocked on the door and came to tell him coffee and French toast was ready and shot Eve a look that could have turned her to stone if they were in biblical times.

Edward stood up, his shoulders hunched. He looked exhausted.

'What can I do for him?' she asked.

'It's not your responsibility to help with Myles. He has a mother and me. You're here to do a job,' he said but he wasn't unkind, more pragmatic.

'I know but I have two brothers the same age and while I don't claim to know anything about parenting, I could be his friend.'

Edward sighed. 'I don't want you doing too much though.

An occasional pop-in might help but if he tells you to go, then go – he has a terrible temper.'

'I won't do anything more than offer friendship, as much as someone my age can offer friendship to a fourteen-year-old boy.'

Edward laughed. 'How old are you?'

'Twenty-seven,' she said. 'Turning twenty-eight.'

Edward made a face. 'God that seems years ago for me.'

'How old are you?' she asked lightly, so as not to seem like she was investigating their suitability as a couple.

'Forty.' He rolled his eyes. 'A walking cliché of a man in a middle-aged crisis. Wife has bolted. An angry teenager, a morose child, a house that's too big and too expensive, and a career that could be on the downhill slide. All I need now is a younger girlfriend and I'll be living out a Nicholas Sparks novel.'

'Or Nicholas Sparks' actual life, allegedly, according to media reports,' Eve said and Edward laughed.

'Let's go and have breakfast,' he said and they walked back towards the kitchen.

'After breakfast you have to write,' she reminded him.

'Absolutely,' he agreed. 'I need to escape into something after this morning.'

'I'm sorry,' she said. 'I was out of line.'

He stopped in the hallway and turned to her, his hand on her shoulder.

'No, you were right to ask. I can see how it looks and it's terrible, yes. You were protecting him. It's something I should have done more of and better. So thank you.'

Eve nodded. 'Okay, thank you.'

They came to the kitchen.

'Do you mind if I head into Crossbourne? I have a few errands I need to run,' Eve asked.

'Of course, take my car,' he said generously as he held the door open for Eve to pass through.

Hilditch didn't look up at them when they sat at the table.

Eve cleared her throat. 'I'm sorry, Hilditch, for flying off the handle and assuming too much about Myles. I was scared for him and I should have known you would be trying everything to help. You've been nothing but welcoming and kind to me since I arrived.'

Hilditch looked at her and nodded. 'All fine then,' she said and poured Eve a coffee and then went into the butler's pantry.

Edward leaned over and whispered to Eve. 'She's a woman of few words but that is as good an acceptance as any I've seen from her after I lose my temper and she ignores me.'

Flora watched Eve eat, clutching one of her baby dolls.

'I'm going to Crossbourne. Did you want to come for a drive?' she asked and then looked at Edward.

'Is that okay? I'm a very safe driver. Never even had a speeding ticket.'

Edward looked at Flora who gave a little smile.

'I think that's a great idea,' he said. 'And when you come home, the tree will be delivered, so you can help decorate it if you like?' He looked at Eve. 'We have one freshly cut from the estate. Hil will bring down the decorations from the storeroom. It might be quite nice if you feel like helping?'

Eve smiled. Perhaps Christmas wasn't a complete loss after all.

'That sounds lovely, thank you for including me.'

Edward nodded and drained his coffee. 'I hope you're good at untangling Christmas lights. I seem to remember they were in a right mess last year and I think I just threw them in the box.'

'I am very skilled at untangling lights and wrapping presents,' Eve said and Edward smiled at her.

'I think you're probably good at most things you set your mind to.'

Eve wasn't sure why this made her blush but she felt the flush in her cheeks and avoided looking at him in return.

Ridiculous, Eve, she told herself. *Be professional.*

'Righto, let's get organised and we can head off,' she said to Flora.

She would do anything to avoid acting like a smitten teenager around Edward right now, even if it meant walking to the village.

She paused and then thought for a moment, remembering her mother's invitation.

'Are you planning on doing your Christmas lunch or dinner here?'

Edward looked contemplative. 'It will probably be just myself and Flora. More than likely Myles won't come down. Hil leaves us some good food and Flora will open her presents and I leave some for Myles outside his door. I will do some writing, but not all day.'

'Serena said I would have to work Christmas Day.' She waited for a moment to see Edward's response.

'Christmas Day? No, why would she say that? I assumed you would be with your family.'

'It's just that it's also my birthday on Christmas Eve,' she said with a shy shrug. 'I'm a Christmas Eve baby, and for some unknown reason, it's my twin brothers' birthday also. It seems Mum only likes to give birth on Christmas Eve.'

'That's amazing.' Edward laughed.

'It's also annoying but we have learned to love it. We usually have a big birthday party for all of us and for little baby Jesus.'

'Is there a baby at your house?' asked Flora, suddenly interested.

'A little pretend one, like your dolls,' Eve explained.

'Then you have to go home. Ignore Serena. I won't mention it to her,' he said. 'It doesn't bother me.'

'Well actually…' Eve paused, wondering how much of an overstep what she was about to ask was. 'My mum asked if you and Flora and Myles wanted to come for lunch and to celebrate with us. It's always a fun day. I mean it's not posh or anything but it's great food and music and maybe Myles can meet my brothers? They play music. Could be a nice connection?'

God this was so embarrassing. Why the hell would Edward Priest want to come to her family's Christmas celebration?

Edward looked at Eve with an expression she hadn't seen before. She couldn't quite place it. He was always so confident and proud, arrogant even, but he looked vulnerable and shy now.

'We couldn't intrude on your day,' he said but he didn't sound convinced.

'It's not an intrusion, it's an invitation.' She smiled.

'I don't think Myles will come.'

'He might not but he also might,' she said.

'I want to meet baby Jesus,' said Flora to her father.

He laughed and looked at Eve. 'Don't we all?'

'The invitation is there,' she said. 'But no pressure.'

Edward started to clear the table. 'If Myles comes then we will come,' he said. 'I can't leave him alone on Christmas Day.'

'Of course not,' she replied trying to hide how pleased she was. 'It needs to be all of you. Come on, Flora, let's get moving. We have shopping to do.'

15

The invitation was so kind that Edward thought he might cry. He used to be a big crier but not many people saw that side of him. After he had watched the film *Marley and Me* he had been inconsolable for weeks. When Flora was born he cried every time he held her, her tiny fingers grasped around his single one. Songs made him cry; sunsets sometimes made him cry. Anything kind made him tear up inside.

That was why he kept such a gruff exterior, his friend Sanjeev the therapist had said. An emotional shield, he called it, and said that Edward had created it to protect himself from being opened up. That's why he chose an unattainable woman like Amber to marry. She didn't know how to open up either so they just stayed closed, crashing about until one of them broke.

Except Eve's heart was so open he could practically see it beating.

Hilditch walked into the kitchen as he finished clearing the table of breakfast dishes.

'You didn't have to do that, Mr Priest,' she said.

'I wanted to,' he said and he swept crumbs into his hand and tipped them into the sink.

'And now you have to write before Eve returns and starts screaming bloody murder.'

Hilditch started to pack the dishwasher. 'She's quick to fly off the handle that one. Reminds me of you.'

Edward wasn't sure that was a compliment as he went to his study to write. Hilditch was correct in her thinking that Eve would call him out if he didn't write, and he didn't want to let her down.

She had faith in him and he wanted to impress her.

He reread what he had written yesterday, looked over Eve's feedback and made a few minor edits, and then settled down into his chair and started to write.

Edward wrote with no distractions. He had his internet turned off so he couldn't fall down a rabbit hole of research and he didn't check emails until the evening.

His mobile phone was set to 'do not disturb' with only Flora and Myles and Hilditch's numbers programmed to be accepted.

If he needed to research something he would make a note on the paper notebook next to him and then look up the fact later and thread the facts through.

There were more research notes than ever with the police rules into a murder investigation but he was enjoying looking them up in the evening.

But as he wrote he found himself thinking of Eve in her cherry red knitted cardigan and her shiny dark hair. She reminded him of the girl in *Amélie* but prettier.

Watch 'Amélie', he wrote on his notepad.

It was kind of her to take Flora out on her errands. He worried about her being at home so much but Amber had insisted on home-schooling her until she had taken off. He wasn't even sure that Amber had even filled in the proper forms to be allowed to do this. As far as the Department of Education was concerned, Flora and Myles didn't even exist in the schooling system. Flora's schooling had become non-existent since then, unless you counted her ability to warm up dolls.

He made another note: *Look into school for Flora.*

He underlined it and looked at the words. Did this mean he accepted that Amber wasn't returning?

So, what happened to Myles now Amber was truly gone? He hadn't adopted Myles, so the child still had a father out there somewhere. What if there was an accident and Myles needed a decision made on his behalf for surgery or a blood transfusion? Was that up to him? Would they have to call Amber? She didn't answer her phone when he called. Sporadic texts at most. Sometimes a picture for Flora. Nothing for Myles.

He leaned back in his chair and looked at the computer screen.

He might ask Eve her opinion, he thought, and then he started to write.

Eve returned from Crossbourne with Flora and carrying a large number of packages.

'Look at you two, doing Father Christmas's work,' Edward said as he stood by the front door watching Eve and Flora come inside.

Flora looked exceptionally pleased as she entered.

'Eve bought me a doctor's set so I can make sure the babies are alive.'

'Excellent idea,' he said and reached down and took a large number of shopping bags from Eve's hand.

'Nice car,' she said, looking back at Edward's Range Rover. 'I only had one accident but the other car is much worse off.'

'Ha ha, verrry funny,' he said. 'Anything in here for me?'

Was he flirting? *God stop it, Edward*, he told himself.

'Maybe, if you're very good,' Eve replied. Was she flirting? He was out of practice and she was looking gorgeous with her cheeks pink from the cold.

'I hope you were writing,' she said sternly.

'I did write. Hilditch said you would be cross with me and I can't have you cross with me.'

She gave him a small eye-roll and a smile. 'Did you email it to me?'

'I did.'

'Then I look forward to reading it.'

Oh yes, she was flirting.

'Daddy.' He heard Flora's voice and he leaned down. She was wearing a stethoscope and she put it to his chest.

'I can hear your heart,' she said. Her little face was very serious as she performed her examination.

'And what is it saying?' he asked and he looked up at Eve who was watching Flora. Eve was so beautiful, he thought. Her eyes were as big as moons and her heart-shaped face was like one of Flora's dolls.

'It's beating very fast,' Flora said.

He felt his eyes sweep over Eve's body. She was small of height but perfectly proportioned, with a lovely figure.

'Is it?' he asked. 'Perhaps I'm just happy to see you and Eve again. I missed you.'

Eve turned to him and their eyes met.

'Did you?' Eve asked. She looked almost surprised at her question.

'I did,' he answered and he was sure he saw her blush.

'Your heart just exploded,' Flora announced taking the stethoscope off his chest. 'You're dead now.'

Edward stood up. 'At least I died happy.'

Eve took the bags from him.

'I have some things to do,' she said. 'Call me when the tree is ready for tonight and I can come and help?'

He nodded as he realised he had an overwhelming urge to kiss her. He couldn't remember when he last felt like kissing a woman. Not since way back when he and Amber were happy. It was an intoxicating and terrifying feeling but he wouldn't kiss her. He would never overstep a boundary like that and besides, she worked for Henshaw and Carlson.

And at no point did she seem like she wanted to be kissed by him.

She turned to him as she walked down the hallway, 'And just so you know, Mr Priest, I am also exceptional at decorating Christmas trees.'

'Naturally,' he said and felt a flicker of desire inside. Oh yes, she was definitely flirting.

16

Eve knocked on Myles's door and waited. There was silence and then the door opened.

'What?' he asked. He wore a woollen hat pulled low down to his eyes.

'Just saying hi,' said Eve as though she dropped in casually all the time. 'And I went into town today and I picked up a few things I thought you might like.'

Myles walked back into his room but left the door open, which Eve took as an invitation.

She looked around the room, which was actually quite nice. Thick-piled rugs covered the stone floor and there were comfortable armchairs that looked to be Danish, which suited the space. There was a double bed, which was unmade, with posters on the wall of various films and albums.

There was a record player and a handful of vinyl records in a small cabinet.

She was relieved to not smell weed or smoke or see anything else that he shouldn't be doing lying around. There were piles of clothes, some folded – thanks to Hilditch – and some in a mess.

'Where's the bathroom?' she asked looking around.

'You passed it on the way up,' said Myles. 'There's a small door that goes down a level. It's the bathroom and a walk-in dressing room.'

'That's a bit cool?' she said.

'Having a toilet? Yeah, I'm really living the dream,' he snapped.

Eve ignored the barb and handed him a bag.

'I went past the guitar shop in town and picked up some things that really helped me when I was playing – just a few things that will bring your playing up to the next level.'

Myles took the bag without thanks and peered inside and then reached in and took out a metal contraption.

'It's a capo. I didn't see one when I came last time,' she said. 'What does it do?'

'Get your guitar, maybe the acoustic,' she said and she sat down on one of the chairs while he handed her the instrument.

She played it and then tuned it slightly. Then she clamped the capo onto the neck of the guitar and started to play 'Blackbird' by The Beatles.

The sound changed and she saw Myles's face light up. 'That's cool.'

'It's very cool, just like your toilet,' she said and she saw him laugh a little.

'You can play in different chords or use the same chords you know in a higher pitch without transposing them, which is hard.' She played a few slides on the guitar.

'Whoa, that's seriously impressive,' he said.

'It's a neat tool, and you can use it on the electric. Go and see what else is in there.'

Myles opened the bag.

'A series of picks in different sizes and types. Some people have their favourite picks but I was never fussy. But it's always good to have one on hand.'

And he pulled out a guitar strap.

'That's a Fender broken-in strap. It's the most comfortable strap you can own, and it looks good.'

Myles touched the strap, feeling the leather and turning it over in his hands.

'That's really nice of you,' he said quietly.

'Anything for a fellow guitar head,' she said. Myles was like an abused dog she had once brought home for her mum to care for. The animal was so desperate for love but so afraid that it took weeks for them to come out from under the china cabinet; but every day Donna or Eve sat on the floor and talked to the animal, read books quietly, or chatted to each other until one day, the dog came out and toddled over and sat in Eve's lap. Patience and slow movements, she reminded herself. Don't overwhelm him. She got up from the chair and placed the guitar in its stand.

'Okay, well I'll leave you to it,' she said and she walked to the door.

She turned around at the last moment before she left.

'Flora, Edward and I are decorating the tree later, if you feel like coming down. You could bring your guitar if you like and we can play some stuff? No stress if you're not up to it. We'll be downstairs.'

She closed the door behind her and let out a deep breath. She felt like she had been treading on eggshells the whole time she was in the room, but it went better than she thought it would. At least he didn't scream at her to leave.

Asking him to join them downstairs was a big call and she knew he probably wouldn't come, but she wanted him to know he was welcome, that she wanted nothing more than his company.

Being a teenager was hard enough without the extra stuff he had to deal with, she thought, and she went into the snug where Flora was administering to her dolls and sat down to edit Edward's work.

Why on earth Amber Priest left this life she couldn't understand, but who was she to question anything anymore?

She had a stupid, useless crush on a writer who was too old for her, who wasn't interested in her and whose life was in turmoil.

She sure could pick them.

17

The sitting room was lovely in the evenings. The rich velvet curtains were closed and the fire was warm in the grate, sharing its warm light with the room. The lamps were on and the cushions were plumped on the chairs and sofa.

Edward had turned on some quiet jazz-inspired Christmas music and the scent of pine from the freshly cut tree was making him feel something unusual. He sat with his feelings for a while, trying to understand what it was that was welling up inside him and then it came.

Hope. He was feeling hopeful for the first time in a long while.

Myles was still with them. Flora was happier. He was writing. They had a plan for Christmas Day and he was sleeping better since Eve had come to Cranberry Cross. There was something so capable and peaceful about her, as though she was ready to manage anything at any time.

He watched her as she focused herself on the Christmas lights in her hands. She was patiently untangling them and slowly winding up the part that was tangle-free. One over the other and back again. Small increments of the lights slowly coming undone.

'You have the patience of a saint,' he said.

She didn't look up at him. 'I like tasks like this. It's like a meditation of sorts, just one movement at a time.'

It was mesmerising to watch her as she worked. Occasionally she looked up at the door and then back to her task at hand.

'Are you expecting someone?' he teased.

'No.' She smiled at him but she still looked back at the door on occasion.

Hilditch had left them with a roast chicken for dinner and excellent roasted potatoes and a lovely salad and cheese plate.

Eve and Edward had drunk some wine and Flora was sitting happily under the tree, sorting through the ornaments.

The fire added a cosy warmth to the room and Edward had been sure to open a window so Eve could get some fresh air.

It was a lovely scene, something Edward had wished he had with Amber, but she would be drunk by now and screaming at Myles to get out of the way and Flora would have cried and the night would have been ruined.

'Do you have a tree at your parents' house?' he asked.

'We have many trees,' she said.

'Many trees? Like the queen?'

'My mum does think she is the Queen of Leeds, so that would tickle her fancy no end.' Eve laughed.

'No, we have a main tree in the living room, and then a light-up tree on the front lawn and a blow-up tree on the roof, with a sleigh, Santa and his reindeers. We have another in the kitchen but a small plastic one and then a small one in the hallway that is from the pound shop, but it's very nice and if you wind it up it plays "Jingle Bell Rock" and turns in a circle. And finally, a small one in the downstairs loo that is also an air freshener.'

She looked up at Edward and laughed at his face.

'Are you serious?'

'I told you Christmas is a big deal in our house. We have no Christmas shame. We aren't one of those houses you see in *House and Garden* with the well-dressed tree in subtle decorations and a handmade wreath on the door. We go all out and we aren't afraid of it. Wait here,' she said and put the lights on his lap and ran from the room.

Edward looked at Flora who was happily talking to a small china snowman hanging by a red satin ribbon.

Within minutes Eve was back and she stood in front of him and waved a foot at him.

'What on earth is that?' he asked.

'These are my slippers that I use for Christmas. They have light-up noses like Rudolph.' He looked down at her feet and laughed.

'I want some of those,' said Flora.

'I think we should all have some,' Eve stated.

Edward shook his head. 'I will never wear those in this lifetime.'

'You will eventually – I tend to rub my Christmas energy off onto people,' she said proudly taking the lights off his lap and settling down on the floor again.

'You do have wonderful energy,' he said. 'It's infectious.'

'Thank you, I got it from my mum. She's the best person I know,' Eve said.

'People with great mothers have a head start in life,' he said.

Flora looked up from her collection of ornaments that she had made around her on the floor.

'When is Mummy coming home?' she asked.

Edward looked surprised at her question.

'I'm not sure, darling. I'll call her tonight and find out.'

Flora looked sceptical but said nothing else.

He wished he had a different answer for his daughter but the truth was Amber hadn't been answering her phone or replying to text messages. He could see she was still partying from the photos she was uploading on Instagram. It would be nice if she put the same focus on her children, but you can't force people to parent, he reminded himself.

'We could make your mummy a Christmas card,' said Eve to Flora.

'Could we?' Flora looked ecstatic at this opportunity to connect with her mother, however remote she was from her daughter's life.

'Of course we can. We can decorate it with sparkles and glitter and cut out pictures from a magazine of all the things you and she like. It's called a collage. We can get some big poster paper if you like.'

'Can we do it now?' Flora asked.

'Let's do it tomorrow. I saw a craft shop in town. We can visit it and get everything we need.'

Edward looked at Eve as she spoke to Flora, incredulous at her ease with Flora and knowing what she needed. How was it so simple with her? Life at Cranberry Cross felt uncomplicated with Eve under its roof.

'The lights are done,' she announced as she got to her feet. 'We start with the lights and then we can put everything else on. Is that okay with you?'

Edward threw his hands up. 'You're the Queen of Christmas; we are simply your subjects. Go forth and make your magic.'

Eve laughed. 'Then you need to come and help me. I'm not tall enough to get these lights to the top, which is where we need to start.'

Edward stood up and held the lights as she pointed to where she wanted them. She only came up to his shoulder so he could see her struggle was real, but in truth he liked helping and he liked being told where to place the lights.

'You're very demanding,' he teased.

'Am I?' Her pretty face looked worried as she looked at him.

'I'm teasing. I like that about you.'

She gave him a slight smile as she unwound the lights for him to drape around the tree.

'I just like what I like,' she said.

'Me too,' he said as he finally wound the last of the lights to the bottom branches of the tree.

Edward stepped back and looked at his work while Eve turned on the lights.

'Looks pretty good, but I need to lift that side up,' he said pointing to one part of the tree.

Eve lifted the lights. 'Up here?'

Edward looked at her, the soft light enhancing her face, which was slightly flushed. With Flora sitting at Eve's feet and the smell of pine in the room, he wondered when he had last felt this content.

If only Myles was here also, he thought. He loved the boy and the boy hated him. He hated everyone but he seemed to loathe Edward. Disdainful and rude, and sometimes cruel to Flora.

The news that Eve had managed to see him again and show him some things she had bought him in town was a surprise and while he was happy, he was also envious of the ease at which she had been able to break through to him a little.

Eve and Flora started to adorn the tree with the ornaments and were in deep discussion of the placement of the precious items.

'My mummy gave me this.' Flora held up a glass angel, the light capturing the bevelled wings and shooting a rainbow across the room.

'Oh a rainbow, how gorgeous,' Eve said showing Flora who spun the ornament in her hand so the rainbow moved around the room.

Edward's eyes followed the rainbow until he saw it stop at the door and Flora dropped the angel noiselessly onto the rug.

'Myles,' he said casually, his heart in his throat. 'Come and join us. I need some support with these two Christmas enthusiasts who are very exacting on the placement of the decorations.'

Myles looked at him, at the tree, at Flora and finally at Eve who gave him a gentle smile.

'No thanks, I came down for food.' He gave the tree one more glance and then turned and left the doorway; Edward heard the door to the kitchen slam.

'What a shame he didn't stay,' whispered Eve to him as she walked to his side.

'No that was good,' said Edward, feeling his hopes rise more than he thought they could in relation to Myles.

'He hasn't come out in weeks. He came to see you – it's a good thing.'

Eve looked at Edward and nodded but she frowned.

'But I won't always be here, so what happens after Christmas? When you've finished your book? I can't be the only reason he leaves his room.'

Edward chewed the inside of his lip and shrugged. 'I guess you'll just have to stay forever,' he said and laughed a little.

Eve went back to her work on decorating the tree but Edward knew she was right. Eve couldn't be the only reason for Myles to come out of hiding. But as he watched her reaching up to hang an ornament, he could see a sliver of white skin on her back where her jumper rode up, and he wanted her with an intensity that surprised him.

He wanted her to stay, to be in his bed, to spend time with his children, to guide him on his work, to challenge him and to love him.

'Do you want more wine?' he asked, trying to keep his voice steady as he watched her.

'No thanks.' She smiled at him and he felt his body respond.

He rushed to the kitchen and saw Myles standing by the sink, illuminated by the light of the refrigerator and picking at a cold roast chicken.

He didn't want to scare him away but he also didn't want to pretend he didn't see him.

'Isn't Eve great?' he said as he opened the butler's pantry door and came out with a bottle of wine.

Myles shrugged.

'She's okay,' he said.

'She likes you very much,' he said.

'Cool,' Myles replied and glanced at the bottle in Edward's hand. Edward couldn't read his tone. He had never been able to read Myles's tone. That was part of the problem, but only part.

Edward looked down at the wine bottle and then at Myles.

'I might have a mineral water instead,' he said lightly and went back into the pantry and put the wine away.

When he came back into the kitchen, Myles was gone. Only the roast chicken carcass was left and the refrigerator door was still open.

The ghost of chickens past, he thought as he put it in the rubbish bin and closed the fridge.

He was lonely, he realised now. Perhaps that explained his attraction to Eve. She was someone new besides Hilditch. Someone younger and more beautiful and completely off limits. That was it, he told himself firmly. That was all it was. Nothing more.

18

For three days Edward wrote for his life. His routine was working and Eve was editing and managing Serena from her perch in New York.

'When can I read it?' she asked Eve.

'Not yet – he said he wants you to have the whole thing,' Eve said as Flora lay on the floor of the snug looking at a picture book of dolls from around the world.

Eve had bought it in town, trying to get Flora's head out of the morbid garden of Cranberry Cross littered with dolls buried in the snow.

So far it seemed to be working. Flora was quite taken with the dolls from Africa and then asked if they were left in the desert for their mummies to find.

At least then Eve could get up the map of the world on her computer and show Flora where Africa was in comparison to Cranberry Cross.

'Make sure he's on track. We can't afford to not have him deliver,' Serena instructed. 'I don't want to have to remind you that the future of your career and many others relies on him fulfilling this contract.'

'I know,' said Eve, trying to keep frustration from her

voice. Serena's threats were becoming tiring, especially when Eve was doing all the work.

'I don't think you do know,' snapped Serena. 'Why not send me at least the first thirty pages?'

Eve made a face at the phone. 'I did suggest that to Edward but he insisted I send you the whole manuscript, he was very insistent actually,' Eve whispered. 'I don't think I should cross him, he was very rude.'

Eve knew Serena well enough to know that Serena loved to hear when authors behaved badly; it probably excused her own bad behaviour.

'Oh dear, he can be such a prick can't he? Do you need me to call him and put the hard work on him?'

Eve rolled her eyes at that comment but kept speaking and appealing to Serena's ego.

'If you want to, I mean, he might be more responsive to you but he was storming about last night and being very loud about his process.'

'Oh not the process spiel again, he is very challenging when he's like that,' sighed Serena.

'Okay, I will leave it for now, but tell him I will want to see some pages sooner rather than later.'

'Absolutely,' lied Eve.

'I have another call,' said Serena. 'I'll call later.'

Eve put down the phone. She had bought some time but she still hadn't told Serena that Edward had changed genres but she knew he had written a best-seller.

But Serena wouldn't have a choice once she delivered the manuscript. It will be too late to do anything but publish it but she needed to make sure that nothing too much was being done in marketing for his other pitched novel.

She dialled Zara's mobile number.

'Hey, babe, how's it going?'

'God, so good to hear your voice,' said Eve.

'How's Priest? Is he as awful as everyone says he is?' Zara asked.

Eve paused, thinking about the change in him from the first night to now.

The night before they had stayed up playing Scrabble, and Eve had soundly beaten Edward; but she suspected he was letting her win, even though he vehemently denied it.

Sometimes he looked at her so intensely she thought she had stopped breathing for a moment, and then he would catch himself and be brusque and dismissive.

'He's fine, not as bad as people say he is,' Eve replied.

'Has he hit on you yet? I heard he had an affair with Serena when his wife left him,' Zara gossiped.

Eve felt her crush shatter and she sighed. 'No he hasn't thankfully.'

There was a frisson between them but now Zara had said that about Serena, she had an instant dislike for him again.

Serena Whitelaw and Edward Priest. Gross.

'I was wondering if you'd started on any marketing for Edward's next book yet?'

'Not yet, bit early. I think Serena wanted to go out with a hard launch, surprise his readers.'

They're going to be surprised all right, thought Eve.

'Great, if they do anything can you let me know?'

'I doubt it. Everything is slowing down for Christmas now, but if anything unexpected pops up, I'll let you know.'

'Thanks, Zars,' said Eve and she put down her phone.

Hilditch did say that Serena had been to Cranberry Cross.

God she was an idiot. Of course Serena and Edward would have slept together. It was so on brand for them.

Sometimes she thought Edward was lonely and unhappy and had been dealt a cruel blow by his ex, but then she thought of Myles alone upstairs and Flora, who never seemed to mention school – nor did Myles for that matter. She thought about this huge house and Edward's lack of ability to do anything other than write and ruminate while looking out the window.

If Serena and Edward had been together then good for them, she thought, but it left a sour taste in her mouth. She felt embarrassed for thinking for a moment that she had feelings for him or that he thought of her as more than just the girl from the publishing house sent to babysit him.

She jumped out of her chair and went to find Hilditch.

'I'm heading into town. I'm taking Mr Priest's car,' she said. 'Flora is in the snug reading.'

Hilditch was in the kitchen, unpacking the dishwasher. 'All right then,' she said to Eve, not looking up.

Eve paused. 'When Serena came to stay, how long was she here for?' she asked.

'Which time?' Hilditch asked and Eve shook her head.

'Doesn't matter,' she said and she went to get Edward's keys and then ran upstairs.

She knocked on Myles's door and it opened.

'I'm getting out of here. I'm stealing Edward's car and I'm going to see something more than this house. Wanna break out with me?' She smiled at him and laughed.

Myles looked at her and then back at his room and then

back to her again. He paused and then let out a deep breath before he spoke.

'Okay, let's do it.'

They started to drive away from Cranberry Cross.

'Where are we going?' Myles asked, his feet on the dashboard.

'Feet off – if we have an accident you'll break your legs and your femur will end up in your stomach.'

Myles made a face and put down his legs. 'That's really gross.'

'It is, yes, but it happens.'

Eve heard herself speak and laughed. 'I sound like my mother.'

'So where are we going?' he asked.

'I want you to meet some people,' she said.

Myles adjusted his woollen hat and turned on the seat heater.

'It's so cold all the time here, even in the summer. I miss the Cali summers.'

'I'm sure you do. It must be nice to have that bone-warming sunshine.'

Myles looked at her. 'Bone-warming sunshine. I like that. I know that feeling when you feel the heat from the sun inside you.'

Eve tried to think when she had last felt that. Years ago when she and Zara went on a holiday to Ibiza. Zara had danced all night and Eve read by the pool all day. It was a perfect time for both. She really needed a holiday, she thought.

Eve turned the radio to a station with popular music and she sang along as they drove.

At times she saw Myles's fingers tapping the beat on his knee and once she was sure she heard him sing a few words.

The drive was not as long as she thought it would be and in an hour, they were in Leeds.

'What is in Leeds?' he asked as they passed a post office.

'You'll see,' she said and they drove through the streets.

Finally she stopped the car and looked at the semi-detached house with a *Beware of the dogs* sign on the gate.

'Let me send a text to Edward,' she said. And she quickly typed.

Out with Myles. Back later.

That's all he deserved, she thought as she opened the car door.

'All right, let's go,' she said and she waited for Myles to come round to her side and follow her to the gate.

She unlatched it and immediately heard dogs barking and she walked up the path and then knocked on the door.

The sound of the dogs barking was thunderous and Myles looked worried.

'They're fine – all filled with bullshit and bluster like Edward.'

Myles laughed as the door opened and there was her mum.

'Pet,' cried Donna and she reached out and pulled Eve into a hug. 'What a lovely surprise.'

Eve hugged her mum for longer than usual and then pulled Myles into her side, her arm around his shoulder.

'Mum this is my friend, Myles,' she said.

'Hello, Myles, how great to meet you. Eve says such good things about you. Come in, come in.'

Inside, Donna took their coats and they followed her into the kitchen where a dog gate held back a number of dogs of various sizes.

'Mum rescues dogs,' Eve told Myles who was looking at them curiously.

'How many do you have now, Mum?' Eve asked as they sat down in the lounge room.

'I have eight but I have two puppies who I am rehoming.' Donna went into the kitchen and returned with the two small dogs in her hands.

'I have a home for this one.' She held up the bigger one. 'But I don't have any takers for this one. His mother didn't want him and I've hand-raised him. He needs some work to trust people.'

She put the dogs down on the floor and the bigger one immediately did a wee on the floorboards.

Donna pulled tissues out of the sleeve of her cardigan and mopped it up.

'This is why I don't have carpets.' She laughed at Myles who Eve noticed smiled back.

'What will happen to him if you can't find him a home?' Myles asked, watching the small dog wander unsteadily around the room.

'I don't know. I really can't have another one here.' Donna looked around. 'I already have too many. Your dad will kill me, Eve.'

Eve shook her head at Myles. 'Dad's just as bad as Mum,' she said. 'He's a big softie at heart.'

'He'll be home soon. He's out with the boys – they had a half-day today. He's picking them up.'

'Excellent, I really want Myles to meet them.'

'Who?' Myles asked, looking worried again.

If she could only soothe his worries away for a while, she thought.

'My brothers, Nick and Gabe. They're looking for a guitarist for their band.'

The small dog jumped up at Myles's legs.

'He wants you to pick him up,' said Donna pointing to the small dog.

Myles leaned over and picked up the puppy who licked his face enthusiastically.

'He likes you,' said Donna fondly and to Eve's delight she heard Myles burst into a peal of laughter.

His stepfather might be an idiot but Myles was a good kid, she decided. The least she could do was help him in her own small way.

19

Edward didn't check his phone while he was writing. He had been so disciplined, he had even left his phone in the kitchen, away from procrastination and temptation. When he finished his session he went to the snug where Flora was still looking at her book, while her dolls were lined up like a creepy doll army along the wall.

'Hello, darling, have you seen Eve?' he asked.

'Nope,' Flora replied not looking up from her book.

Hilditch was out in the van, which wasn't in the driveway, and then he noticed the car wasn't in the driveway either.

He wandered into the kitchen and checked his phone.

Eve was out with Myles? Wonders never ceased.

He texted back quickly.

That's great! Looking forward to hearing about it when you both return.

He saw she'd read the message and had started to type. He sat in his chair, smiling as he waited for her message but then the typing stopped.

He waited a bit longer and still nothing. He wasn't sure why he felt disappointed she hadn't replied but he did.

Stop being needy, he thought. She was doing a nice thing for Myles, not him.

He wandered back to Flora who was sitting at Eve's desk in the snug, typing on her computer.

'You shouldn't be touching that,' he said and walked over to shut the lid and saw an instant message from someone called Zara.

No news on Priest campaign. Think they are pushing the new author Serena is signing in NYC. Maybe she will sleep with him as well? LOL. Hope The Priest isn't hitting on you. I know you have a soft spot for a silver fox. Zars xxx

Edward shut the machine.

'Don't touch Eve's things,' he said crossly.

'I was helping,' said Flora, her eyes filling with tears. 'She's so nice to me.'

Edward caught himself in the moment and reached out for Flora and pulled her into a hug.

'I know you were, darling, and you're such a good help but computers are silly things and very sensitive. How about we go into my study and I can give you a nice notepad, one of my good ones with the ribbon bookmark.'

This seemed to please Flora and she picked up a doll and walked with him to his study.

A new author? No marketing campaign?

Serena sleeping with him?

Eve liking older men? He wasn't that much older, was he?

Twelve years? It wasn't like he was Hemingway with Adriana Ivancich. That was a thirty-plus-year age gap.

He touched the side of his head where his hair was greying. Was he a silver fox? More like a used-up old pelt, he thought as he went into the study and looked for a notebook for Flora.

'Here you go,' he said, finding a fresh one with ribbon intact.

Flora looked unimpressed at the black book until he opened the inside and showed her the soft blue paper with small dots on the page.

'These dots are fun to join up and make pictures,' he said to her and opened the book and took a pen and started to join then.

'I want to do it,' said Flora. 'Can I sit at a desk like you?'

'Of course,' he said and he put an overstuffed feather cushion on a chair and set her up at the ladies' writing desk.

'Here are some coloured pens. Be careful with them.'

Flora looked at the pens with awe. She was only usually allowed coloured pencils.

'Am I your helper now, Daddy?' she asked as she looked through the colours on offer.

'Yes, of course you are. You're my assistant.'

Flora put her doll on the desk and set to work on her notebook.

Edward sat down at his desk again.

There was nothing else to do except write, he thought and he read what he had written that morning.

Why not write a little longer? he thought and he settled down in his chair.

Eve would be thrilled with his output when she returned, he thought, as he cleaned up the words on the page before he started the next part of the story.

He was writing for her – he realised that. He wanted to entertain her, thrill her, and leave her satisfied at the end. It was all for Eve and he wondered if she knew yet.

Myles sat opposite Gabe and Nick in the garage where they had set up their fledgling band equipment.

There was a drum set on an old rug. An electric piano with a microphone and an amp but no guitar.

'Evie,' Gabe yelled. He was the singer, he had told Myles.

Myles heard Eve call back, 'What?'

'Can we use a guitar?'

'Yeah,' she said and Gabe ran to go inside the house.

'She keeps her old guitars here. They're a bit crap but they'll do,' said Nick who was possibly the coolest person Myles had ever seen.

He had an earring in each ear. One was a diamond, and one was a black cross that dangled when he moved his head.

His hair was shaved on the sides and he had a small mohawk, spiked like a cool dinosaur. Myles wanted to tell him but he thought it might sound a bit stupid.

Instead, he looked at his hair and said, 'Cool hair.'

'Cheers, mate,' said Nick. He was taller than Gabe and they looked similar but not totally identical. They had such different styles. Gabe was all preppy and clean-cut, but he had a tattoo behind his ear, which he said his mum had lost her shit about when she saw it. It was a little barcode, which when scanned showed his birthday on an app.

Myles immediately wanted one but could imagine Edward saying no. His mum would let him but that wasn't a good thing. She didn't care what he did.

Gabe returned with a guitar and a lead and handed it to Myles.

'This hasn't been played for a while. Not since Evie was last up here. It'll need a tune.'

Myles took his phone out of his pocket and opened an app and played a note. It was really out of tune but he eventually got it to sound less like it was being played underwater.

'What do you want to play?' he asked, suddenly nervous. What if they thought he was a shit player?

'You start to play something and we'll join in,' said Nick sitting at the drum kit.

Gabe moved behind the keyboard and played a chord.

Myles thought about all the albums he had listened to, all the videos he had watched when learning the chords for his favourite songs, the obsession with his favourite guitar players, Jimi Hendrix, Jack White, Jimmy Page, B.B. King but nothing came to mind. Instead he played a chord, and then another one, and then he found the groove and played in the garage with brothers he didn't know.

He heard Nick find the rhythm and they played together, repeating the riff, then Myles found some more notes and then Gabe joined in on the keyboard.

There was something inside Myles that clicked for the first time in his nearly fifteen years of life. He felt like he belonged, as though he wasn't on the outside anymore. There was something that connected the three of them and Myles had started it.

He hadn't learned how to make friends easily or keep them, not with his home life. When some people at school had found out his mum used to be a model, then they wanted to come to the house, but there was no way he could risk them seeing his mother when she was drunk. Then he started to keep to himself more and more until he stopped attending school altogether, and since Edward wasn't his legal guardian and Amber was in America, there wasn't anything the school could do about it until Amber returned.

But this moment in Eve's parents' garage, with the coolest boys he'd ever met, made him want to never leave.

They played a little longer and then Gabe waved at them to stop. 'Do you know any Arctic Monkeys?' he asked.

Myles breathed a sigh of relief and nodded. '"Do I Wanna Know?"' he asked and Nick started to play the beat and then Myles joined in and played the iconic guitar riff.

Gabe's voice soared over them, even without a microphone and Myles nearly stopped playing as he took in the sound. It was warm and rich and with just the right amount of rasp.

The song finished and Myles grinned at the brothers.

'Hold up, you didn't tell me that you could sing like that. It's insane,' he said to Gabe.

'You should hear Eve sing,' Gabe answered. 'She's like Stevie Nicks and Adele mixed into one voice.'

'Really?' Myles couldn't imagine Eve singing.

'Yeah, she was super cool until she became a dork,' Nick joked.

'Let's do another,' said Myles, and he started to play another Arctic Monkeys song and the twins joined in. This time Nick sang harmonies.

Eve wandered out to the garage with the puppy in her arms and watched them finish the song.

'You wanna join in, Evie?' Gabe asked.

Eve laughed. 'No, the pipes are a bit rusty now.' She looked at Myles. 'We need to head off soon,' she said.

Myles stood up and took off the guitar. He leaned it carefully against the chair then went to Eve and took the puppy from her hands.

'Hey I was thinking...' he said.

'Oh? Do I want to hear this?' She laughed.

'I think I should take the puppy. I mean it needs a home.'

Eve stroked the dog's head. 'But a dog can't live in a tower – it's not a canine Rapunzel. It would need to be toilet-trained and taken outside regularly and walked.'

Myles looked down at the dog in his hands. 'I can do that,' he said.

'You think you can suddenly change everything for this little one?' Eve looked sceptical but he knew he could. He felt it like it felt right when he was with the twins playing music.

'Can Myles come back, Evie?' asked Gabe. 'He's good. Not as good as you but he's good.' He smiled at Myles. 'No offence but she was really good.'

Myles laughed. 'None taken. She showed me a few things on the guitar – she is good.'

'Maybe Myles doesn't like either of you,' she teased. 'The three unlikeables.'

'That's a cool name for a band,' said Gabe.

'It's a better name for the band than Baked Beans,' Nick stated.

'It's really cool,' said Myles. 'The Unlikeables,' he repeated as though trying the name on like a jacket.

'Are we all in a band now?' said Gabe excitedly.

Myles grinned and the puppy licked under his chin.

'I think we might be,' said Nick.

Myles looked at Eve. 'Can I be in the band? And can I keep the dog? I promise I'll be responsible. Please?'

Eve looked uncertain for a moment but then she reached out and touched the dog's little paw.

'I need to talk to my mum first. And you should call Edward and ask him. And be nice about it – the more pleasant you are the less chance you have of putting people offside. That's how relationships work, you know?'

He rolled his eyes. 'Yes, Evie,' he said and she frowned at him.

'Only people who love me call me Evie.'

Myles shrugged, 'No drama,' he said and he kissed the top of the puppy's head.

'I already have a name for him,' he said to Eve.

'Oh yes, what's his name then?'

Myles looked down at the little dog who was nestling into his jacket for warmth.

'This is Jimmi,' he said. 'In honour of Jimi Hendrix, Jimmy Page and Jim Halpert from *The Office*.'

'Excellent choice, mate,' said Nick.

'Agree,' said Gabe.

Eve sighed and put her hands in her pockets. 'I'll speak to Mum and then you can call Edward if she agrees.'

Eve came back with Donna's blessing.

'Your turn to ring Edward,' she said and she took the puppy from his arms.

Myles walked away and pulled his phone out of his pocket.

'Come back next week. We're free on the weekends after midday. I work at the shop down the road and Nick does the paper round,' said Gabe.

Myles nodded and smiled at them.

'Good jamming with you,' he said and he walked outside, wondering how in one day his world could seem so different.

2 1

'Do you think dogs dream?' he asked Eve while she drove them home.

'Of course they do,' she answered. 'My mum read a study stating they dream like we do, of the people we love, but dogs probably dream of playing and eating more than us. Perhaps they don't process trauma or hard things in their sleep but they definitely have dreams.'

Then Myles was silent for a while.

'I have shit dreams – that's why I don't sleep much.'

'That's hard, really hard. Sleep is so important. That's where we empty our brains of all the stuff we don't need, like we put everything away for a new start the next day.'

'I try to sleep and if I do get to sleep I don't stay asleep for long. That's why I stay up, so I get so tired and then my body just gives in.'

Eve nodded. Slowly, slowly, she reminded herself.

'What do you dream about?' She kept her voice casual as she asked such a loaded question.

'My mom,' he said. His voice was flat and he looked out the window.

'Do you miss her?' she asked.

'Fuck no,' he cried and the dog stirred in the back of the

car. 'Shh, it's okay, buddy,' he whispered to the dog, or was that to himself. She wasn't sure.

'Oh okay, you and your mum aren't close?'

He snorted. 'My mother is an abusive bitch who Dad kicked out because she drank so much and the last time she did she hurt Flora and he'd had enough.'

Eve was shocked.

'Not that he kicked her out when I was being abused but hey, it's clear Edward never gave a shit about me. But I have nowhere else to go, so that's why I'm stuck at the stupid house.'

Myles was quiet for a while.

'You know she once said I was her biggest mistake,' he said.

Eve frowned. 'That's a terrible thing to say. I'm so sorry.'

He shrugged. 'It is what it is. She said heaps of shit to me, mostly when Edward wasn't around. It wasn't until she was drunk and pushed Flora over that Edward did something. He will do anything for Flora but not for me.'

Eve knew better than to argue with him about this. It would be invalidating him to try, and she didn't know the truth; only Myles and Edward knew that, and maybe Amber Priest.

'Do you ever hear from her?' she asked.

'Nah, she's partying in LA. She doesn't care about Flora either; she only cares about herself.'

'Do you like Flora?'

He turned to her and frowned. 'Like her? Not really. She's really annoying with her dolls and stupid games.' He paused for a moment. 'I love her though, if that makes sense. I wouldn't want anything to happen to her, which is why I told Edward that Mom had pushed her over and cut Flora's head open.'

Jesus, Eve thought. *What the hell had been happening in that house?*

'I get it. I love my brothers but they really fucking annoy me sometimes.'

Myles laughed. 'They probably say the same thing about you.'

'Probably.'

They drove on and Eve turned up the tunes and they listened, and hummed along as they came into Crossbourne.

'Lucky Mum had everything for Jimmi,' she said as they turned off and drove towards the house.

Donna had been generous with Myles, giving him the dog bed and food and a leash and a very handy book on how to care for a puppy.

'Your mom is amazing,' he said, reaching around to pat Jimmi's body.

'She is. You can borrow her if you like?' Eve smiled and Myles smiled back.

'Can I go there next weekend? I want to take my guitar.'

Eve turned up the driveway to the house. 'If Edward says yes, then it's fine with me.'

Myles made a face. 'I don't have to ask him. He's not my dad.'

'You asked him about the dog,' she said and then saw his face.

'You did ask him didn't you, Myles?'

Myles didn't answer and Eve sighed. 'This isn't going to go well,' she said. 'Don't lie to me ever, okay?' She was furious with him.

'I'm sorry, I just knew he would say no and I already love him.' Myles's voice sounded like it was about to crack.

When they arrived at the house, Eve stopped the car and looked at Myles.

'Good luck with this one.' She sighed and then got out of the car.

Myles clipped on the leash and let the puppy do a wee and then walked inside as Eve followed him. He stood outside Edward's study for a moment and looked at Eve.

'Go on, show him,' she encouraged, hoping Edward wouldn't overreact.

He knocked on the door and she heard his voice.

'Is that you, Eve? Myles with you?'

Myles opened the door and Eve followed behind. *Please don't be an idiot*, she thought as Myles walked into the study. The last thing Myles needed was Edward shooting down his stepson's dreams. Eve held her breath, waiting for Edward to explode but it didn't happen.

'A puppy,' squealed Flora.

'Oh wow,' said Edward. 'What a fine little dog. Did you get him today?'

Edward had lifted the dog from Myles's arms and was showing him to Flora.

'Yes, from Eve's mom. She didn't have a home for him, so I though…' Myles paused. 'I thought we could give him a home. I've named him Jimmi.'

Edward held the dog up and looked into his eyes. 'Pleased to meet you, Jimmi. Welcome home. I can't think of a better man to show you the world than your new owner Myles.'

He handed the dog back to Myles.

'I won't lecture you on all the responsibilities of dog ownership. I assume Eve has already done that?'

Myles gave a little laugh. 'She has and her mom did also.'

'Take him out for another wee – he's sniffing,' said Eve and Myles walked to the door.

'You wanna come, Flors?' he asked and Flora looked as though her world had turned from black and white into technicolour as she ran from the study.

'Take your coat,' called Edward after Flora.

He and Eve faced each other. 'A dog?'

'He was supposed to call you and ask, but he lied and I will deal with that, but he was so smitten. I think he thought you would say no.'

Edward frowned. 'I wouldn't have said no. I think all children should have a family dog, but Amber disagreed. It will be great for him and you are the perfect person to help him with little Jimmi. Are you okay?'

'Fine thanks. Get some words down?' she asked.

'Yes, I wrote two thousand five hundred and thirty-three words,' he said, looking proud of himself.

'Send them to me and I'll get to work,' she said and she turned to leave the study.

He grabbed her hand. 'Eve, what's happened?' he asked.

'Nothing, I just have things to do,' she said and she gave him a thin smile and left the room.

She would never have this conversation with Edward Priest. The man was a flirt, probably slept with anyone who was interested and assumed she was the stupid young girl from the office who was looking for a leg up with a leg over.

She headed to the snug and opened the door and saw her laptop closed. She had left it open when she left the house. She had thought about it when she and Myles left, because she thought the battery would be flat when they returned.

She opened it up and Zara's message flashed on the screen. She scanned it quickly and then closed the laptop again.

God, she hoped Hilditch or – even worse – Edward hadn't seen it. That would be so embarrassing on so many levels. No, it was best she kept this experience professional with Edward. Nothing more than editing his work.

22

The morning sun shone brightly, promising warmth like Edward's smile and interest, but it was all a sham, Eve thought as she stomped around the grounds of Cranberry Cross. She was trying to stay out of Edward's presence as much as possible. For the last three nights she had begged off dinner with him and had eaten one night with Flora and the other night with Myles in the tower, sharing a pizza and crooning over Jimmi, and once in her room.

The more she avoided spending time with Edward, the more keenly she felt him trying to connect with her. Asking her what she wanted for dinner, if she wanted to have lunch with him in Crossbourne, if she wanted to come to a movie with him and Flora.

She was polite but distant. If he was entangled with Serena then she wanted nothing more to do with him than working on his book.

And he seemed to have slowed down on his commitment to the word count of fifteen hundred words per day. He'd delivered eight hundred words the first day and then six hundred the second day, and then five hundred the third day.

She wasn't sure if he was blocked or doing it on purpose, but she wasn't his muse and if he couldn't deliver then that was on him, she had thought as she'd watched Flora digging in the snow under a bare-branched oak tree.

'Any luck with your baby-finding mission?' she asked the little girl as she approached.

Flora stood up, and squinted as she looked at Eve and the sun behind her.

'No, I've lost one of my babies,' she said looking more curious than worried.

'I was sure I put her here but we've had more snow and now she's really deep.'

Eve looked around and saw some gardening equipment in the distance, leaning against a wheelbarrow.

'Then we'll need to dig,' Eve announced and stomped through the snow and onto the gravel path where the snow was melting.

Flora followed her, her little feet leaving marks behind Eve like a baby duck following her mother.

'Here you go,' said Eve, looking into the wheelbarrow and seeing a trowel and handing it to her.

'A little spade,' said Flora proudly.

Eve picked up a large spade and went back to the tree where Flora claimed the doll was buried.

'Here?' she asked.

Flora was already bending down and digging with the trowel, flinging snow with abandon.

'Okay, here it is,' Eve answered her own question, and she put her spade into the snow and dug in deeply, tossing the snow over her shoulder.

Flora watched her and laughed. Soon they were throwing the snow over their shoulders and Flora was screaming with laughter.

Eve couldn't help but join in. It felt good to be doing something physical and Flora was such a joyous spirit.

'Look out.' Eve heard Edward's voice and she turned. He was standing to the side, his hands in the pockets of his navy peacoat, looking annoyingly handsome.

'We're looking for my doll,' said Flora, trowel in hand.

'The doll must be in deep,' he said, and Eve turned her back on him.

She was the one in deep. Why did he have to be so handsome and have such lovely children and such a great house and why, oh why, did he ever sleep with Serena?

'Eve, can I talk to you?'

Eve stuck her spade in and put her foot on the top and then lifted the snow. A naked plastic doll was on the end of the spade, sliced through the middle but hanging off the end of the spade.

'Oh God, I've killed it,' she said without thinking. But Flora didn't seem fazed at all; instead she reached over and pulled the doll from the spade.

'You can't kill something that wasn't even alive, silly,' Flora stated matter-of-factly as she assessed the damage.

'I'm taking her to the hospital,' she said to her father.

'Wise idea,' he said as Flora ran towards the house.

Eve picked up the spade and the trowel and walked past Edward to put the items back where she had found them.

'What's wrong?' he asked her.

'Nothing,' she said, trying to infuse some warmth and nonchalance into her voice.

'That's not true. You're avoiding me.'

Eve gave a false little laugh and hated herself for sounding so insincere.

'I'm fine. I'm just trying to keep professional boundaries,' she said turning to him.

'Did you cross a boundary I wasn't aware of?' He seemed genuinely confused.

'I think maybe taking Myles to my parents and getting the dog,' she lied.

Edward shook his head. 'Let's walk,' he said.

Eve didn't want to walk anywhere with him and not this close with his lovely soapy scent and worry-lined face that she wanted to smooth with her hand.

Instead, she walked with him along the paths, cleared of snow by the gardeners, while a blackbird sang somewhere in the distance.

She said nothing as they walked, waiting for him to fill in the space.

'I don't think you crossed a boundary with Myles. He's been the best I've seen him in days since you took him to your parents'. He's been talking to your brothers on the computer. He's bringing Jimmi into the other rooms, and talking to Flora, helping her connect with the dog. You worked a miracle.'

Eve watched a robin on a tree, flitting from one branch to another.

'There's a robin,' she said pointing at it.

'When robins appear, loved ones are near,' said Edward.

'Isn't that about the dead?' she asked.

'Yes, I think so,' he answered and they stood and watched the bird for a while until, with a shake, it flew away.

'Any dead relatives you're expecting a message from?' she asked with a laugh.

'Nope, I mean my parents are still alive, so maybe a grandparent? What about you?'

'Are your parents still around? That's nice. Do they see the children?'

Edward shrugged. 'They live in Spain. It's been hard to see them lately with everything going on. And Amber, well she didn't like them very much so yes, it was difficult to connect with them the way they wanted.'

'A shame for Flora not to know them well,' she said. 'And Myles.'

They turned and walked towards the house.

'Yes, Myles was always welcomed and cared for by my parents but Amber drove a wedge in there.'

'That's hard,' she said.

'I feel like you're avoiding me and it's not just about Myles and your family.'

'No, not at all,' she lied.

She would fly away with the robin before she admitted to him that she had once held a candle for him.

'I worry and when I worry I can't write,' he said.

Eve looked at him as they walked. 'You have to learn to push through that feeling. Writing should be an escape.'

'I never have learned how to separate very well,' he said. 'Perhaps I have a boundary issue with my publishers and editors.'

Eve wanted to roll her eyes. 'No doubt,' she said as they got to the house. Eve kicked the snow off her boots and opened the door.

'The only advice I can give you is to never shit where you eat,' she said with a sweet smile and she walked inside.

'What do you mean?' He seemed confused.

'I mean, don't get into a personal relationship with your publisher or editor, because it will never end well. You will find you have crossed more boundaries than Genghis Khan and all that is left is destruction and drama.'

Edward frowned. 'I'm lost. What are you talking about, Eve?'

'You, me – it's not going to happen,' she said.

Edward seemed shocked. 'I didn't think it was. I thought we were friendly, that's all. I'm sorry if I gave you that impression or if I made you feel uncomfortable.'

Now Eve felt stupid and presumptuous. 'I mean, sure, I just… I guess, being here.' She stumbled over her words.

'Did you think I was making a move on you or something?'

'It does happen,' she said.

Edward stopped walking. 'I have simply enjoyed having another adult here who I can talk writing with and who seems to care about everyone here. It's just lovely, Eve, and I and the children are so grateful for your company.'

His sincerity was real and Eve felt silly for assuming his need for connection was more than that.

'I'm sorry for assuming your intentions were anything other than friendly.' She laughed. 'Intentions – I sound like Elizabeth Bennet.'

Edward put his hands in his pockets and hunched his shoulders.

'No intentions, I promise,' he said. The watery sunlight made him seem very pale and she saw how tired he looked.

'Anyway, you go and have some thinking time and I'm going to do some work. You're doing really well,' she said and she saw Edward give a small smile.

'We're doing really well,' he said with an emphasis on the

first word. 'It's mutual, Eve, we could be a great team.' He paused. 'Editorially I mean.'

Eve nodded. 'Of course, I didn't think you meant otherwise. Thank you.'

Edward opened the door, allowing her to step through first. Now they were so formal with each other that Eve felt embarrassed.

She was so used to younger men crossing boundaries with her that Edward's almost chivalrous behaviour was taken as something more.

Eve took off her coat and hung it on the peg near the kitchen door.

'To work then,' she exclaimed as though going into battle.

'Once more unto the writer's desk, dear friend, once more,' Edward said and he disappeared down the hallway.

23

Eve's phone rang as she was deep into a crucial chapter of Edward's book. It was annoying how easily he told a story. Short, crisp sentences with an exceptional yet relatable vocabulary that allowed him to say so much. His book was a page-turner and, at times, when Eve read it she forgot she was supposed to be reading like an editor, not as a reader. The pace was thrilling, and the character insights made her want to be friends with the main character.

The phone rattled her and she took a moment to mentally come back into the room.

'Zars,' she said, happy to see her friend's name on the screen.

'Hey, guess what?'

'What?'

'Claudia's pregnant.'

'Oh wow, lovely,' said Eve, trying to remember who Claudia was.

As though reading her mind Zara went on. 'She's the editor in young adult and they're moving Peter from fiction there as he wants to work in YA – God knows why, so much angst or too many dragons – anyway, so there is a spot for a new editor and they're recruiting in-house.'

Zara took a breath.

Eve sat up straight in her chair.

'Oh God, okay, I have to go for it.'

'Yes you do and Serena promised you would get the next editing gig, remember? She said it when you didn't get Rami's role.'

Eve snarled thinking about Serena's double-cross. Rami was junior and had started a year after Eve, and yet she was promoted even after Serena had said Eve should go for the role.

Serena had said it was because she had too much work for Eve to do and she would be sure to get the next opening on the fiction team – and Rami would only be getting romance anyway, which Eve didn't like.

This wasn't true but Eve hadn't argued. Eve was happy to edit anything other than Serena's schedule for her teeth cleaning, waxing and eyebrow threading.

'Okay, when is the email going out?' she asked, opening her work email and scrolling through the demands from Serena that she had been ignoring for three days.

'Tomorrow morning, so get your CV ready. This is your time to shine, woman. Later.'

Zara hung up and Eve stared at the computer screen for a moment. To get out from under Serena. To have her own list. To grow and nurture authors whose work she cared about. To champion from acquisition to best-seller list. *Oh please make it so*, she prayed to the goddess of junior editors, whoever that was.

And then she wouldn't have to do jobs like this, working with handsome and charming authors who pretended to be interested in her to only find out he was interested in her boss.

No, she wasn't ever going to do anything like this again once she got the promotion.

She searched through her folders and found her CV.

It was old and she hadn't updated it since her last attempt at a promotion; but two years later, she had runs on the board. Even if Serena took credit for them she would know that Eve did them when it came time to assess her application. Surely Serena wouldn't pretend that the work she had done was hers when Eve was going for this role?

But she knew Serena better than most. Of course she would take all the credit unless Eve appealed to Serena's vanity.

That was the only way to work a woman like Serena. Tell her she was her mentor, that Eve, the little fledgling was ready to leave the nest and she couldn't have done any of it without her lovely mistress Serena.

Even thinking about the load of rubbish she would have to write in the cover letter made her scowl but needs must, she thought and she opened a new document and started to type.

When she had finished she sat back and read it again, correcting a few typos and spacing.

Who said she couldn't write fiction as well as edit it? She laughed. It was the perfect letter for her application. Respectful, admiring, subservient and with just enough smarts to make Serena think she had taught Eve all she knew.

Once she updated her résumé, then it would be ready to send off the moment the email was released to the company.

She pressed save and then closed her laptop.

She was ready; she could feel it.

24

Edward lifted up the bottle to fill Eve's wine glass.

'No thanks,' she said. 'I'm not drinking. I need to keep my head clear.'

The kitchen door opened and Jimmi ran in and jumped up at Edward as Myles came in and sat next to Eve.

Edward put the wine down.

'I probably shouldn't either. I need to keep getting those words onto the page or Eve Pilkins will have my head on a silver platter.'

'Why a silver platter?' asked Flora. 'Why not a gold platter? Or a china plate? Or even a cutting board?'

Myles laughed. 'What about a pizza box?'

'Would it have to be rolled flat?' pondered Flora. 'We could put your head under the car wheel.'

'Enough,' said Eve laughing. 'You two are so gruesome sometimes.'

'They really are my children,' said Edward laughing along.

Eve noticed Myles glance at Edward and then look down at Jimmi who was sitting under his feet.

'Righto, what's Hil left us for dinner?' she asked cheerfully.

'Poo on a stick,' said Flora and then she laughed loudly.

'Flora, please,' Edward said sternly but Flora was still laughing to herself.

'You're such a loser,' said Myles but not meanly.

'I know.' Flora laughed and Myles joined in.

'She's nuts,' he said to Eve.

'We're all a little bit nuts; that's what makes us interesting.' Edward lifted the lid of the cast-iron pot.

'A lovely chicken cassoulet and some crunchy bread and chocolate pudding for dessert,' Edward said. 'I'll be mother and serve.'

It was hard for Eve not to imagine what it would be like if this were her life. If these were her children or Edward were hers. She tried not to but it was as though her mind went to the place she shouldn't, and she was suddenly fantasising about a life she would never have. She didn't even want that life, did she?

'Eve?' Edward's voice broke through her thoughts. 'Plate?'

She handed him her plate and he served her dinner.

'Can I see the twins on the weekend?' Myles asked Eve.

She looked at Edward and then at Myles.

'I have no idea. Can you see the twins on the weekend?'

'What do you mean?' Myles looked confused.

'I mean, I can't give you permission, only Edward can, and if he says yes, and the twins are free, then I guess you can, but I'm not the person to ask.'

Myles sighed and looked at Edward. 'May I please go and see the twins on the weekend?'

Edward passed the bread around. 'Sure, I can drive you,' he said.

'Oh, you don't need to do that,' Eve said quickly.

'Why not? I should meet these boys he's spending time with. God knows what their family's like.'

Eve laughed. 'Yes, they are certainly an unusual bunch. The older sister is a real piece of work I've heard.'

Edward laughed. 'Why don't we take him to your family's house and then we can head into Leeds and do some Christmas shopping?' he suggested.

'Cool,' said Myles, and he started to eat his dinner with some level of enthusiasm.

Flora nodded. 'I need a new doll. My other one can't be stuck together.'

Eve made a face. 'Sorry about that.'

'It's okay,' said Flora. 'She had other problems as well. These things happen.'

Edward ran his hand through his hair and shook his head.

'I see what you mean about *The Turn of the Screw* thing now,' he said to Eve in a low voice.

She smiled back and they held eye contact for a moment longer than Eve expected and she knew she was blushing. Why the hell did she blush so much around this man? He must think she had a faulty internal thermometer. She had told him she wasn't interested in anything more than a professional relationship and he had said that was all it was, so why was she acting like a smitten schoolgirl around him?

Edward shifted in his seat and she felt his foot touch hers and then move away quickly.

'Is Jimmi under the table?' Edward asked, reddening.

'No, he's with me.' Myles looked down at the dog under his chair. 'Why?'

'Thought I felt him,' said Edward quickly and he and Eve ate in silence for the rest of the meal, while the children chattered enough between them for it not to be too noticeable.

After dinner, Edward took Flora to have her bath and put her to bed, and Eve cleaned up the kitchen and put on the dishwasher.

Myles sat in the kitchen, feeding Jimmi tiny pieces of chicken.

'I think Edward likes you,' he said.

'I like him. He's a nice man,' she answered, as she rinsed out the cast-iron pot.

'No, I mean *likes you* likes you.'

'Don't be silly – he's just being polite.'

'Edward isn't polite to anyone, so I think he's into you.'

Eve shook her head. 'He's just being kind because I'm working on his book, that's all. We have a good professional relationship. Not everyone who gets along well is in love with each other.'

Myles sighed and patted Jimmi. 'Sometimes I wish you were my mom.'

Eve was silent. She would never say that she wished she was his mother also, and Flora's, and that she and Edward were together and that living at Cranberry Cross was some obscure fantasy of a literary bucolic paradise that would never exist in reality.

'You have a mum,' she said gently. 'And although it might seem like she's far away…'

'She is far away; she's in America,' he scoffed.

'I mean mentally, emotionally, I think she loves you very much.'

Myles rolled his eyes. 'I know exactly who my mom is, yet every adult I know tries to convince me otherwise. As though I'm stupid. They want her to care because it makes them feel better about the fact my mother hates me, because it means they look at themselves and wonder if their mother loves them or if they even love their own children.'

Eve put down the washcloth and dried her hands on a tea towel and sat down opposite him.

'I think that's the smartest thing I've ever heard anyone say about anything and I have worked with a lot of smart people.'

Myles shrugged.

'No really, I think you're right.'

She sat back and thought about what he'd said. He was right. People didn't want to hear what children say let alone their opinion on parenting by their parents. Some parents were shitty by nature and Amber Priest seemed to be one of them, addiction or not.

'I know Edward loves you,' she said.

Myles shrugged again. 'Maybe but it doesn't matter. I have Jimmi now.' He leaned down and kissed the dog's head.

'It does matter,' Eve said. 'You matter to Edward and Flora, to Hil and to me, and now to the twins. They have been annoying me about you, wondering when you're coming back.'

Myles looked up, his eyes sparkling. 'Really? I mean I

talk to them a bit but I didn't want to ask them if they like me cos that would be lame.'

'They like you, you big loser.'

'Takes one to know one,' he said and they smiled at each other.

'You're a good person,' she said. 'Jimmi is lucky to have you.'

'And Edward is lucky to have you,' said Myles and he paused. 'We all are.'

Eve looked down at her hands, afraid he would see her tears. Everyone in this house was desperate for love in a way that made her heart ache. She might be the child of bus drivers and went to a state school and worked through school to pay for any extras but her house was filled with love. She had parents who listened and who tried to improve their own lives so they could provide more for their family. It wasn't that Edward didn't provide but he was emotionally stunted in a way white men who grew up with money often were. He didn't have to try to understand because his money was enough of a bargaining chip. He thought he could solve everything with money. Myles's depression, Flora's loss of her mother, Amber's addiction. If he just stopped for a moment and saw the emotional needs of those around him, then he might not be in this mess.

But it wasn't her problem, she reminded herself. None of this was her problem and once the book was delivered she would be able to take her promotion and never work with Edward Priest again.

So why did that make her feel so sad?

25

Edward clipped Flora's seatbelt tight in the back of the car, as Myles put his on and clipped Jimmi into his special seat between them.

'Jimmi has his own belt now,' said Flora patting the puppy's head.

'He does,' said Edward. 'All three of my babies lined up, safe and secure.'

He saw Myles wince.

'Not that you're my baby anymore, Myles.' He laughed.

'I was never your baby,' Myles mumbled but Edward heard.

He got into the driver's seat and adjusted the rear-view mirror.

'I know, that's a big regret of mine – not knowing you as a baby. I think you would have been one of those wise babies, who came into the world knowing things already. Unlike your sister who is definitely a new soul.'

He could see Myles was looking out the window. 'Shame we won't ever know,' Myles said and Edward wished he hadn't brought it up. He was trying to let Myles know he loved him like his own flesh and blood but he couldn't seem to do it very well.

Eve got into the car. 'Gosh sorry, I had to send an email.' Her face was flushed and she was breathless as she clipped her belt securely.

'Sounds important,' he said.

'It is.' She smiled mysteriously and wiggled her eyebrows at him and he laughed.

'Is it about me?' he asked and heard how pathetic he sounded.

'Not everything is about you, Mr Priest.'

'I know, it was a stupid question.' He turned on the car and they drove down the driveway.

'Myles? You want to choose the playlist?' she asked.

Myles connected his phone and soon guitar music was playing in the car.

'Who is this playing?' asked Edward.

'Santana,' Eve and Myles said in unison.

'You two are really into music.' Edward laughed again.

Myles played his favourite tunes all the way to Leeds, and Eve talked about some of them to Edward: why they were important guitar pieces, when they were written and who was playing them.

Edward didn't really care about the music as much as he wanted to hear Eve's opinion on everything. He could listen to her read the election rolls, he thought as she clapped in time to some songs and sang along to others with no vanity or shyness. She had a good voice and sometimes she and Myles would sing loudly to a song they both loved and he could see Flora bouncing in her seat in time with them, keen to be a part of the car chaos.

At times Edward wondered if this was what it was like to be a family, remembering Amber did nothing with them.

How many times had he wished to go out like this, and she would tell him she wasn't up to it, or felt unwell?

They arrived in Leeds, and Eve directed them to her parents' house.

'Dad and Mum are both home today,' she said happily as he parked the car.

Edward opened the door and what felt like nerves hit him. He hadn't been nervous since he was a teenager but, now, he felt his stomach flipping and his muscles were tense. What was he nervous about? Meeting Eve's parents? How ridiculous, he told himself as he helped Myles with Jimmi.

Eve was already at the front door of the house and then two people were hugging her.

He was jealous of them for an instant.

'Edward, these are my parents, Donna and Sam Pilkins. Mum, Dad, this is Edward Priest.'

Sam Pilkins was a small man with a wiry frame and a nose broken long ago. Edward noticed his big hands when he shook one of them and the piercing look Eve's father gave him.

Sam was probably fifteen years older than Edward but he looked like he could outdo him in any physical sport.

Donna was an older version of Eve with dark hair but cut short and an open heart-shaped face and a happy smile.

'Edward, what a great son you have.' Donna hugged him and he laughed and turned to Myles.

'He's a good kid, I know.'

Myles rolled his eyes but didn't seem so off-put, and not when the twins came running downstairs.

'Come inside,' said Donna taking Flora's hand.

'Would you like to see a new kitten I have?' she asked the child who nodded vigorously.

'Look but don't bring it home,' said Edward firmly, following them into the house.

If he expected a simple, humble home, he was mistaken. It was an ode to Christmas décor with lights, trees, decorations on every conceivable surface.

'We really love Christmas,' Eve whispered and he felt her nearness intoxicating.

'I can see that,' he whispered back.

'I think it's the combo birthday and Christmas energy that makes Mum hyped about this time of the year.' She laughed.

'We're going to the garage,' said Myles, Jimmi following him along with the other dogs in the house. 'Sam is showing us a new set-up for the amp he did for the band.'

Flora was in the kitchen, looking into a box with Donna pointing out the new kitten.

Edward walked around the living room, looking at the photos of Eve and the twins through various stages of their lives.

'You look like you had a happy childhood,' he said to her.

She sat on the sofa. 'Yes, we did. Simple but we were encouraged to follow our interests. Mum and Dad weren't given the same opportunity. Mum should have been a vet, and Dad would have been an amazing teacher. But they both finished school early and worked because they had to. Met while driving buses and fell madly in love. Had me. Then had to wait thirteen years before Mum had the twins but here we are.'

Edward sat in an armchair and thought about his father. Upper-middle class, university-educated, banker, married a girl from his circle and that was it. No struggles really, but also not great happiness. He wondered, at times, if his parents should have stayed married, their emotional distance so apparent to him growing up.

Now they seemed to have a great companionship but he wouldn't have ever said it was a grand love affair.

'Daddy, can I stay here with Donna? She said I can feed the kitten his bottle.'

Edward looked at Eve who shrugged and threw her hands up. 'How can we compete with giving a kitten a bottle?' she asked.

'We can't,' he said and looked at Donna who was in the doorway.

'As long as it's okay with you?'

Donna smiled at Flora. 'It's perfect. I love the company of little ones. I miss my lot being this age. And she can feed him while I fold the washing.'

Edward saw the joy in Flora's face and wondered if he had ever seen her as happy as she was in that moment.

'So, it's you and me and the Christmas shopping?' he said to Eve.

'I guess it is.'

His stomach flipped again at the thought of having Eve all to himself for a few hours.

'And you're all coming for the birthdays and Christmas Day?' Donna asked.

'If that's still fine with you?'

'It's more than fine; it's perfect,' said Donna as Sam came inside. 'Isn't it, Sam?'

'What?' Sam's gruff voice answered.

'That Edward and Eve and the kids come here for Christmas and the birthday party?'

'I expected Eve to be here anyway, but no skin off my nose if the others come,' he said and came and stood over the chair where Edward was sitting.

He looked up at the man, wondering what he was doing.

'You're in Dad's chair,' said Eve with a laugh.

'Oh gosh, sorry.' Edward jumped up and gestured for Sam to sit down.

Sam sat with a harrumph and opened the newspaper on the small table next to him.

'Righto, we're off then,' said Eve cheerfully. 'Back soonish maybe.'

'No rush pet,' said Donna and she patted Edward on the shoulder as they walked to the door.

'Don't mind Sam – he's very protective of his Evie. Hasn't liked any of her boyfriends yet.'

'I'm not her boyfriend,' he started to say but Donna smiled at him and screwed her nose up.

'Shh, off you go now. Drive safely.'

And she pushed him out the front door and towards her daughter who was already waiting by the car.

Why could everyone else see it except Eve or didn't she want to see what he was feeling? He didn't understand but he wanted to and maybe this trip would help him make it clear to her how he felt, if only he was brave enough to take his chance.

26

Leeds was busy with shoppers and families visiting Father Christmas and ice-skating at Millennium Square.

Edward bought them coffees and they watched for a while, laughing at the attempts, falls and admiring those who could actually skate.

'I haven't done something like this in a long time,' said Edward. 'I usually do the shopping online or give Myles money.'

'That's not very festive of you,' she said.

'I'm not usually very festive.' He laughed. 'But now I know it's a certain someone's birthday, I am all in, as Myles says.'

He turned to her and she saw the look in his eye. He wanted to tell her something but she wasn't sure she wanted to hear it.

'Excuse me?' Eve heard a voice and she turned.

An older woman and man stood next to them.

'Are you Edward Priest?' she asked.

Edward shook his head. 'Sadly not, I wish I had his money – or money for every time someone asked me that.'

Eve tried not to laugh as he spoke.

'Oh just as well then, Dave here used to be a big fan but

his last book went on and on, like he wanted to tell us all how smart he was. "Just get on with the story," Dave said. Didn't you, Dave?'

Dave nodded in agreement. 'At least now we don't have to lie. Have a lovely Christmas.'

The couple wandered off and Eve burst into laughter.

'That was more brutal than the Goodreads review I got that read that they thought I was writing my books with AI technology until they realised that AI software had more self-awareness.'

Eve screamed with laughter. 'Stop, it's too funny.'

Edward leaned over the railing and looked at the skaters below.

'It's a tough gig, this entertaining people.'

'Do you want me to feel sorry for you?' Eve teased. 'I know what your royalties are, so I will find it hard to feel sad for you. But Dave? He deserves more. He works hard, he is married to that woman, he deserves the escape and adventure and instead you deliver him a dry history lesson.'

Edward groaned. 'I know, that's why I changed genre. Our Dave isn't wrong. It was a boring book to write so it would have been equally boring to read.'

'Unlike your new crime novel, which will soon become the greatest detective series since Dublin Murder Squad.'

Edward tapped the plastic lid of his takeaway coffee with his fingernail. 'I was thinking, do you think I need to give my detective, Anna, a love interest? I was thinking she could have a husband who is tired of her always working so late and have some tension at home?'

Eve groaned and put her head down onto her hands. 'Spare me.'

'What? What do you mean?'

Eve turned to him. 'You know, I watched this TV show a year or so ago, and it was about a woman who was a detective and she was investigating a serial killer, and one of the things I liked the most about the show – and it was a really good show by the way. I'll try and remember the name and you should watch it.' She paused. 'What I liked about it was that it didn't fall to some patriarchal trope of the man competing for the woman's time. The husband of this detective was totally on board with her solving this crime. He said he was all over taking care of the kids and the home while she did the police work because it mattered to the community. It was more important than his bloody ego.'

Edward's eyes widened.

'So don't fall for this trope that so many men write. You know what would be great? If she was either single and absolutely cool with it and had new lovers often and always, or she was happily in a relationship with a really supportive partner – male or female – who brings her cups of tea when she's working late and folds the washing and tells the children that Mummy is actually making a difference to the world. Why isn't mass murder enough drama? Why do we then have to show women supposedly neglecting their duties as a mother? Or a wife?'

He was silent for a moment.

'You're right.' He walked to the rubbish and threw his coffee cup away and then came back to Eve's side.

'You're so right that it's embarrassing to hear to be honest. I'm embarrassed for every man who has ever resorted to that trope. It is insulting.'

Eve smiled and patted him on the arm. 'When you know better you do better, Mr Priest.'

'Do you think my writing is sexist?' he asked.

She shrugged and made a face. 'It's a bit sexist, but not overtly like a James Bond book but more dismissive. Women often serve a purpose in your books to work as an exposition device but they're archetypes. The wise older woman or the sassy, beautiful waitress. They aren't even main characters; they merely point the way for your main character to go to next. And he never says thank you to them.'

Edward put his hand up. 'Between you and Dave's wife's review, I'm feeling a little tender now.'

'Come on, tender man, let's go shopping,' she teased. 'I'll buy you a notebook to write down your feelings about this new personal awareness.'

'You know every writer is a sucker for a new notebook,' he said and he wished she would tuck her arm in his and they could walk through Leeds showing off their love to the city.

Instead, her hands were firmly in her coat pockets, a warm scarf around her neck, partially covering her mouth, and a woollen hat on her pretty head, her bob cut framing her perfect face.

'Do you have a list?' she asked.

'I'm not really a list sort of a person,' he said, standing out the front of a bookstore. 'Shall we see if they have any of my books?'

'Get over yourself.' Eve laughed but Edward walked into the store and headed to the fiction section.

'Oh look they have four of the last one and two of the ones before that.'

'Okay, feeling better now, Duke Needy?'

Edward looked at the spines of the books on the shelves.

'You know, you never get tired of seeing them in store. It's still my biggest thrill. Like the first time Serena took a chance on me and published *The Stained-Glass Mirror*.'

'That's still a stupid title,' she said, picking up a copy of a new book she had been meaning to read.

'It is, but Serena titled it so you should tell her,' he said. 'We had an argument about it but it did make people think and she knew what worked for this market.'

Eve walked away at the mention of Serena's name. She had sent her application for the job off before she had got into the car to come to Leeds and hoped Serena would see merit in the application.

But now she was with Edward and she had almost forgotten she was supposed to be keeping boundaries strong and instead they were shopping like a married couple while her parents looked after his children.

'I might get Myles a book about guitars,' he said as he came to her side.

'Boring,' she said.

'Rude.' He laughed.

She turned to him.

'Did you and Serena have an affair?' she asked, hurdling over the supposed boundaries she had just been thinking about.

'What?' He laughed.

'My friend at work said that you and Serena were lovers.'

'Lovers? That's a very old-fashioned term.' He smiled at her, his eyes catching hers then searching her face.

'Okay, she said that you two had sex.'

He frowned. 'Why do you want to know?'

Eve regretted the question immediately, but she also couldn't pretend it didn't annoy her. But Edward owed nothing to her, not even an answer to the question.

'I don't, forget I asked. It's just gossip.' She picked up a photography book of dogs catching treats. 'This will be good for Mum.'

'Would it matter to you if I had?' he asked.

His face was close to hers and she opened her mouth, trying to speak or breathe; she wasn't sure when she was this close to him.

'Edward Priest, what an honour to have you in our store,' said a loud voice and Eve saw a man behind him. 'Would you consider signing the books of yours we have on the shelf? We usually have more but yours sell so quickly, we can't keep up.'

Edward turned to the man, his face calm, impassive. 'Absolutely, I would love to.'

Eve paid for the book for her mother and went and waited as Edward signed the books and took photos with the staff and a few people in the store who knew him.

As he signed the last book, Eve saw Dave and his wife walk into the shop.

Eve started to giggle as she saw the look on Dave's wife's face.

'He's not Edward Priest,' she said loudly. 'He's an imposter. I hope you didn't pay him.'

Edward looked at Eve who was now wiping tears from her eyes.

'Let's get out of here,' he said and he took her arm and they ran from the store like shoplifting teenagers.

They ran up Briggate, laughing, her hand in his as he pulled her into a side street and then down into a laneway, and he pushed her up against a wall.

His mouth hovered around hers, as though looking for permission.

'I never slept with Serena. I would never sleep with Serena. We were not lovers.'

Eve looked up at him, wanting this to be true.

'I have not been with any woman since Amber left. I haven't wanted to be with any woman until you, Eve Pilkins, came into my life and turned it upside down.'

He took a deep breath and paused.

She could feel him against her body. Her hands wanted to touch him, her mouth to kiss him; she wanted everything in that moment.

But she ducked down and out from under the bridge he had made with his arms.

'Eve,' he pleaded.

She shook her head. 'Not until the book is finished,' she said huskily. 'I won't be that woman. I don't want people gossiping about me the way they do about Serena.'

She looked at him. 'I've applied for a promotion at work, and if I get it, I want it to be because of my work. I don't want people to think I got it because I slept with our biggest author.'

Edward nodded. 'Okay, I understand that, I do. But it still doesn't mean I don't want to kiss you.'

She felt like her knees were going to give way but she knew she had to live by her values or she would never forgive herself.

'Then finish the book,' she said.

'And when I do, then you will disappear back to London,' he said.

'I don't know what I'll do, Edward,' she said and then she stepped forward and kissed his cheek, slowly, lingeringly.

'Don't try and read the last page before the story is finished. Let's just wait and find out what happens in the end. The fun part is how we get there, and you have to finish your book first.'

Edward's mouth kissed her chin, and her cheeks, and her ear and then her neck and she leaned into him a longer moment than she should have, but she couldn't pull herself away.

'You promise we will get a happy ever after?' he whispered to her.

And for a moment, her mouth found his, and they kissed, in a laneway in Leeds ten days before Christmas.

'Anything is possible,' she whispered back.

27

The memory of Eve's mouth on his was distracting Edward from writing. The feel of her body against him was interrupting his thoughts. The need to touch her again was causing him to get up from his desk chair and look out the window to see if she was in the snow with Myles or Flora.

The shopping was successful but mostly because they decided to agree on everything and, sometimes, they touched hands over a suggested gift and he felt electric shocks through his body.

He could have sworn on a Bible that Eve's mother knew something had happened when they went back to her parents' house. She had a small smile playing at her mouth whenever he looked at Eve or asked Eve a question or told her parents what a wonderful editor Eve was and how she had helped him enormously.

The trip home after they picked up the children from her parents' was thick with tension. All he wanted to do was put his hand on her thigh as he drove but Myles and Flora talked constantly all the way and sometimes she twisted in her chair to talk to them and he couldn't concentrate with her nearer than before.

He didn't know if he had ever been as distracted as he was by Eve.

'Concentrate,' he said aloud, willing himself to sit down and write.

A knock at the door relieved him from his angst. 'Come in,' he said, hopeful it was Eve but it was Hilditch.

She came inside and closed the door.

'You okay?' he asked.

Hilditch sighed. 'I'm fine but I don't think you will be when I tell you what I just found out.'

Edward gestured for her to sit down but Hilditch shook her head.

'Amber's coming back.'

Edward sat down instead. 'What? How do you know?'

Hilditch raised an eyebrow. 'She messaged me to tell me it was a surprise and that she would be back for Christmas lunch.'

'Holy hell.' Edward sighed.

'I told her that I don't believe in surprises, which I don't, and that I would be telling you. I would expect a call any moment.'

As though summoned by Hilditch herself, his phone rang.

'Christ on a bike,' he said and he saw Hilditch laugh a little.

'You sound like Miss Eve.'

He looked at the screen on his phone. 'Los Angeles area code.' He put the phone down. 'I need to think. I'll call her later.'

'You can't have her back here,' she said with a warning in her voice.

'I know, but she's the mother of the children. I can't ignore that.'

Edward sat for a moment. 'We're going to Eve's family for Christmas,' he said firmly. 'Amber can wait in line.'

Hilditch paused. 'She said she wants to take the children back to Los Angeles.'

Edward laughed. 'Over my dead body she will. She's not fit to be a parent.'

But Hilditch shook her head, 'Unless you decide to do something about this in court, then she does have a right even if she isn't fit to parent.'

'I don't have time for her right now,' he said. 'Maybe she can come and see the children after Christmas and we can try and find time for her to visit?'

'You think Amber is going to be satisfied with a visit?'

Edward put his head back against the chair and closed his eyes. 'I pay for everything, because I've realised I pay her to stay away from us all.'

He looked at Hilditch. 'For the first time Myles is eating dinner with us, he's playing with Flora, he isn't screaming at me. He has friends.'

But Hilditch snorted at him.

'That's not because Amber is away, it's because Eve is here. She's the glue in all of this.'

He nodded at her words.

'I know.'

'So what happens when Eve returns to her life?'

Edward couldn't bear to think about it. He needed to finish the book and then he could be with Eve but Amber coming back to Cranberry Cross was not ever in the way he had plotted out his and Eve's ending.

'I need to write,' he said to Hilditch. 'But thank you for telling me. I'll call her and work it out.'

Hilditch left him alone again and he picked up his phone and texted Amber.

Hil tells me you're coming to town. We have plans for Christmas and won't be here until the new year. Please let me know when you wish to see them. They don't need surprises from you. We also need to discuss the divorce and the children staying on with me full-time. You can visit them when I'm here but you can't have them until I know you are sober for a year and have regular drug and alcohol tests. This is not negotiable, Amber.

Ed

He pressed send and heard the whooshing noise as it made its way to Amber. This was the right thing to do. No matter how much Flora yearned for her mother, it wasn't who Amber could be or had ever been. And he knew forcing Myles back to try and connect to Amber was fraught and would set him back in his trust of adults.

He moved back to his desk and looked at the paragraphs he had written.

Onwards, he told himself and he started to write.

28

Edward came into the living room and sat down with a tired sigh.

'She wanted me to read four books and tell her the story of when she was born and then asked a lot of questions about how she was made and her birth that frankly I was unprepared for,' he said.

Eve looked up from her book and laughed. 'Do you need me to talk you through it?'

Edward made a face at her. 'No thank you, I'm well aware. I was there, remember? It's funny though, she won't ask me about these things for ages and then all the questions will come at once, and they are more evolved than the last round.'

'That's called growing up,' Eve said.

'True,' he agreed. 'But I feel like Myles was born knowing everything about the world and more.'

'But Myles had to learn early,' said Eve. 'He didn't get to slowly discover the world can be a shitty place. Amber showed him from day dot probably, even before you were in their lives.'

Edward stared into the distance. 'You're right,' he said.

Eve went back to reading her book.

'What are you reading?' he asked, peering at the cover.

'A Scandi crime book, pretty good but gruesome.'

'It's the cold and no darkness for parts of the year – that's why they write cruelty so well, makes them angry,' said Edward.

'You're generalising. Don't forget Moomins came from Finland, and they're very whimsical.'

'The hippopotamus trolls? Ah yes, Flora has a picture book of them. Weird little creatures.'

He was silent for a while.

'Is crime your favourite genre?'

She put her book down. 'No, I like anything really, well maybe not sci-fi but that's because I don't have the patience to mentally teleport my mind into another galaxy.'

Edward smiled. 'But you can transport yourself to the fjords running with blood and villains hiding in the forests?'

'Quite easily,' she admitted. 'What about you? What's your favourite genre to read?'

Edward thought for a moment. 'I think it's historical fiction, but I will be honest with you... I stopped reading a few years ago. I just didn't have time and I think it's really affected my writing.'

Eve nodded. 'That makes sense. I think writers need to stay relevant in their style and see what else is being written. Also good writing can be motivating to try and replicate in your own work.'

'That's a good point.'

'What about your favourite film? Is there one you could watch once a month and not get sick of?' she asked.

'God, films are another thing I have left to my former life.

I loved Hitchcock films, and I also loved *Notting Hill*,' he said, looking a little bit sheepish.

'*Notting Hill?* The romcom with Julia Roberts and Hugh Grant?' Eve asked, trying to make sense of his admission.

'What? It's a great film. And Julia's smile, I mean, there's nothing like it is there?'

Eve started to laugh loudly, feeling tears in her eyes. 'You, Edward Priest, like a romcom movie?'

He leaned forward, speaking in a conspiratorial tone. 'I like lots of romcoms, as you call them.'

'Oh yes? Tell me your top five then,' she challenged.

'Only five?' he scoffed.

She lifted her head to meet his challenge. 'I am a seasoned romcom watcher with my flatmates, so tell me what you have and I will tell you if you have any taste or not.'

Edward ran his hand through his hair.

'That's a very Hugh Grant thing you do with your hair,' she teased.

'Thank you,' he said and she laughed again. 'Okay let me think.'

'*When Harry Met Sally. Sleepless in Seattle. Four Weddings and a Funeral.*'

'Good start,' she said.

He thought for a moment. '*Groundhog Day.*'

'Oh perfect, that is a good one,' she agreed.

'*Moonstruck.*'

'I haven't seen that,' Eve admitted.

'Then you have lost,' he said throwing his hands up.

'What? Why? Because I haven't seen one of them?' she asked.

'Yes, one of the best with Cher and Nicolas Cage and New York as the backdrop.'

'We should watch it,' she said suddenly and she took the remote control and turned on the television.

'Is it on?' he asked. 'That's a coincidence.'

Eve laughed hysterically.

'What?' he asked, seemingly offended.

'I'm going to rent it online and play it through the TV. It's called technology, old man.'

It was Edward's turn to laugh. 'Fair point. I've realised I don't read anymore, watch films or keep up with technology. I really am in stasis. Thank God you're here to bring me into the new world.'

Eve found the film and pressed play. 'Okay, let's see why you think this film is so good then.' She sat back on the sofa and curled her legs up next to her. 'Come and sit next to me.' She patted the seat next to her and Edward came to her side.

'So I guess the writing schedule is on hold tonight if this movie is playing?'

She laughed. 'We must have some play, otherwise all work makes us very dull.'

'It won't be dull. But I can't promise I won't get distracted and try and kiss you,' he said, nuzzling her ear as the music started.

'You can kiss me afterwards,' she said. 'I promise.'

She leaned her head on his shoulder, the scent of his cologne and his wool jumper soothing as Cher took her through New York and falling in love.

Please let nothing ruin this for us, Eve thought as she felt Edward's lips on the top of her head.

It was perfect right now. She never wanted this time to end.

29

The sound of Jimmi barking and feet running down the hallway welcomed Eve as she came inside the house.

Flora had tied a pink ribbon to his collar and was holding on to the end of it.

'Myles said I can use this as an indoor lead,' she announced, 'and since he's spending the night at the twins' house, Jimmi is going to sleep in my room with me.'

Eve patted the dog on the head. 'Jimmi will love being in your room. Where will you put his bed?'

She and Flora walked towards the snug, the dog leading the way.

Edward's door opened, and their eyes met.

'All okay?'

'All is fine,' she said with a smile. 'Go and write or there will be no supper.'

Edward growled at her and closed the door.

'Any babies buried in the garden today?' she asked Flora as they went into the snug and Jimmi jumped onto the sofa.

She thought about telling him off but the sofa was very comfortable and got the best of the light in the morning.

'I haven't buried any babies lately,' said Flora. She sat

on the ground facing Jimmi, stroking his head. 'I think I'm growing out of that now.'

Eve nodded and turned her head away so Flora wouldn't see her smile.

'I understand. I was really into horses for a while and then one day I woke up and thought, Horses, schmorses, who cares?'

'What did you like instead?' asked Flora.

Eve thought for a moment. 'The guitar. And books.'

Flora sighed. 'I don't know what I'm into now but I like being inside more than I used to, especially when I hang out here with you and since Myles has been nice to me. And also because of Jimmi.'

Eve understood Flora even if Flora didn't understand herself yet.

No child should feel unsafe in their own home, yet Flora had for so long.

Eve checked her emails and answered a few, but there was nothing from Serena about her application. Not even an acknowledgement of receipt. And Serena had stopped asking to read the pages. Something else had diverted her attention and it nagged at Eve. Something was going on and she wasn't sure what but with Serena, it was rarely good.

She wondered if she should send off an email to human resources and ask them how the vetting of the candidates was going but she thought that would be too pushy.

'We should take Jimmi outside to go for a wee,' said Eve, needing to get away from her computer.

'He did a wee before, in the hallway. Hil was cross but

then she patted Jimmi and said that sometimes when you have to go you have to go.'

Eve laughed and moved to the sofa with Jimmi.

Flora climbed up onto Eve's lap and curled up, her breath blowing onto her neck.

Jimmi rolled onto his back, his big feet dangling in the air.

Eve closed her eyes for a moment. This was peaceful, she thought, and wondered if she was feeling content or sleepy or both until she didn't have to ask herself. She was asleep.

Edward read through the chapters Eve had edited. It was cleaner than his original version and she pushed him to write in detail, the sort of writing he liked, walking the reader through the red herrings, the murders, the evidence, the fake alibis and false witnesses.

He had the ideas and could put the words into order to tell a story, but Eve made it come alive.

Picking up his phone, he dialled a number on speed dial.

'Serena, how are you?'

'Edward, how's the book going?'

'That's why I'm calling, actually.'

'Don't tell me Eve isn't up to it? She can be very capricious. Don't worry, I will be looking at it closely in case she's missed things.'

Edward laughed. 'No I'm actually calling to say she's amazing and this book is a testament to her skills.' He paused knowing Serena needed flattery first. 'It's clear she learned from a master.'

'You're too kind,' she cooed.

'I don't want anyone else working on my books at Henshaw and Carlson now,' he said.

'But I look after you, Edward.' She sounded miffed now. Not the impact he was after.

'I know you do, but she can stay on my books can't she? With you?' He hoped that was enough to keep Serena happy but also for her to see that Eve really was exceptional and he didn't want to lose her input into his novels.

'Darling, if you want Eve to stay on your books under me, then it shall be. I won't let her go anywhere. Consider her chained to you for as long as you keep writing.'

'You're fantastic, Serena, thank you.'

He heard her start to say something but he quickly interjected. 'I have to press on, Serena, but have a lovely Christmas. See you in the new year hopefully.'

He hung up from the call and gave himself a mental pat on the back. Eve would be thrilled when she learned he had ensured she would stay on as his editor. It really was an ideal situation for all of them.

30

Eve adjusted Flora's woollen hat as Edward and Myles came inside, Jimmi firmly in Myles's arms.

'He doesn't like the snow,' he said to Eve. 'And he gets scared at night.'

'Maybe he needs little snowshoes and a tiny dog torch,' Eve said patting the dog's head.

'Can dogs wear shoes?' asked Flora.

'They can but I don't think they find them very comfortable,' Eve replied.

'Go and put Jimmi in the laundry with his bed and then we can head off,' said Edward.

'I've never been to a night market. It's so exciting,' said Flora. She patted her little purple purse that was strung across her body. 'I have ten pounds to spend. That's the most money I've ever had. I could buy the whole market.'

Eve smiled at the child, as she felt Edward's hand on her back. 'You set?' he asked.

She nodded.

Soon they were in the car on their way to the Christmas market. It was a cold but clear night and there was a hum around Crossbourne as they arrived.

'Is it usually this busy?' she asked Edward as he finally found somewhere to park the car.

'I have no idea. I've never been,' he said.

'Never been?' Eve was shocked. How could you not visit a Christmas market this close to your house? She didn't understand why people didn't love Christmas and all the trimmings. Even if you weren't remotely religious, there was something nice about a holiday where you got to give people presents and eat lots of delicious food.

'Why not?' she asked as she felt Flora's mitten-clad hand slip into hers.

'I don't know. I think I became so caught up in what was happening at Cranberry that I couldn't leave the place. I hated to be there, but I couldn't leave in case something happened.'

Eve nodded. 'I understand. But that's over now, right?'

Edward looked ahead. 'Hopefully.'

Before Eve could ask what he meant they turned a corner and the market came into view.

Flora gasped and stopped. 'It's so beautiful.'

Eve wasn't sure what to expect but the market exceeded all expectations.

The market stall tents were all in red and white with striped awnings and pointed tops, looking a little like Santa hats, with jolly gifts beneath them.

Rows of column heaters lined the pathways, glowing and welcoming, while rows of Christmas lights were strung across from tent to tent.

A large fire pit was surrounded by stools made from tree trunks and signs suggesting shoppers sit a while and indulge in a mulled wine and roasted chestnuts.

There was a roaming folk band playing Christmas songs and Christmas elves handing out sweets and little presents to children passing them by, while singing with gusto to the adults.

The market was filled with scents of burning pine and apple wood, chestnuts, popcorn and sugar.

And everywhere she looked were items on sale that made her smile.

'I could do all my shopping here,' she said to Edward.

He smiled at her. 'Look at you. You're so excited.'

Flora pulled her hand to look at the handmade wooden toys on sale.

Within an hour, Edward was carrying bags of wares and following Myles, Eve and Flora, as they stopped and looked at every stall.

'I feel like Tenzing Norgay,' he said as he put another bag across his shoulder.

'God, Mum would love it here,' Eve said as they stopped at a table and sat down.

'Cider?' asked Edward.

'Lovely,' Eve replied.

Myles and Flora watched some jugglers as Edward came back to the table with some cider and chips.

'You should bring your mum next year,' Edward said as he sat opposite her.

Eve ate a chip. 'I should,' she said carefully.

'I mean,' Edward said, 'you might be here again for Christmas.'

Eve felt a smile playing at her mouth. 'I might,' she said.

'Unless I get asked to move to outer Timbuktu to work on a tardy author's book.'

'Oh don't say that.' Edward shook his head. 'What a state I was in and look how it's all humming along now. You are truly a miracle worker, Eve.'

He looked into the fire for a moment and then turned back to her.

'It's more than the books though – you know that?' He paused. 'You never need to speak to me about writing again. I just want to be with you.'

'I think my days of being at Serena's beck and call are soon to be over.'

'Why?'

He leaned forward to hear her better.

'I've applied for a promotion, an editorial role,' she said. 'I think I'm ready and I deserve it now. I'm tired of being Serena's beck-and-call girl.' She laughed.

'Oh, Eve, that's fantastic,' he said. 'You really are great and have such a good ear for dialogue and eye for detail. They absolutely have to give it to you.'

'I hope so. I mean, it's everything I have worked for.' She paused. 'But it might mean I come up on weekends or something. I don't know how it would work.'

Edward looked at Myles and Flora laughing as Flora danced to the band.

'I never thought I would have this,' he said gesturing around him and to her. 'You gave it to me. I want you to have your dreams also. I will fit in with you and your life. I want to be your support now.'

Eve shook her head and laughed again. 'How is this happening?'

'What?' he asked.

'This.' She waved between them both. 'How did this happen? We hardly know each other and we're speaking like it's inevitable.'

He shrugged. 'Because it is.'

'And what about the children? And their mother?'

She saw Edward's shoulders straighten and his jaw twitch. 'She doesn't count anymore. She made her choice.'

Eve said nothing but knew nothing was that simple. Parents made mistakes. They made bad choices but it didn't mean they didn't love their children, nor that they couldn't change.

Sitting in the market felt otherworldly. As though they were in their own personal romance novel, where none of the realities of the world existed. It would be easy to think that there would be no obstacles or troubles ahead. No pain or loss or struggles. But life wasn't a Hallmark movie and Eve knew that Edward ignoring Amber couldn't last forever.

'I'm not their mother,' she said suddenly, surprising herself.

'Pardon?'

'I'm not their mother.' She looked at Flora and Myles. 'They have a mum. And I don't want to be their mother substitute. Whatever happens with Amber, they must have a choice also. You can't decide for them; they need to be consulted.'

Edward was silent for a moment. 'She says she's changed.'

'You heard from her?'

'Hil did. She said she's coming back.'

Eve nodded, feeling sick in her stomach. It was the right

thing for her to want to see her children but it also felt upsetting.

'I told her we're away until new year and then we can talk but she can only visit them with me there.'

Eve let out a slow breath. 'That's good.'

'Is it?' Edward looked at the children. 'Myles is coming out of his shell for the first time. Flora's stopped burying dolls in the snow. I can write freely without half my mind being held hostage by Amber's behaviour.'

Eve nodded. She understood, as much as she could, but she was also aware their lives were very different. She was on the career path and he was trying to keep his children safe.

Shaking the mood off her, she lifted her glass of the sweet liquid.

'To better times ahead,' she said and Edward lifted his and they touched glasses.

'To us,' he replied.

To us, she repeated in her thoughts. But how would an 'us' work in the future?

It seemed impossible and yet inevitable. She would have to wait and find out their ending.

31

It was Christmas Eve and Edward had been writing for days to meet his deadline. His bottom was sore from sitting for so long. He forgot to drink water, only realising when his lips were stuck together. He forgot to go to the bathroom until his kidneys hurt.

He ate cheese and pickle sandwiches and drank coffees as Hil handed them to him but he often forgot to finish them, and there were half-drunk cups around his desk, despite Hil trying to whisk them away when she delivered the food.

But he was so deep in the story, he had no idea what was happening outside his desk.

He typed like a man possessed, moving through scene by scene, wanting the reader to get to the pivotal moment in the plot at a good pace without being too rushed.

He wanted them to feel the world in which his detective lived. To taste the cold black tea she drank from the cup made the day before. The way she washed her underarms at the sink in the police station bathroom. How she ignored her terminally ill mother's phone calls. How she walked the path of the murderer daily, trying to find the link to understand who he was. It felt like the first time in his writing life that he was fully immersed in the character and he knew part of the reason he could be so deep in the development was because of Eve's presence. She was always around but not intruding. She could be found in the snug, reading or talking to Flora or Myles. Perhaps finishing off his edits and chatting with Hilditch in the kitchen. She was just there. Present, steady, calm.

There was something about her presence in any room that warmed him. It made his nights more cheerful when once he avoided them with wine and misery.

But he was torn. He wanted to finish because he needed to tell the story but he also knew that Eve would go back to her life once it was done, no matter what vague promises they had made to each other.

One kiss might have been enough to cement a marriage in the 1700s, but he and Eve were strangers with an intense attraction.

He had come out of his study to sing happy birthday to her with the children and Hilditch and had apologised for not organising a present from him.

Eve had laughed and told him a finished manuscript would be enough but still, he understood why Amber had felt so neglected. It wasn't an excuse, it was a lack of good time management, he thought as he walked through the house. He noticed the scent of the pine decorations and the lights of the Christmas tree twinkling from the snug.

Eve had put a tree in the living room, the kitchen, the study and the snug and Edward had to admit he liked them all.

'Knock knock,' he said as he tapped on the open door of the snug, where Eve sat peacefully reading.

Eve looked up from her book. 'Who's there?'

'Me,' he said confused.

'You knocked and said "Knock knock".' She laughed. 'I thought there was a joke.'

'No jokes,' he said and he moved beside her and sat down, lifting her feet onto his lap.

'I've finished,' he said, rubbing her socked feet.

'For the night? Well done,' Eve said looking at the pages of her book.

'No, I've finished, finished.'

'Finished? Like done, done? The end? Denouement? Fin?'

Edward let out a huge sigh. As though he had been holding his breath for weeks.

'Yes, it's done.' He turned to Eve. 'I am so grateful to you, Eve. For the book, the kids, for me. For it all.'

Eve smiled and gave a small laugh. 'You're silly. You wrote the book; I just gave you a kick up the bum. And as for the kids, well Myles needed some friends and Flora needed to know she mattered. Sometimes a stranger is best at pulling the threads together.'

He took her hand in his.

'And today's your birthday,' he said. 'And I haven't done anything for you.'

'Yet.' She smiled and he felt his stomach flutter and moved her dark hair behind her beautifully shaped ear. He had never noticed people could have lovely ears until he met Eve.

'It is,' she replied.

The tension in the room was palpable.

'I do owe you a present,' he said.

'You really don't. My work here is nearly done,' she said.

'Are you leaving?' he asked.

'Not yet, as according to Hil, the bus will be a few days because of the bleedin' snow,' she said in Hil's accent.

Edward laughed and he stroked the palm of her hand with his thumb.

'So when the buses start running again, you'll head off?'

'I still have to do the final edits,' she said. 'But then, yes, back to reality.'

Their eyes locked on his and his need for her was as intense as the exhaustion he felt, but he wanted her more than anything he had ever desired.

'Come to bed, Eve,' he said, and he took the book from her hands and laid it on the table.

He stood up and pulled her to her feet and waited while she paused and put her feet into her reindeer slippers.

'I can't wait to take them off first,' he whispered in her ear just before he kissed her neck.

'Never,' she said as she arched to take his kiss down her neck and onto her collarbone. 'I will be naked but I will never take off my Christmas slippers.'

Edward dipped her in his arms and kissed her.

'Let's go, birthday girl. I am going to unwrap you like my own special present.'

Eve kissed him back but then pulled away.

'I have a present for you, and I want you to open it.'

She went to the tree and reached under and pulled out a box. She came back and handed it to him.

'It's your birthday, I should be giving you your present,' he complained but Eve shook her head.

'This means a lot to me, so if you can open it, it will make me happy.'

Edward shook the box. 'How can I argue with that?'

He tore off the paper and saw a simple white box. He lifted the lid and then burst into a loud peal of laughter.

'Oh, Eve. You didn't!?'

Eve smiled and then clapped her hands. 'I did, so put them on.' Edward lifted a reindeer slipper with a glowing red nose from the box and put it on the floor and kicked off his sneaker. He slipped one foot into the shoe and then put the other on.

'Okay, I admit, they're comfortable and cute but if you ever, ever tell anyone I am wearing these, I will never forgive you.'

Eve kissed him and their pointed reindeer toes touched.

'Come to bed, Evie Pilkins, please. I want you and your silly slippers in my arms when we wake on Christmas Day.'

'Only people who love me call me Evie,' she teased.

'And only people who love me call me Ed – my parents because they're my parents, and my agent, because of all the money I've made him.'

Eve laughed and kissed him.

'Formal names only, noted,' she said and then she ran from the room and up the stairs.

'Come on then, Mr Priest, don't keep a girl waiting.'

'Coming, Miss Pilkins. Ready or not.'

32

Trying to explain Christmas Day at the Pilkinses' house was impossible. It was best you just sat and absorbed it all like the sponge in Donna's trifle and when you'd drunk enough, you just joined in with the chaos, Eve had explained to Edward as they arrived at the house.

As welcoming as the Pilkinses were the first time he met them, Edward was still nervous about spending the day with Eve's family.

'Stop worrying about it,' Eve told him repeatedly but he seemed more anxious than necessary. 'Is there something else I should know about?' she asked him before they set off for the drive to her parents' in Leeds.

'No, no,' he had said but he kept checking his phone until they were on the road.

But as soon as they were driving his mood seemed to shift and he sang Christmas music loudly to the playlist Eve had plugged into the car from her phone.

Eve would turn occasionally to see Myles and Flora singing along and then she would look at Edward and wonder if this could go on forever. And now she was seeing her family. She reminded herself that sometimes things do work out for the best, even when you don't think they have any possibility of sorting themselves out.

'What sort of fare will we be partaking in at the Pilkinses' today?' asked Edward as they passed the snowy landscape.

Eve laughed. 'I don't know if I should tell you. It might be too much and you'll head home to the leftovers at Cranberry Cross.'

'Oh God, what are we talking here? Stuffed mushrooms and jellied eels?'

'No, we're not barbarians,' she said. 'Think Christmas and birthday combined.'

'A Christmas pudding with birthday candles?' he teased.

'Just wait and find out, you impatient and impudent man.'

The Pilkinses' house was lit up like Bond Street, with coloured lights on the house, the fence, the garage, the trees and a blow-up snowman on the roof. Edward parked the car and the children ran up the path to the front door as soon as the car stopped. Across the front of the house was a huge banner reading *Happy Birthday to Eve, Gabe and Nick*.

'It's astonishing you all have your birthdays on Christmas Eve, I mean what are the odds on that?'

'One in five hundred thousand,' she answered as she lifted a large sack of presents from the back of the car.

'Really?'

'Yes, we did the maths years ago.' She laughed again as Edward took the sack from her and another from the car.

'Wow,' said Edward as he looked over the fence. Signs lined the path to the front door with slogans reading, *Santa*

Stop Here, Elf Resting Place, Reindeer Parking Only and more.

'I told you my family loved Christmas,' she said as they walked up to the door.

'I feel bad about you not spending last night with your family for your actual birthday,' he said quietly.

She turned and looked at him. 'I don't. Spending it in your bed was a far nicer option.'

She could see Edward blush and she bit her lip from trying not to laugh at her shyness when she knew how he had been with her in bed. He was by far the best lover she'd ever had. There was more than just desire but, at times, she wondered if she loved him or if he loved her. But that wasn't possible after such a short time, was it? This was real life, not a fairy tale.

'Happy birthday.' Eve heard and saw her mother on the top step by the front door.

'And Merry Christmas to you,' called out Eve as she and Edward walked up the path.

'Hello, Edward,' Donna said and kissed him on the cheek. 'Pop those under the tree in the living room,' she directed him.

As soon as Edward was inside the house, Donna hugged Eve.

'You have a glow about you,' she said and looked closely at Eve's face. 'Have you and Edward declared your undying love for each other and the printed word?'

Eve laughed but she knew she was turning red. 'Mum, be quiet,' she whispered.

Donna raised an eyebrow, something Eve had never been

able to do and was jealous of. 'Don't show off with your curious eyebrow gymnastics and be all judgey.'

'I'm not being judgey, I just think you two have a strong connection. A mother knows these things.'

Eve hugged her mum again. 'I am so lucky to have such a great mum.'

'Thank you, darling.'

Donna and Eve went inside the house where Myles was larking with Gabe and Nick while Flora was sitting patiently on the floor next to the presents.

'Eve?' Flora asked.

'Yes?' Eve set down her bag and coat on the coat stand.

'Do we open the presents before or after lunch?' she asked.

Her dad laughed. 'Sounds like you as a little one, Evie.' He turned to Edward. 'She would be straight up in the morning to start opening the Christmas presents without taking a breath, even though she'd spent the night before opening birthday presents.'

Edward bent down to Flora. 'It's rude to ask about the presents,' he said. 'We will open them when the Pilkins family is ready.'

'No it's totally fine,' said Donna. 'Why don't we open the birthday presents and then Flora and Myles can open one Christmas present each before lunch.'

Flora gave a little fist pump into the air with a quiet but impassioned, 'Yes.'

'Drink, Edward? Donna's made mimosas.'

Edward shook his head. 'No I won't, maybe just the orange juice and less of the bubbles? I will have to drive home later and day drinking makes me tired.'

'Mummy liked to day drink bubbly drinks,' announced Flora.

The room was silent. Eve looked at Edward who appeared shocked.

'Okay, so let's do presents,' said Eve quickly. 'Flora, would you be my helper for the presents?'

Flora jumped up quickly. 'Yes please.'

Eve handed her a box. 'This is for Gabe from you and Myles.'

Flora walked solemnly over to him and put the box on his lap.

'Happy birthday. I hope you like it, even though I don't know what it is.'

The tenseness in the room from the mention of Amber dissipated as Gabe tore into the paper.

'Oh wicked, a mini synth for the keyboard.' He lifted the box up for the room to see.

Flora handed Nick his present who opened it as fast as Gabe.

'What in the world is this?' he asked turning the box over in his hands.

'It's a rhythm watch, with a headphone port, so you can be the most in-time drummer in Leeds.' She smiled.

'That's amazing,' said Nick and she knew he meant it. 'Thank you.'

Eve shook her head. 'I didn't choose it; Myles did all the work and research. He really believes in your talent.'

Myles looked pleased but embarrassed at Eve's words.

'Yeah, well done,' Nick said. 'Good choices, mate.'

Eve opened her presents from the twins, which were an

assortment of sweets, notebooks, a tote bag with Penguin classic books printed on the fabric.

'I love all of these,' she said.

Her parents gave her an oversized mohair cardigan with pearl buttons and a red heart on the back.

'Oh wow, I adore this,' Eve said and she stood up and pulled it on immediately. 'It's so warm and gorgeous. Thank you.'

Flora and Myles gave Eve a new pink suitcase.

'The wheels work,' said Eve as she pushed it back and forth.

'So you can come and visit and stay,' said Flora, climbing onto Eve's lap.

Eve nestled her nose into Flora's hair. 'I can't wait.'

It was Edward's turn and he stood and went to the tree and picked up a slim box.

'Happy birthday, Eve, from me,' he said and handed it to her.

She opened the beautifully wrapped present and saw the logo on top of the box.

She lifted the lid and there was a Dupont pen in black enamel and gold.

'It's inscribed,' said Edward. She picked up the pen and read the words.

Eve Pilkins – Editor

She looked up at him and smiled. 'Thank you,' she said. 'That means a lot that you think I can do it.'

'You are doing it, you did it. You edited my book and it's

exceptional, just like you,' he replied and leaned down and kissed her cheek.

'Happy birthday, children,' Sam Pilkins said and blew a party horn over and over. 'Now it's time for Christmas lunch and then we will do birthday cake and then pudding, so I hope you haven't eaten any breakfast, because you're about to have the feast of your lives.'

33

Edward sat on the sofa with Flora by his side.

'I'm so full I'm going to chunder,' she said.

'Flora, that's revolting. Where did you hear that word?'

Eve walked in holding a plate of birthday cake and Christmas pudding and custard.

'What word is revolting?'

'Chunder,' said Flora with an eye-roll. 'Gabe said it outside in the garage and then he farted,' Flora reported.

'Wow, we really are showing our best selves today,' said Eve as she sat next on the other side of Edward.

'Is that cake and pudding? On the same plate?' he asked.

'Yes and it's delicious. So don't start with your fancy pants taste.'

'Not the combination but where are you putting it? I am stuffed full.'

Eve closed her eyes as she chewed. 'Don't yuck my yum. I'm enjoying this.'

Sam Pilkins was sitting in his recliner chair, his eyes closed, hands on his stomach.

'I'm with Ed. Cake and pudding together is disgusting, like that turkey stuffed duck thing they have in America.'

'A turducken,' said Eve. 'A chicken, inside a duck, inside a turkey.'

'How do they get inside each other?' asked Flora, her face confused.

Before anyone could answer Myles and the twins came into the room in their coats, their faces ruddy from being outside.

'We want a present from you for Christmas Eve,' Myles said.

'I gave you your presents. I'm not made of money you ungrateful little twerps.' She laughed.

Gabe stepped forward. 'No, we want you to do something for us.'

Eve looked at them, mischief all over their cold faces from being in the garage.

'No,' she said putting up her hand.

'Come on,' said Nick. 'You said you would anytime.'

'Not today, Satan.' Eve shook her head and ate another piece of cake and pudding as an end to the conversation.

'Please, Eve. Please?' Myles looked at her with such intensity that she wondered if it was what she thought they were asking for.

'Gabe and Nick talk about how great you are, please?'

'What do they want you to do?' whispered Flora.

'They want me to sing,' she said.

'Oh yes, yes, this is perfect, I want to hear and see also,' Edward said.

'Go on, love, I haven't heard you in a while. I miss it,' Sam said from his chair, eyes still closed.

'Dad, I thought you would be on my side.'

'I'd like to hear you sing a song,' said Flora quietly and put her hand in Eve's.

The touch of the soft skin of Flora's hand in hers, the way her little fingers curled around her hand and her face looking up at hers felt like a shock of love. A deep wave of wanting to always keep the child safe wasn't like anything she had felt before.

'I will sing if you join my band with me,' she said to Flora.

'But I can't play guitar,' said Flora.

'No but you can play the tambourine and sing along with me, can't you?'

Flora nodded excitedly.

'Righto, get your coat. We'll have a practice first and then call you out. Tickets will be twenty pounds to go to the animal shelter where Mum volunteers. And Edward Priest will be paying for all of them,' she said and caught his eye.

He laughed and nodded. 'Naturally.'

'We will call you when we're ready for an audience,' Eve said as she helped Flora into her coat and hat and mittens.

Eve adjusted the microphone on the stand and jumped up and down to keep warm. Then she strung the guitar strap over her shoulder and fixed the instrument to feel comfortable.

She turned to the boys behind her.

'You ready?'

The boys nodded, Gabe and Nick with huge grins on their faces. Myles looked nervous but excited.

Flora stood next to Eve, a tambourine in hand and a Santa hat on her head, excitedly shaking it.

Eve put her hand on Flora's shoulder to quieten her.

Edward and her parents sat on lawn chairs outside the garage, her mum wrapped in a large red blanket.

'Ready?' She turned to the band and then Nick started playing the drums, finding the beat, and Eve started playing a riff and then they were off. Flora danced around in front of them as Eve started singing 'Last Nite' by The Strokes into the microphone and caught Edward's eye and winked as she burst into the chorus.

She saw his mouth drop open as she sang, and then laughed into the guitar solo, closing her eyes and giving it her all. She loved playing but this was enough, and playing with her favourite people in the world made it even better.

They banged out the song and Flora gave a little tambourine solo at the end to an enthusiastic round of applause from the audience.

'You're amazing,' said Edward to Myles. 'All of you,' he said, looking at Eve.

'And I've never seen such an enthusiastic tambourine player. I loved the high kicks with the beat at the end.'

'They were karate kicks,' corrected Flora.

'Yes, I should have called them that. I didn't notice they had a self-defensive theme to them.'

Eve laughed as she undid the strap and lifted it over her head and handed the guitar to Gabe.

'You happy now? I'm freezing, I have to go inside.'

Gabe hugged her. 'You're the best.'

Edward walked back to the house with her.

'You made all my teenage rock fantasies about hooking up with the coolest lead singer come true watching that,' he whispered in her ear as he opened the door for her to step inside.

'You're funny,' she said and she felt him pull her into the laundry and close the door.

His mouth was on hers and her arms slid up around his neck.

'I'm utterly smitten with you, Eve,' he said. 'You're the most talented, cleverest, sexiest person I know.'

'You need to get out more,' she said as she kissed him back.

A knock at the door interrupted them and Eve slid it back and saw her mum.

'Sorry to interrupt, but I know you wanted to head off before it gets really dark as there's snow coming.'

Eve turned to Edward.

'I have a present for Flora,' she said. 'I wanted to give it to her as we left.'

Edward narrowed his eyes. 'Okay?'

'You'll love it, I promise,' she said. 'Go and wait with Flora in the living room.'

Edward left and Eve and Donna arranged everything and then went into the living room where Flora and Edward were sitting on the sofa.

'I have a present for you,' said Eve. 'Well it's from Mum and I.'

Donna came in behind her and handed Flora a small wicker carrier basket and put it on the coffee table.

Eve watched Flora lean forward and look into the basket and then gasp.

'The kitten,' she cried. 'You said she had been promised to a new home.'

'I know. Yours,' said Donna with a happy smile.

Flora had been disappointed when she had arrived to learn the kitten wasn't in the kitchen.

Now her day was made.

'A kitten?' asked Edward but he had reached into the basket and was cradling the small animal while Flora stroked its head.

'It's a girl kitten, Daddy,' Flora said.

'What will you call her then?' asked Edward.

Eve smiled at them both as they chatted about names.

'He's a lovely one, that Edward Priest,' whispered Donna. 'He's perfect.'

Eve watched the way he listened to Flora, a different parent from the man she had met weeks ago.

'No such thing as perfect, Mum – you taught me that – but he's close. Pretty close.'

34

Three days after Christmas, Eve finished editing Edward's book. Instead of telling him immediately, she sat at her desk in the snug and wondered how she would explain it to Serena. The company was expecting the usual *Edward Priest* epic novel filled with adventure and far-flung places that his average reader would think of visiting in their lifetime.

Instead, he had written a book about a feminist female detective investigating a serial killer in Sheffield. Serena wouldn't like change and Eve knew trying to sell in this genre would take a strategy that showed her the financial opportunity, but if Eve couldn't position this correctly, then she might see it as Eve failing at the task Serena had set her.

Finally she took a deep breath and started to write the email. It took seven versions before she was satisfied with the words and she attached the manuscript and pressed send before she chickened out.

She had done what she could with the argument for publishing Edward's book and giving it the same level of support they would give his other work, but because it wasn't Serena's idea, there was every chance she would refuse to even read it.

Eve closed the laptop, otherwise she knew she would be refreshing her email every ten seconds waiting for a reply, and she walked to the study to tell Edward.

Flora was sitting on the rug playing with the kitten.

'How is Christmas?' asked Eve as she wandered in and sat in an armchair.

Flora's decision to name the cat Christmas was accepted by the family when she announced that this was her favourite Christmas ever. Who could argue with that? Edward had agreed.

'She's good. She liked chasing the mouse with feathers up its bottom.'

'Poor mouse,' Eve said as she rubbed her eyes that were sore from staring at the computer for so long.

'You okay?' asked Edward looking up from his own computer.

'Just sore eyes,' she said. 'They're dry.'

'Go and water them,' said Flora.

'Good idea,' Eve said with a smile. 'I've finished,' she said to Edward.

'Finished?' He frowned.

'The first edit. I've done all I can now. It's good. In great shape. If I read this from a new author I would commission them immediately.'

Edward jumped out of his chair. 'You've finished? This is amazing. Did you send it to Serena yet? Has she said anything?'

'I sent it to her a little while ago. She won't have read it yet, so hold your horses.'

Edward came to the side of her chair and kissed the top of her head.

'You're amazing, Eve, thank you.'

She looked up at him.

'I'm just doing my job.'

He frowned at her.

'Are you okay?'

The truth was Eve didn't feel okay. Finishing the book meant their time together was over, at least in this form. At Cranberry Cross she didn't need to navigate the tube or stand in a packed train to get to work. Didn't have to deal with running around after Serena and her petty requests, or watch her take credit for Eve's work.

'Fine, just tired.'

'Did you want to have a rest? I think Hil's out so we could grab the children and head into Crossbourne for a late lunch?'

Eve nodded. 'I might actually. And hopefully we'll hear back from Serena tomorrow and she'll love it.'

'From your mouth to Serena's ear,' he said as she held her hands out for him to pull her to her feet.

'I will have a nap and a shower and come down at one-ish?'

'Perfect,' he said and then hugged her.

'Thank you, Eve, for everything. I adore you.'

She laid her head against his chest for a moment and then pulled away.

He hadn't made any real overtures about their future yet besides the suitcase, but she wanted to have the conversation. How would it work? What if she won the promotion? How would that affect them?

The questions whirled in her head as she headed upstairs to nap in her bed.

She'd been spending her nights in Edward's bed but now she needed to have her own space.

Within minutes of lying down, she reminded herself to check her phone was turned up as she felt herself falling asleep. Perhaps she had already turned it up, she hoped, as she slipped into a deep sleep, her eyes feeling relieved to be closed and not staring at a screen.

Eve woke with a start. She heard something outside. It wasn't the sound when she first came to Cranberry Cross, it was more obvious and very female.

'You lying piece of shit,' she heard and she rushed to the window and looked out to see Amber Priest smashing Edward's car with a hammer.

Where on earth had she found a hammer? Eve wondered, watching as Edward stood to the side and Hilditch was talking on the phone.

Calling the police, Eve assumed.

She was in two minds as to what to do. She should try and find the children and see they were okay and not near the drama, but she had the feeling she should stay away from Amber and her hammer.

Thankfully the children made their own decision and her door opened.

'It's Mom,' said Myles, his face stormy and drawn, Jimmi trotting in behind him. She hadn't seen that look in him since he had met her brothers and then Jimmi brought extra light into his world.

'Why is she so angry?' Flora asked, Christmas the kitten in a small basket lined with baby blankets.

'I don't know, darling,' said Eve, gesturing for them to sit on her bed.

She went back to the window and peered out again just as Amber looked up and saw her. Their eyes locked, then Eve stepped back from the window but it was too late.

'Who is that?' screamed Amber.

'No one, she's from the publisher's. She's helping me with work,' Edward said.

'Like Serena Whitelaw did? Is extra special attention part of the reason you stay with that company? Do they hire for their sexual skills and their proofreading? A double whammy hey? How many women have you fucked from there now? Three? Does she make it four?'

'Shut up – the children will hear you.'

Oh, Edward, thought Eve as she walked to the door.

'Let's go up to Myles's room, hey? Then we don't have to hear this fighting.'

The three of them trudged up to the tower and Eve closed the door. There was no sound of the chaos downstairs but they sat in silence on the floor.

'Do your parents fight much?' asked Myles.

Eve thought for a moment, trying to remember her childhood.

'Not fighting like that. Maybe disagreeing but about silly things, like putting the rubbish out and the twins being naughty when they were little.'

She waited, trying to think.

'The only time I remember a serious fight was when I got into a new school, a posh one and I had a scholarship, and Dad wanted me to go but Mum didn't. She said that I would be fine at whatever school I went to and it wasn't fair to the boys if I went because they couldn't afford the fees for them on the money they made.'

Flora was playing with the kitten, not paying much attention, which Eve found odd. She had seemed like she'd yearned for her mother this whole time, and now she was removed. Perhaps the idea of her mother was more comforting than the reality, which made sense after seeing Amber outside with the hammer.

'So what school did you end up going to?' asked Myles, interrupting her thoughts about Amber and Flora.

'Oh, the local school. I told Mum I didn't like the uniform of the posh one, and they said they wouldn't let me wear double piercings in my ears.'

Myles laughed. 'I get it. Is that where Gabe and Nick go now?'

'Yeah, it's a good school. I didn't need to be surrounded by people who I couldn't hang out with on the holidays because they were going to fancy resorts and skiing. I just wanted to hang out with my friends and the band we had and to be a dork and read books. I had a nice life with Mum and Dad. I didn't need to try and pretend that I was anything else.'

'Do you think Edward would let me go to that school with them?' Myles asked.

Eve didn't show her surprise. Instead she shrugged and acted casual, as though he wasn't asking about something important that could change his future.

She knew he would remember this moment and even more so if it worked out.

'Maybe, I mean it's a bit of a hike. Maybe you could stay at Mum and Dad's a few times a week. I don't know, I mean anything is possible. We just have to work out a way.'

Myles hugged Jimmi and she could see him hiding his face from her.

'I don't want to be with her. She doesn't love me; she hates me.'

She could hear the crack in his voice and she felt his pain, wishing she could fix it all but knowing only one person could fix it.

'And Edward hasn't adopted me, so he doesn't have any rights for me. I looked it up online.'

Eve sighed. No child should have to look up custody laws to try and predict their future.

'Let's not go there yet,' she said and touched his arm.

'You're here, you're safe with me and Flora and Jimmi, and Edward will sort out your mum. She sounds sick, so maybe he can get her some help.'

'She's been in rehab so many times,' he said.

'What's rehab?' asked Flora.

'It's like a hospital for people who need extra love,' Eve said.

'She can come to my doll hospital. Christmas likes to lie with the babies when they're in their beds.'

Eve's heart broke hearing Flora's offer.

'You're a very kind person, Flora.'

Flora nodded. 'I am, except when I'm hungry and then I can be a right pain, Hil says.'

Eve smiled and lay on the rug. 'Myles? I think we need to hear some Fleetwood Mac.'

Myles got up and found the album and put it on his record player. The needle hit the vinyl, the comforting crackles came through the speaker and then the sounds of Stevie Nicks and Lindsey Buckingham singing 'I Don't Want to Know' came through the speakers. Eve sang at the top of her voice, remembering the harmonies like the alphabet.

Edward hadn't denied he had slept with Serena to Amber. She accused him of being with other women from the publisher's.

Was she just one in a long line of women he'd used and discarded once they were of no use to him?

She pulled her phone out of the back pocket of her jeans where it was digging into her and looked at the screen.

Seven missed calls from Serena.

Multiple texts.

'Shit,' she said and jumped up.

'You said shit,' said Flora excitedly.

'Get over it – shit isn't even a swear word anymore,' said Myles to Flora.

'It is to me. It's a swear word until you're in big school, Daddy told me,' Flora argued back.

'Hang on, I need to make a work call. Don't leave here,' she told the children and she went out into the stairwell, thankful there was phone coverage.

She looked at the texts.

Call me. Where are you? Call me now. Eve, this is not okay. Eve? Call Me Now!

Eve took a deep breath and then dialled the number, hoping today wouldn't get any worse.

35

'Amber, put the hammer down,' said Edward.

'No, I won't. I hate you.' Amber was storming around the car still, hitting it at odd intervals.

'You said you were away. You were here the whole time. I could have seen my children at Christmas.'

'Not with a hammer you won't,' he said.

She smashed a back light as a comeback.

'Amber, you know this behaviour is just going to mean you don't get to spend time with them. It isn't good for you or them. No one is going to let a parent be around their children when they are breaking property, being violent. Come on.'

Edward had seen Amber like this before but it had been so long since he'd seen an episode, he had forgotten how terrible it was.

She seemed out of herself more than ever this time and he wondered what she was taking.

He couldn't smell alcohol, so he wondered if it was drugs causing this chaotic paranoia.

He glanced at Hil who was still on the phone but who was clearly listening with one ear.

'Don't look at Hil. She turned my children against me, you old witch,' Amber said.

Edward noticed how thin she was, thinner than when she was modelling. She looked tired and sad and drawn, and he wished above anything else he could fix whatever was troubling her but she never told him her past and he was so bewitched by her beauty and American confidence, he had taken her on, warts and all, and thought he could fix her. He'd thought he would adopt Myles and they would all live happily ever after.

Except now, he knew it wasn't ever a realistic plan. Amber was broken before he even met her and Myles had suffered the most.

He would never let Amber parent Myles again and certainly not when she was like this.

A police car drove up the driveway and Amber turned towards it. She threw the hammer at them, missing it only by an inch.

'Jesus Christ, Amber, stop it,' Edward yelled as two police got out.

'What's going on?' asked one of them, a woman who looked at Amber and then to Edward to answer the question.

'He won't let me see my children.' Amber pointed at Edward.

'And rightly so if you have a hammer and are using it for anything other than home repairs,' said an older male policeman standing in front of Amber.

'Do you want to press charges?' asked the policewoman looking at the damage.

Edward looked at Amber. 'Yes, I do, and I don't want

her anywhere near this house. Not until she gets her life together.'

Amber lunged forward at Edward but the policeman stopped her and held her back, lifting her from the ground so her feet kicked at the air.

Edward could feel his temper rise and the thought of his children inside the house, hiding from their mother yet again.

'How many times do you need to try, Amber? I would never keep you away from the children but I can't let you be around them like this. It is so damaging, more than what you're doing to yourself, it's changing them. It takes everything to bring them back every time you're like this and one day, but there will be a time one day, if they're around you long enough, they won't come back. Myles was nearly ready to hurt himself. Flora is obsessed with death, trying to find her mother through macabre games she's inventing. You have to get better or else you don't get to be in their lives.'

Amber looked enraged but he realised she wasn't listening or comprehending anything he was saying.

'Take her away and get her some help,' said Edward to the police.

'We will have to take a statement,' said the policewoman.

'Can I check on my children first?' he asked.

'Yes, go. We'll take her to the station and then if you could come down to give the statement when everything is okay here?'

'Fine, fine,' said Edward and he ran inside.

The need to see his children and Eve was overwhelming as he searched through the house.

They weren't in the snug or his study or the kitchen and

he thought for a moment and then realised the safest place was the tower.

He opened the hidden door and started to climb the stairs to his future.

Eve was standing outside the door to Myles's room.

'Eve? Are you and the children all right? I'm so sorry, that was awful. How much did they see?'

Eve looked at him and then at the phone in her hand.

'They're okay – they're in there.'

'Okay, I'm going to talk to them now. The police are taking Amber to the station. I'll head down soon and make a statement.'

Eve said nothing as he opened the door and walked in to see the children.

She could hear them talking and she closed the door for privacy and went down to her room and pulled out her old broken pink suitcase and threw her clothes into it, not bothering to fold them. She searched under her bed for her Christmas slippers and piled all her toiletries into a plastic bag and dumped them in her case.

A last search of the room revealed a hair tie and a pink sock with a hole in the toe, which she threw in the rubbish bin.

She carried her suitcase downstairs and checked the study, and found her notes on the book, which she put on Edward's desk.

Her laptop was in the snug along with some books and the tote bag the twins had given her for Christmas, which she placed her last items inside.

She thought for a moment and then left a box on the desk.

She wouldn't take anything with her that he'd given her, not now. Not after everything he had taken from her.

Eve went to the front door as the police car drove away and Hilditch was coming inside.

'Where are you going?' asked Hil, looking at the suitcase.

'Home,' said Eve, taking out her phone and ordering a taxi.

'Home? Why? Is everything okay?' Hilditch looked confused.

'Everything is perfectly clear thanks, Hil.'

'Where are Edward and the children?' Hil looked behind Eve down the empty hallway.

'In the tower,' she answered. 'Oh great, the car is two minutes away. That's lucky isn't it? Considering we're in no-man's-land.'

Hilditch looked at Eve closely.

'What's happened? Was it because of Amber?'

Eve shook her head. 'It doesn't matter.'

'It does. Edward and the children have been happier than they've ever been since you arrived.'

Hilditch had always been polite, sometimes verging on warm but this was unlike anything she had offered Eve before.

'It's not my sole reason for living though,' she said, trying but failing to keep the bitterness from her voice.

'I didn't suggest it was,' said Hil. 'But you seemed happy too.'

Eve shrugged as she pulled on her coat and beret that hung in the hallway and pulled her suitcase outside. 'I was,' she said. Then she turned to Hil, who was standing alone in the doorway. 'Tell me, how many different women did Edward have stay here from Henshaw and Carlson?'

Hil shook her head. 'None besides Serena. She was stuck here because she booked the wrong train back and couldn't get a driver because of a roadblock.'

Eve rolled her eyes. Knowing Serena, she would have probably felled the tree with a withering look on her way up to Cranberry Cross to ensure she couldn't get back and would have to stay.

'So who was Amber talking about?' asked Eve.

'I honestly don't know,' said Hil. 'But why don't you stay and ask him yourself? You shouldn't leave without speaking to him about this.'

Eve heard herself give an ugly laugh just as the taxi pulled into the driveway.

She walked towards the car as the driver opened the boot of the car for her suitcase.

'I'm not leaving because of other women. I'm leaving because Edward Priest just lost me my job.'

She lifted the case into the car and then went to the back seat.

'Tell the children I'm sorry I couldn't say goodbye. It wasn't them. It was never them. I was their protector for a while but I am not their mother. They have one, and a father. They need to do their job now.'

Eve got into the back seat and closed the door of the car, just as she saw Edward coming towards Hil, the children by his side.

'Go,' she told the driver and turned her face away from Cranberry Cross so they wouldn't see that her heart was broken, and Christmas was now ruined for her forever.

36

'Darling, I love the crime novel, just love it,' Serena said as soon as she answered Edward's phone call. 'A huge shift for you but good on you for being courageous enough to move with the times. Your last book didn't sell as well as the others. I think people's world vision is becoming smaller since it's such a risk to travel now and so expensive. I offset my flight to New York by planting fifty trees in Surrey. We must do what we can, don't you agree?'

'Why did you fire Eve?' Edward was seething as he paced in the study.

'What, darling? I didn't fire her. She resigned.'

'Why? Why did she resign?'

'Darling, I don't know why – you know these millennials. They switch modes like they're playing a computer game. They just move on, no loyalty; always in it for themselves.'

Edward looked out over the empty gardens. Nothing on the trees, no one on the paths, no birds in the sky.

'She was going for a promotion. She told me about it.'

Serena sighed. 'Yes, I know. She was close – I told her that. But once you told me you wanted her to stay on assisting me, so I could work on your books and she could assist us, then there wasn't any chance she could move departments. Not when our biggest author wants her to stay where she is.'

'Serena, Jesus, that's not what I said.'

'Oh didn't you, darling? I can't remember. I'm very busy. Don't worry about Eve. There are a thousand Eves out there. I have a lovely one who has a double degree from Cardiff. She's fabulous and has a penchant for crime also. Her father is a silk, so she knows all the inside information. She's working in reception but I can promote her today if you want?'

Edward couldn't believe Serena's words. He knew she was ruthless but this was Machiavellian.

Eve hadn't answered her phone and he had tried to follow her car but the police rang him and said Amber's lawyer was on the phone and they needed his statement as soon as possible.

'Serena, I need you to listen to me.' He spoke slowly, and quietly. He couldn't afford to lose his temper at this moment.

'I need you to bring Eve back, and I need you to give her the promotion she is due.'

'Darling, I don't think so. To be honest, she wasn't a great assistant.'

'She's not meant to be your assistant. She's an editor. She studied at Leeds, she knows story inside out, she has an exceptional eye for dialogue and detail. She's remarkable, and might I say it, Serena, she's better than you realise?'

Serena started to interrupt but he went on.

'You bring her back or I will pull the novel and find a new publishing house.'

Serena's voice changed. 'Edward, if you do that you will

owe us over five hundred thousand pounds to buy back this book.'

'Oh, Serena, I won't just buy back this book, I will take all my books,' he said as he lifted the lid of the box Eve had left in the snug. The pen he had given her for her birthday. It was telling that she had left it on the desk. She wouldn't be an editor while under Serena's command at Henshaw and Carlson.

'That will cost you millions – more than you can afford,' she stated. 'You would be ruining the company and your reputation.'

'I don't give a shit about my reputation, Serena, or the money. I will sell every last thing I have to make sure I get what I am worth and Eve gets what she's worth. Do you understand?'

Serena was silent.

'I'll make the call now,' she said after a moment.

'Goodbye.'

He put down the phone and collapsed into his armchair.

A few minutes later the children came into his study.

'Is Eve coming back?' asked Myles pointedly.

Both of them looked at him expectantly.

'She's calling Eve now,' he said wishing he could fix their sad faces.

'Will you have to sell Christmas?' asked Flora, looking at the cat who was attached to a pink satin leash.

'No, sweetheart, never.' But he looked around the house.

If he had to buy back his catalogue, he could sell the house.

He dialled another number.

'Tom? I want you to be prepared for what I'm about to tell you.'

Tom Keltner had been his agent since he started and Edward's loyalty to him was legendary. Tom's agency had grown with Edward's success but they were, above all, good friends.

'Okay,' Tom said.

Edward explained the situation, as he watched Flora lie on the sofa, and put her head on Myles's lap. He patted her head while he texted on his own phone.

Probably talking to the twins, Edward thought, but wouldn't ask if he had heard anything about Eve. He didn't want Myles being the go-between in the relationship. That wasn't fair.

Tom listened and took down some notes.

'Let me do some maths,' he said. 'I know anyone would be thrilled to have you and the detective novel sounds great. Send me over a copy. I know Kristin Scott Thomas's agent is looking for something more gritty after *Slow Horses*. She was great in that.'

Edward finished the call and looked at the children.

'Well this won't buy the baby a new dress,' he said. 'Let's go and do something.'

'What baby?' asked Flora looking around the room suspiciously.

'It's a saying,' said Edward with a smile. 'Meaning we need to get on with the day instead of wasting time.'

'Get on with what?' asked Myles. His voice was tight and he looked as angry as he had ever seen him.

'Whatever we want,' Edward said, trying to keep his tone light.

'Why? We never did anything before Eve came, and now she's gone we'll go back to it again. Stop pretending we're a family. I'm not your kid and you're not my dad and she's not my sister.' Flora sat up and looked at him.

'You're my brother to me,' she said.

'I don't want to stay here anymore.' Myles stood up.

Edward sighed. 'I understand that you're upset and so am I, and Serena and I'm working on trying to find Eve to explain but you don't have anywhere else to go right now but here. So sit down and stop making things harder than they are.'

Myles held out his phone. 'Actually I do have somewhere to go. I'm going to Eve's parents' house. They said I can stay as long as I like and I can go to school with Gabe and Nick.'

'What? When did you talk to them about this?'

'I spoke to Eve about it when she was in the tower with me, when Mom came to the house. She said she thought it would be good and I could live at the Pilkinses' house.'

'No, she said you had to ask Daddy,' Flora corrected.

'Shut up,' Myles snapped.

'Don't speak to her like that,' Edward warned.

'Or what? You'll lock me in the tower like you did last time?'

'I never locked that door, Myles. You were free to come and go as you pleased. You chose not to.'

'Why would I?' Myles said, and he walked to the door and snapped his fingers for Jimmi to come to his side.

'I'm going to their house later. I can get the bus.'

'Not with a dog you can't,' said Edward.

'I can so. Gabe said I just call him an assistance dog and they'll let me on.'

'Myles, come on,' said Edward but Myles shook his head at him.

'I don't want to be here anymore. The Pilkinses make me feel like I belong, which I don't feel here. Goodbye,' he said and Edward heard him calling Jimmi as he went to his room.

'Can I take Christmas on a bus?' asked Flora.

Edward groaned and closed his eyes.

He would get on a bus soon just to escape from it all. *Dammit, Serena, you absolute devil.* If she couldn't fix this then he would have to fix it himself – whatever it took he would do it. Not to try and get Eve back but because she deserved more than the crumbs Serena had thrown her.

And that's when Edward knew he loved Eve. Because for the first time in his life, he wanted someone else's happiness more than his own.

He thought about Amber and the long times she had been alone while he travelled the world on some whimsical, self-indulgent research trip. Or the lack of interest he took in her life, her dreams; God, he didn't even know if she had any. He had been a terrible husband. He didn't deserve to have Eve in his life if this is how he treated the mother of his child.

Eve had shown him how to be present, how to honour his talent, how to push himself as a writer and as a parent. So why wouldn't Myles want to go and live with the people who raised Eve? Perhaps he should go there and be reparented by the Pilkinses. They would do a better job than the lesson in manners and disconnection Father and Mother had given him.

He would let Myles go, because the child needed to know

he was wanted somewhere. And because he had suffered the most.

He texted Myles.

I will drive you, he wrote.

He could see the three dots on the screen as Myles typed.

You won't see Eve, if that's why you're doing it. She's not there.

I wasn't planning on it, he typed back. I will drop you off and that's it.

K, came back the reply.

Another loved one lost, he thought as he put down his phone.

Whatever else could happen? Bad luck always came in threes, Hilditch had said to him. Whatever it was, it couldn't be as bad as this, could it? He could only hope, he thought to himself as he went to organise Myles.

37

'He asked Serena if I would stay on working on his books, as she's his main editor and because he's the most successful author there. So I would be stuck getting Serena's coffee and protein bars for the rest of my time at Henshaw and Carlson.'

Eve was lying on the sofa at her flat, with Zara and Anita on a chair each. There was a large bowl of crisps and an empty wine bottle on the table and another one being opened by Anita.

'But you know Serena bends the truth according to what she wants and needs,' Zara said as she held her glass out for Anita to refill. 'How can you trust her words?'

'I can't,' said Eve. 'But I can't trust Edward's right now either. He needed me for his book, his children, himself. But it's too much too soon.'

Anita ate a crisp and thought for a moment.

'I think it's good you resigned,' she said.

'You do? Why?' Eve sat up, desperate to hear something good about the situation she was in.

'Because you need to find your way without Serena or Edward. They both have their careers. You're still finding yours and you need to do it alone.'

Eve nodded. 'You're right. I need to stand on my own two feet. If I'm with Edward everyone will assume anything I succeed at is because of him, and if I stay with Serena I'll never get anywhere.'

'Are you going to talk to Edward?' asked Zara.

Eve shook her head. 'It's too complicated. I like him, a lot, but with his ex and the kids, and now his stepson is staying with my parents, it's just so messy.'

Her friends nodded and Zara held out the bowl of crisps.

'Can I offer you a prawn cocktail crisp for your troubles?' she asked with an apologetic shrug.

'Wow, you really know how to treat a lady.' Eve laughed a little as she took a snack.

'So what now?' asked Anita.

Eve looked at her friend and sighed. 'I guess I have to find another job.'

Eve's phone rang and she saw Serena's number on the screen.

'That's a no from me,' she said and switched her phone to silent.

'Maybe she wants you to come back,' Zara said.

'I would eat a beehive before I worked for her again,' Eve said and drained her wine and held out her glass for a refill.

'Okay, so that's a definite no.' Zara laughed.

'I'll look for a new job tomorrow but tonight, we can order a curry and watch shitty TV and finish this wine. Deal?'

'Deal,' said Anita and Zara in unison.

'And it's New Year's Eve tomorrow,' said Zara. 'We can go to the costume dress-up events at Stars Niteclub and spend a stupid amount of money on drinks and talking to underwhelming men at the overcrowded bar and then be bitterly disappointed, if you want?'

Eve laughed. 'That sounds like a special sort of hell for the desperate and lonely.'

'Hey, don't knock my plans,' Zara said with a chuckle and then she paused, her face serious. 'You know you can come. I know you won't like it but it's something to do, isn't it? Just in case you're depressed and feeling shitty about being at home alone on New Year's Eve.'

Eve reached out and held her friend's hand. 'You are beautiful and lovely and above all, you're a good friend and even though I would actually prefer to be eaten by wolves than attend that event, I am grateful you're thinking of me.'

'If you go, you might feel like you're being attacked by wolves,' said Anita. 'I have a Little Red Riding Hood outfit you can borrow.'

'Oh, Grandmother, what big ideas you have. No thanks. I worked for a wolf for the past three years, I am done,' Eve said decisively. 'Now let's order a curry that I can eat with my big teeth.'

That night Eve lay in bed, reading the many text messages from Edward.

He claimed he hadn't asked Serena to keep her as an assistant. He told her he would pull his books if she wasn't given the job as editor. He said he missed her. The children missed her.

She didn't reply to him because she didn't know what to say yet.

Something about what Anita had said about finding her own way without Serena or Edward resonated with her.

She was tired of being in service to Serena and even Edward. She needed to look after herself first.

A text from Serena came through as she was thinking.

> Call me back, urgently. You can have the editorial job. Please.

Eve had never heard or seen Serena say please in the whole time she had worked for her. *Please* was a foreign word to Serena's mouth, along with *thank you, great work*, and *well done*.

Eve had two choices. She could ignore the texts or she could be honest with her.

She thought for a moment and then typed.

> Hi Serena, I won't be coming back to Henshaw and Carlson. I hope everything works out for you there. Please don't contact me again.
>
> Eve

It was final. It was done. There was no going back now. Serena wouldn't like being told no but it wouldn't matter what Serena offered her now. Eve was done with Henshaw and Carlson.

But she didn't know what to say to Edward. He had so much chaos in his life and watching Amber with the hammer was too much. She had agreed to help him with a book, not become his children's stepmother.

Edward needed to work his life out before they reconnected again and Eve needed to get a job off her own bat.

She turned her phone off and then her light and closed her eyes. It would get better, she told herself, it always did. It was just hard to see it when you were in the middle of the storm.

38

Edward sat in the living room of the Pilkinses' house. Sam stared at him as though he was the worst person in the world and Donna's voice had an icy tone as she spoke.

'Myles doesn't want to return to your house,' she said. 'He said he wants to stay here, but we're not his legal guardians and apparently his mother is not available to assist in any of the practicalities right now.'

Edward rubbed his chin as he thought.

Eve wasn't returning his calls. Sam and Donna had told him they wouldn't be discussing their daughter with him at any time. Myles wasn't speaking to him and Flora was back to burying dolls in the melting snow. He had found the card that Flora and Eve had made for Amber. A large piece of poster paper with pictures drawn by Flora of Amber and her together, with all the dolls around them. Inside Flora had written, obviously helped by Eve, her plans for her mother's return including breakfast with Hilditch, playing with the dolls, skiing, (none of them skied) and eating chocolate. It seemed like a reasonable plan except he knew Amber wasn't coming to do any of those things with Flora anytime soon.

'Amber is attending a hearing tomorrow. There is an

injunction order on her and it will be extended tomorrow. I haven't heard from her since she came to the house, so that's good.'

Donna's face relaxed a little. 'The poor woman, she sounds so unwell.'

Edward was silent, remembering that was what Eve had said about Amber also. The Pilkins women immediately went to compassion instead of judgement. It was something he needed to do more of but it was hard with Amber. She was unwell but she was also destructive and difficult, and he often wondered if her being in the children's lives added anything positive to their day-to-day experiences. Myles was antisocial and the scars of his abuse were evident. Flora was behind in her schooling and friendless and more than likely depressed, Sanjeev had said when he called him.

'I can get you the names of some great child psychiatrists who deal with trauma,' he had offered but Edward wasn't sure how he felt about it all. If he was honest with himself, he was actually terrified about what they would say about him and his inaction with Amber for so long.

'I can sign off on anything Myles needs. I am his legal stepfather,' he said.

'They start school next week,' Donna said. 'You will have a bit of running around to do for that.'

Edward nodded.

'And what about Flora? Where is she going to school?' Donna asked.

'I was thinking the local school in Crossbourne.'

'They'll have to do a school assessment,' Donna said. 'It seems like she's missed a lot of learning.'

Edward was silent in the face of the criticism. She was

right. Both children had missed out on so much because of his and Amber's dysfunction.

Flora wandered into the room and sidled up to Donna.

'Can I stay here too?' she asked.

'You can stay the night but not forever. Your dad and Christmas need you at home.'

Flora had left Christmas at home when they came to visit Myles. Jimmi had jumped all over them excitedly, but Myles had said hi to Flora and ignored Edward.

'Can I stay the night, Daddy?'

Edward thought about it for a moment. He had to go to London tomorrow to meet his agent and the heads of Henshaw and Carlson. It might be nice for Flora to be with the family instead of rattling around Cranberry Cross with Hilditch.

He looked at Donna who nodded. 'It's fine with me,' she said. 'It's Thursday and tomorrow I have the day off so why don't you come and get her on Saturday or Sunday. We can pop into Asda and pick up a few things for your stay,' she said to Flora who looked thrilled.

'What about Christmas?' she asked.

'Hil can feed her,' Edward promised.

Flora ran from the room to tell the boys, he assumed, and he sighed.

'I know this is a mess but I'm trying to fix it.'

Sam cleared his throat. 'You're a successful writer, Edward but that doesn't mean you're a successful father. You have to make a choice. I chose to stay in the job I had for so long because my home life was more important to me than my work life. I could have gone further up the bus company and then Donna wouldn't have had as much support at home and she couldn't have done all her work with the rescue animals. I would rather have less money than less time with my kids.'

Edward was silent for a moment. 'It wasn't about the money, really. I was just...' he searched for the word '... selfish,' he finally admitted.

Sam nodded. 'Men usually are,' he said and then he picked up the paper, signalling his life lesson to Edward was over.

He stood up and put his hands in his pockets. 'I'll go and say goodbye to the children.'

Donna followed him to the back sunroom, where the boys were lounging and playing on their phones, while Flora was watching the fish in the tank.

'I'm coming back for you on the weekend, Flora,' he said.

'Okay,' she answered not looking away from the fish.

'Bye, Myles, I'll sort out the school stuff on Monday.'

Myles shrugged. 'Whatever.'

Gabe and Nick looked at Edward sympathetically. 'Bye, Mr Priest,' they said.

'Edward, please call me Edward,' he said and he left his children in the best care he knew right now.

'Thanks, Donna,' he said to her at the front door.

'It's okay – you all need support,' she said.

He paused, knowing he shouldn't ask about Eve.

'When you speak to her, tell her I said thank you. For everything.'

Donna's face gave away nothing. 'Drive safely, Edward, and good luck for court tomorrow.'

Eve didn't want to see him anymore and why would she? He had nothing to offer her really. He was too old for her, too selfish, and he had a complex home life.

He didn't blame her, he thought as he drove back to Cranberry Cross. He wouldn't date himself either.

Hilditch was in the kitchen when he arrived home.

'Flora's staying there for a few days,' he said, sitting down at the table. 'Probably best while I sort this mess out.'

Hilditch looked up at him. 'Good idea,' she said. 'She loves Donna. The grandmother she never had.'

'She does have two grandmothers but they're not really into being grandmothers,' he said.

He imagined leaving Flora at his parents' house. They would probably try to teach her bridge and how to make a good Pimm's fruit cup.

And Amber's parents, well he had never met them. Amber claimed they'd disowned her but he had never bothered to find out more. He wondered if they knew the struggles she'd had over the years, or if she had two children.

'Did you leave the woodshed open or was Flora playing in there?' Hil asked as she peeled some eggs.

'Woodshed? No, I haven't been out there.' Edward shook his head.

'Odd. There were some of Flora's blankets out there and the fire bucket was outside the shed. Flora shouldn't play in there. There're things to start fire with like the accelerant and fire bricks.'

'I'll make sure I tell her,' said Edward. 'But she doesn't like it much anyway, says there are spiders.'

Edward went to his study and read his emails.

Nothing of any importance.

God he missed Eve. He thought about texting her but she didn't want to hear from him.

He sat in his chair and looked out over the gardens.

The only thing he knew how to do was write, when he felt like this, he thought, and then he opened a new document and typed at the top of the page:

Book Two – Detective Anna Tilson

For Eve, he wrote and then scrolled to a new page.

39

Eve adjusted the sleeves of her blazer and smoothed out an invisible crease on her pant leg.

She had sent her résumé out to every publishing house she could, having saved all the contacts in her laptop from working at Henshaw and Carlson. It was the least the company could do after Serena blew up her career there.

She had had two phone calls with initial interest and then they called her back, and she'd received one invitation to meet for coffee in London with a small independent house that was getting a good name for prize-winning fiction and having a diverse list of authors.

The managing director was a man called Jasper Harris who, according to the trade magazines, was a champion of women writers, LGBTQI authors and authors of colour, diverse topics and excellent new crime fiction. Eve hoped that this was actually true and that it wasn't all bullshit.

Serena was listed as the female mentor of the year in one of the largest publishing magazines for the past few years and Eve knew what a lie this was. Serena never lifted anyone else up besides herself.

Jasper had suggested a cosy little café on Great Ormond St in Bloomsbury, just near his office and she was relieved not to see anyone she knew as she arrived. The publishing world in London was large in nature but made smaller by gossip.

Jasper arrived in a rush, with a trench coat over one arm and a large bag of what looked to contain fruit in the other hand.

'Gosh, sorry, Eve, I've been rushing around. My assistant is pregnant and she's craving anything citrus-flavoured so I popped out and grabbed her a selection of things that will hopefully ease the cravings. She works mostly from home but is in today doing some sorting before she goes on leave.'

Eve wasn't sure she heard correctly. 'You're getting fruit for your assistant?' she asked. 'That's a surprise. Not many bosses would do that for their staff.'

'I think you might find you're framing that opinion based on Serena, not normal human beings.' He laughed as he sat down and put the bag of fruit on the spare chair.

'How are you? I'm so pleased you wanted to meet with me,' he said. 'I know we're not as big as Henshaw and Carlson but we really are wonderfully committed to publishing excellent books.'

Eve smiled. 'I know about your company and the books you're publishing. It's wonderful for me to meet you also.'

'Let's get a coffee each and then we can get stuck in,' Jasper said.

Soon they had their drinks and Jasper leaned forward over the table.

'Before we start,' he said. 'I have to tell you that Serena has been calling everyone, telling them not to speak to you.'

Eve felt her stomach drop. 'Excuse me?'

Jasper sighed. 'Yes, she seems to think you're going back there soon.'

Eve shook her head. 'I'm not.'

Jasper nodded. 'I know you think that but she doesn't accept it and Serena, well she can be a bully to those outside her office also.'

Eve massaged her temples for a moment. 'So why are you talking to me then?' she asked him.

Jasper laughed. 'Because Serena, the wicked witch of publishing, has never scared me. I'm an outlier anyway. A gay man who publishes black writers, queer writers, graphic novels. I am not ever going to be a real threat to her or the big houses but I love what I do and we have seven staff now, all full-time and I'm looking for a new editor. Someone to build up their own list.'

Eve took a sharp breath. This is what she wanted. She needed to be away from the big publishing world for a while. She wanted to nurture new authors, connect with agents, help mentor and support people like herself. She wanted to find great books that had passionate readers.

'I would love to be considered,' she said. 'I know I don't have a lot of credits on my résumé because I was Serena's assistant, but I did a lot of editing I just can't claim because they're her authors.'

Jasper laughed again. 'Oh I went to university with Serena. She was always getting juniors to do her work. I expected nothing less from her. Old habits die hard.'

Eve shook her head. 'Okay that makes me feel better then.'

'Did you work on the last Edward Priest book?' he asked.

Eve felt her body stiffen. Was this interview only happening because Edward had set it up? Because Jasper wanted him to join his list of authors?

'Not much,' she said. 'A little, I've worked on his new one. It's coming out next year.'

'Thank God,' said Jasper. 'Terrible editing. Sloppy. I wasn't sure if it was because Serena was lazy or because Edward Priest was in that state of his career where he felt his words were untouchable.'

Eve's shoulders dropped with relief. 'Perhaps a bit of both, but he was quite amiable on the one I worked on. I was ruthless and he accepted all my suggestions.'

Jasper stirred his coffee. 'That's good to hear. I've always liked Edward. He was good to me when I started my house, sent me some great quotes for new authors to use on their books. And I could tell he read them. Not just paying lip service. You know if Edward Priest tells you he will do something, he will do it. And he hasn't got a lying bone in his body. He can be a rude prick but at least he's not a liar.'

Eve was silent as he spoke.

'I must give him a call someday. It's always hard when publishers call authors though. They think you're after them to join you. Edward is a terrific writer. I think if he came out of the rut he's in and wrote something he cared about then he would be brilliant and exciting. Not that my house could afford him.' He chuckled. 'It would be nice to have someone like him on the list so then I could get more authors looked at by other houses – you know, a rising tide lifts all boats et cetera, but I will have to find my own Edward Priest. They're out there somewhere.'

Eve nodded. 'Finding the talent is such a good feeling, when you read something that cuts through the rest. Nothing quite like it.'

Jasper nodded enthusiastically. 'I agree, it's thrilling.'

He then looked at her for a moment that was longer than comfortable.

'You look exhausted though.'

'Thanks.' She half-laughed.

'Take some time, Eve. I will wait. Take a few weeks, recover from Serena. She's a lot.'

Eve smiled. 'She is. Thank you.'

Jasper stood and picked up his bag of fruit.

'I need to head back but call me in a few weeks? Unless someone more exciting picks you up.'

'I will, thank you, Jasper,' she said, grateful for his time and respect. He seemed like a good person, which was a relief after working with Serena.

After he left, she ordered another coffee and drank it while thinking about what she wanted. Jasper's job sounded fantastic but was it too literary for her? There was something about commercial fiction that she loved. How they were often a reflection of the social and cultural zeitgeist, they were written to sweep the reader along and to be, above all, entertaining.

She didn't know what was next for her but Jasper was right. She was exhausted from everything, not just Cranberry Cross. She needed to rest and read for pleasure and to work out what she wanted for a time instead of helping other people meet their goals.

It was both an exhilarating and terrifying feeling but she

knew, if she didn't work this out now, it would follow her for the rest of her life.

She finished her coffee and walked out of the café, ready to find what she was meant to do next with her life on her own terms.

40

The lift opened on the top floor at Henshaw and Carlson, and Edward stepped out to see his agent Tom waiting.

'How are you, my old friend?' Tom extended a hand, which Edward took and then pulled him into a hug.

'I need to see more of you; I'm a shit friend and a shit client.'

'Where is this coming from?' Tom slapped his friend on the back.

'I'm just atoning – it's a new thing I'm working on. Having some realisations that I might be a bit of a selfish bastard.'

'Took you long enough to realise, but that's what we love about you. You don't mean to be one, you were born like that. And so was your father and his father and all the fathers on the Priest side before that.'

Edward laughed because it was the truth, but it only took one person to change the path of their family lineage.

'Shall we talk before we go in?' asked Tom. 'They've given us a room, which I assume isn't bugged.'

'I think you're joking,' said Edward as they walked into the small side meeting room and he closed the door.

'How did you go with the hearing?'

'It was fine. They extended the injunction on her and they

managed to find her parents, who she estranged, not them. They're willing to take her in if she goes back to America. I have offered to pay for her ticket.'

'That's a good outcome I suppose, but let's talk about this deal. Serena didn't get your editor back. Apparently, she's refused to even speak to her. Not a surprise but knowing Serena she will be making it hard for her to get another job.'

Edward sat down. 'Why the hell did you let me stay with her for so long?' Edward asked. 'Did you know she was this bad?'

Tom laughed. 'Of course I did but she was on your side; she made you a lot of money. That pile you live in came courtesy of Serena and her deals.'

Edward knew he was right but it still made him embarrassed that he had refused to see what Serena had pulled in his career to make him as famous as he was.

'You can't have it both ways,' Tom said.

'So if you buy back the rights to your books, it's twenty million pounds,' he said.

'Twenty million? God, do I have that?'

'In cash? No. But you could sell the house; might take a while to offload it but it would solve it and then I would need to find you a new home for those books and the new detective one.'

Edward felt nervous, like he had when he sent his first book out to agents who were open to submissions years ago.

'Do you think someone will take me on?' he asked.

Tom roared with laughter. 'God you writers are an insecure bunch aren't you? So bloody needy. Yes, I think with your multiple publishing deals and a movie deal and more, someone will take you on.'

Edward stood up. 'Well then let's go and buy back my freedom.'

'Let me do the talking,' said Tom.

'I'll try,' Edward replied.

'Try very hard. You get personal; I'm making this about the business, okay?'

'Okay,' said a chastened Edward.

Edward shook Tom's hand after the meeting.

'You did well,' said Tom to Edward.

'At keeping my mouth shut?' Edward laughed.

'Yes,' said Tom as they walked to the lift and Tom pressed the button. 'You head off and I will organise the paperwork with their lawyer. Call you later?'

'Thanks, Tom,' said Edward as the doors opened.

'My pleasure, I love a bit of cut and thrust. You were becoming my most boring client, so it's good you've given me something to do.'

Edward was still laughing when the doors closed.

The lift travelled for a few floors and then the doors opened and a young woman stepped inside. She looked at him for a long moment and then turned away.

People didn't always know his face unless they were avid readers of his books but the way the woman looked at him wasn't as a fan but more curious. She looked as though she was about to speak and then stopped herself.

Maybe a friend of Serena's, he thought, and then it dawned on him.

'Do you know Eve Pilkins?' he asked. 'She used to work here.'

The woman turned to him.

'I know Eve. I live with her. I'm Zara,' she stated. 'And I know who you are.'

Edward sighed. 'She won't believe I wasn't with Serena.'

Zara nodded. 'I know but she spent years working with someone who lied to her daily and about things that affected her career and her life. She doesn't know what to believe now.'

'How can I convince her?' he asked.

'You can't – that's not your job. She will have to work out how she feels about everything but right now she's exhausted. She's edited a book under incredibly difficult circumstances, she's given everything and more to you and your children, and she is burned out from Serena.'

Edward was silent. Zara was right of course.

'How can I help her?' he asked. 'With no agenda, I just want to make sure she is safe and feels better soon. Her happiness means more to me than anything.'

The lift stopped and the doors opened and Zara put her arm out to stop them closing.

'You can't do anything. This is for her to solve but I will tell her I saw you. That you were asking after her.'

She stepped out of the lift and Edward let the doors close. This was as close as he had been to Eve in days and yet she was still so far away. He leaned his head back against the cold metal and closed his eyes.

He wanted only the best for her and he wanted to be his best for her, even if she never spoke to him again.

The lift opened and Edward stepped out and walked into the street, without a publisher for the first time in twenty years, ready to start a new chapter in his life.

41

'Did he look okay?' asked Eve when Zara told her about the quick conversation with Edward in the lift.

'I don't know, what does he normally look like?' Zara asked. 'He looked like a rich white dude whose shoes cost more than my rent this month.'

Eve sighed. 'He said he wanted to make sure you were happy and that he didn't know how to prove he wasn't with Serena.'

Eve shrugged. 'It's not about that now really. I mean it's hard to know the real truth, but I need time away from them all – him, Serena, Amber. It's chaos at Mum and Dad's with Myles and Flora, but Edward is heading there tomorrow to get Flora, Mum said. Poor little thing. She must be so confused about everything.'

Eve poured water from the kettle into a hot water bottle and gently tipped it so the air escaped and tightened the lid.

Zara was silent.

'What? What do you want to say?' Eve asked.

'Nothing,' Zara said and turned away.

'You know, for someone who works in marketing, you're pretty bad at lying,' Eve said hugging the hot water bottle to her chest.

Zara turned to her. 'I believe him,' she said. 'After he left, I found out he's pulled his catalogue. I'm not supposed to know but you know Henshaw and Carlson, such a gossip factory. Anyway, he's pulled the books. The board offered to fire Serena but he said they should have fired her anyway for being so unethical in her bullying and lying. Quite a few other staff and authors have come forward about Serena. It's a PR nightmare for them. Serena is denying it all and screaming blue murder now, but it's too late. She's been exposed and is, right or wrong, the poster person for bad behaviour in publishing.'

'Great, so she'll be sullying my name even more.'

'You're missing the point, my self-involved friend. Serena is being held accountable for the first time in her career. And Edward has walked. He doesn't have a publisher and he has to pay a shit-ton of money to the company, which is hard cos who has cash anymore? Not that I would have his money, but twenty mill they're saying.'

'He doesn't have that sort of cash,' Eve said. 'He said the house at Cranberry was a huge expense and he would have to write forever just to pay for the upkeep.'

Zara shrugged. 'I don't know how he'll pay for it but it's happening and it's because of you.'

'Gee thanks,' Eve said.

'I'm just telling you what I heard and what he said to me. Use the information however you wish, but I thought you should know.'

Eve hugged her friend. 'Thank you. I'm going to sleep on it and see how I feel tomorrow.'

'Always a good idea,' Zara said.

Eve went back to her room, climbed into bed and opened

her book. She was rereading her favourite children's books. Tonight she was reading *Five Children and It*, an old-fashioned tale but it always made her laugh. She thought how much Flora would like the story of the children and the sand fairy but then closed the book. She couldn't seem to get the Priest family out of her head. Everything always came back to them. The song she heard that she thought Myles might like, the story about Serena from Jasper, the book for Flora.

What was she doing? She thought as she lay and looked at the ceiling. She missed them, she loved them all, especially Edward.

Why was she running away because his life was complicated at the moment? Life was always complicated in its own way. Everyone had a turn, her mum always said, and this was Edward's turn – and she'd left because she was scared.

This was the first time she had been honest with herself. Deep down she knew Serena was lying and Edward was telling the truth. But she had used it as an excuse – that she could not face the children and Edward because of Amber.

She jumped out of bed and found Zara in the kitchen, making ramen.

'I left because I was scared of Amber. I hadn't seen anything like that before.'

Zara looked at her friend. 'Imagine what it was like for those kids then.'

Eve burst into tears. 'I'm a horrible person. I just left them all.'

Zara held her. 'You're not horrible, you were scared.'

Eve nodded. 'I was. And I'm not qualified to help them. What could I do?'

Zara rubbed her arms. 'You did the right thing. You took them away from the events and you stayed with them until Edward could be with them.'

Eve gulped as Zara went on.

'And you're not supposed to be qualified for this sort of thing. You're not a social worker. No one is supposed to be qualified for that. Ever.'

Eve wiped her eyes with her dressing gown. 'I wanted to go back and be super successful and show him who I am without him or Serena.'

'You absolute goose,' said Zara. 'Just be yourself and then the people who are looking for you will find you. Don't try and be a mini-Serena in your ambition or anything else. Be yourself and be truthful to that. Then it will work out; it always does.'

Eve looked at her. 'Have you ever thought about writing a self-help book for young women in the corporate world?'

'I have actually,' said Zara. 'But get a job first and then we can discuss my advance.'

They hugged again and Eve went to bed, settled in to sleep. She needed to talk to Edward but not when she was like this. At least she understood her response now and surely Edward would understand, wouldn't he?

42

Edward woke with a start. He had a headache, which was unusual for him, and then he smelled the smoke. He looked around his bedroom and then pulled on his slippers that Eve had given him and opened the door to the hallway. Smoke came bellowing into the room.

'Jesus Christ,' he said, covering his face with his T-shirt.

He went back to his bedside table and called 999.

'Fire,' he said, pulling on a jumper and finding a scarf to put around his neck.

'There's a fire, Cranberry Cross,' he said, giving directions to the house. 'Send help immediately. There's no one else in the house. I'm leaving now,' he said and he slipped his phone into the pocket of his tracksuit pants and covered his face with the scarf.

He covered his face, tightening the scarf as much as he could around his nose, and he opened the door and ran.

The hallway was dark with smoke and he fell over a table leg and crashed to the ground.

He got up again but his head was pounding. The smoke smelled acrid, inorganic, but he couldn't describe it exactly. He could hear crackles behind him and the hallway walls felt like they were closing in on him.

The stairs were there but he could feel heat now and he realised the fire had started downstairs. He turned to head back to his room and see if he could wait for help – keep the door closed and lean out the window – but the sound of windows shattering told him that wasn't going to happen. He had to make a choice.

He stood for a moment and then he heard a sound.

What the hell was that?

Christmas. Jesus, Flora's kitten. He couldn't leave it here to die. He listened again and heard it coming from the left of him. His eyes were burning from the smoke but he found the door to the tower.

Christmas must have been locked behind it all night. He found the notch and opened the door, reached in and felt the kitten rub against his hand. He snatched it up and put it down his jumper, gasped the clean air in the stairwell for a moment, and then fixed his scarf back in place. He thought about the way out from where he was. Down the stairs, then to the right and past his study and then to the foyer and outside.

A normal journey would take less than one minute; now he wondered if he would ever make it out.

He opened the door to the hallway again and his eyes watered as he cradled the kitten beneath his jumper and made his way to the stairs.

One at a time, holding on to the wooden banister, he made his way down, the stone wall on one side radiating heat.

Christmas mewed as he took one step at a time. The last thing he needed was to fall down the stairs as well, then they were done for.

Sirens sounded and he felt relief as he knew help was coming.

Nearly there, he told himself as he took the next step.

And then he heard it. The laughter from above him. The hysterical screams of his name followed by laughing.

He turned and looked up. Squinting, he could just see the outline at the top of the stairs.

'Amber,' he cried and she lunged at him, which was the last thing he remembered.

43

Eve woke with a start. She had dreamed of Edward. He was trying to call her but he couldn't make a sound. She was trying to hear him but she couldn't get close. Anxiety flooded through her and she texted her mum.

What time is Edward coming to get Flora?

Not sure yet, why?

I might come to yours. I want to talk to him.

Good idea.

She thought about calling him but she didn't want to have this conversation over the phone. They needed to face each other and decide what their future looked like and what they were worried about. She knew Edward had as many concerns as she had, but they were different.

And she wanted to see Flora and Myles.

With renewed purpose, she showered and dressed, and collected some things in an overnight bag and left for the train to Leeds. She had two and a bit hours' uninterrupted reading time, she thought gleefully, and picked up her copy of *Five Children and It* and the first book in the Narnia series to take on the trip.

Soon, with a coffee and a croissant in hand, she was settled in her seat and she turned her phone on silent and opened her book.

The city disappeared and the countryside began, but Eve was faraway in the countryside of Kent with the children and It, making wishes and causing ruckus.

After an hour, Eve checked her phone, hoping Serena had still avoided texting her, especially now she had been fired from Henshaw and Carlson. But there was a call from her mum and a text and one from Hilditch.

Why would Hilditch call her? she thought as she dialled her mum back.

'Hi, Mum. Is something wrong?'

Donna paused. 'Where are you, pet?'

'On the train to you,' she said. 'About halfway. Nearly at Grantham.'

'Okay, love, I'll meet you at the station.'

'Mum, what's happened?' she asked. 'Hilditch from Cranberry Cross called me also.'

'I'll tell you when I pick you up,' said Donna.

'Mum, I'd rather hear it from you than from Hil, whatever it is that's happened. Is it the children? Edward?'

Donna took a breath that to Eve felt like it went forever.

'Please, Mum,' she said.

'There's been a fire at Cranberry Cross.'

'Oh no, thank God the children were with you.'

Donna didn't say anything.

'And Edward? Is he okay?'

'Oh, lovey, he's been taken to hospital, that's all I know but it's bad, Hil said when she called me. Really bad. Amber was there also. They think she started it.'

'Jesus Christ,' Eve said, feeling her mouth become dry. Her head was throbbing with an intense headache she hadn't experienced before. She felt like she couldn't breathe and was being suffocated.

'Is he alive?'

'Hil said yes,' Donna said. 'But Amber didn't make it.'

'No, God, no, that's terrible. Those poor children.'

'They don't know yet. I was hoping you could come and talk to them with me.'

'Of course,' said Eve as she stared unseeingly at the passing landscape.

'I was coming to tell him that I understand now, why I ran away, why I didn't want to believe he was telling the truth.' She thought for a moment. 'That I love him.'

'And you will tell him,' Donna said firmly. 'I'll pick you up and then we will go to the hospital and see how he is and then we can tell the children the whole story.'

'Thanks, Mum,' Eve said, thinking of Amber and her pain and anguish. 'I'm lucky to have you. Thanks for looking after the kids – they're lucky to have you also.'

'Shh now, just get here safely.'

Eve rang Hil, who didn't answer.

'Please let him be okay,' she said to whatever gods might be listening as she willed the train to go faster but knowing it was an impossible task.

There was nothing she could do but try and stay calm until she arrived in Leeds.

Her phone rang and she saw it was Hil's number on the screen.

'Hil, what's happening? Mum told me. I'm on my way now.'

'It's terrible, Eve. He's inhaled so much smoke – they're doing all they can but they think he has burns inside his respiratory tract and the accelerant was poisonous.'

Eve dug her fingernails into her leg to try and focus on what Hil was saying but felt like she was floating above the train. How could this be happening?

'What are they doing for him?' she asked.

'I don't know now. I'm outside; he's surrounded by doctors and nurses. It's just terrible.' She was distraught and Eve knew Edward needed someone steady to relay information and news.

'Just stay there, Hil – you're all he has by his side right now and I know he relies on you and cares about you as much as you care about him. I can't think of anyone better and more capable and calm to be with him.'

She was sure she could hear Hil breathe out slowly, as though Eve had given her permission to get herself together.

'Thank you, Eve, I'll go and speak to the nurses and see what's happening and I'll let you know.'

Eve held on to the phone, glancing at the screen every other second to see if there was news. At least Hil was there, she thought, trying to find something positive in the moment.

The rest of the trip was an exercise in patience and staying in the moment. Every time the train slowed she thought she would lose her mind and when it moved faster, she wished it would fly to the hospital.

At last the train arrived and Eve sprinted off the train with her bags and ran to her mother's car, which was idling on the street with Donna in the driver's seat. Eve threw her items into the back seat and jumped into the car.

'Any news?' asked Donna as she drove right on the speed limit to the hospital. 'And don't ask me to go faster; we don't need us in the ED too.'

Eve knew her mother was right but it felt torturous to get so close and still not be there.

'It's a twelve-minute drive; I can make it in ten,' Donna said as she expertly overtook a bus and gave it a honk and a wave.

'That's Davey – he's doing my shift,' she said and Eve turned around and waved at the man in the driver's seat.

'I spoke to Hil but she hasn't let me know anything since. It's been over an hour,' Eve said. 'I hope that doesn't mean anything other than her phone ran out of charge.'

'Don't go there, love,' said Donna and she pulled up at the front of the accident and emergency department. 'Off you go, and I'll find a car park.'

Donna had barely stopped the car when Eve had run inside and she went to the desk.

'Hi, I'm Eve Pilkins. I'm here for Edward Priest,' she said to the nurse who was staring at a computer screen.

She looked up at Eve who saw her face change.

'Wait here and I'll get someone for you,' she said and disappeared behind a door.

Within seconds the nurse was back and she buzzed Eve inside.

'I'm just taking you to the family room,' she said, 'where Mrs Hilditch is waiting.'

'How is he? Any change?' she asked the nurse as she trailed behind her.

'I don't know – I'm not looking after him,' she said but not unkindly as they came to a wooden door with a *Family Only* sign on the front of it. The nurse knocked at the door and then opened it and gestured for Eve to go inside.

Hil sat on a sofa, a box of tissues in front of her, several already used and on the floor.

'Eve,' she cried and she jumped up and pulled Eve into a hug.

'It's terrible,' she said. 'He's on life support but they don't think he will make it.'

Eve sat on the sofa. Any hope she held on the train had dissipated the moment the words came from Hil's mouth. What had she done? She had wasted time, precious time, worrying about her career and Serena and past lovers. All so ridiculous now she looked back on it. And how would she tell the children their mother was gone and would take their father with them?

No, it wasn't going to happen. Not while she was here.

She stood up and walked out of the room and found a nurse who was wheeling an empty wheelchair along the hallway.

'I'm here to see Edward Priest – he's in ICU. Can you take me?'

The nurse looked at Eve with surprise.

'I can take you to ICU but I don't know if they'll let you in yet. They're still working on trying to get him settled.'

Eve shook her head. 'I'll wait for as long as it takes,' she said. 'I'm not going anywhere.'

44

For the first three days Eve didn't leave Edward's side.

The children came to see him at the hospital and Eve told them that their mum had died in the fire.

'What about Christmas?' asked Flora, as though Eve hadn't mentioned her mother had just died.

Eve looked at her mum who leaned forward.

'I don't know about Christmas, darling. She was a little kitten and all that smoke would have been hard for her.'

'Did Mom start the fire?' asked Myles, as ever, straight with a punch to the gut.

'I don't know – the police are looking into it,' Eve lied but she knew Myles could tell she was skirting around the truth.

'We will need to bury Christmas,' Flora said, her bottom lip trembling. 'It's not nice for her to be alone in the house.'

Myles reached out and pulled Flora to him.

'They will find her, Flors, I promise. And I'll call them and tell them to give her a proper funeral, okay?'

Flora started to sob and she buried her face into Myles's shoulder. Eve saw his tears and felt her own as they sat together in the family room.

She looked at Myles and shook her head. 'I'm so sorry,'

she said to him. 'I wish this had a different ending for your mum and your dad.'

'Maybe if you hadn't left then this wouldn't have happened,' he hissed at her.

Eve felt Donna bristle but she nodded.

'I know, I thought about that also. But maybe you and Flora would have been in the house and me – or none of us. It's impossible to know anything other than where we are now, which is here and we have to stay connected and kind to each other while your dad tries to get better.'

Myles looked out the window over the car park.

'He's not my dad,' he said almost to himself.

Flora pulled away and held his face in her tiny hands.

'But he is your dad,' she said. Eve could see her eyes searching Myles's.

'He loves you; you make him laugh. He said you were the sort of person he wished he was as a kid. He called you cool and said he would never be cool. He told me he thinks you will do something amazing one day. He told me when you were little you used to sit on his lap and read his palm. He told me that you used to say that the line down the middle was the road you had to walk to find each other.'

If Eve had ever seen evidence of a higher power in life, it would have been in that moment. Flora spoke beyond her age and knowledge. It felt otherworldly but so right and she knew Myles felt it also.

His sobs broke Eve as he fell to the floor, and Eve and Flora moved to hold him and rub his back.

They said nothing as he cried but, as his tears eased and his breathing slowed, he slowly sat up.

'When can I see him?' he asked.

'You can sit with him now if you like,' said Eve and Donna nodded that she would look after Flora, while Eve took him to Edward's bedside.

'There's a machine breathing for him,' Eve said as they waited for the doors to the ICU to open. 'And lots of wire and leads.'

Myles didn't respond but as they walked inside, she saw him pause before he went to Edward's side.

'Dad, it's me, Myles,' she heard him say and she stepped away and moved to the side of the wall where she couldn't hear or see.

This moment wasn't for her to witness.

She looked at her feet, still wearing the same sneakers from when she arrived three days before.

She hadn't showered and was living on vending machine snacks and coffee but she would be by his side until the story was finished. No matter how it all ended.

'They're taking him off the ventilator today,' Eve told her mum as she buttered some toast. 'So I'm going to shower and head in to see him. His parents are calling but they can't come yet as his mother has had a hip replacement and can't sit to fly. But she's very nice and so is his dad. It's obvious they love him but they're just a bit...' Eve tried to find the word.

'Posh?' asked Donna and Eve made a face. 'Yes, that's it, like they're not quite going to let their guard down to say they're worried sick or are feeling desperate about it all. I can hear it in their voices but I can't imagine you and Dad being so distant.'

'We don't know other people's families or their responses to things,' said Donna. 'We are open with our feelings but just because some people don't say them aloud doesn't mean they don't feel them deeply.'

'I know, it's just weird,' said Eve as she spread apricot jam on her toast and ate it as she packed her bag for the hospital.

It had been a week of Edward on life support and slowly he was being weaned from the sedation drugs to try and get him off the ventilator.

Eve was at the hospital every day and it was only Donna who could get her to go home and shower and sleep, reminding her that Edward would need Eve to be strong and well while he recovered.

Hilditch was coming to spend the day with Flora, and Myles was getting ready for school when the doorbell rang.

'I'll go,' said Eve to her mum who was flicking through the news on her iPad.

Eve opened the door and saw a fireman with a box in his arms.

'Hi?' Eve said.

'Hello, I'm from the Crossbourne crew that went to Cranberry Cross. The housekeeper said the family are staying here?'

'That's correct,' said Eve.

The fireman handed her the box.

'This was found with Edward Priest when we got to him. We thought you might like to know it's survived.'

Eve looked into the box and amongst a white towel was the little white kitten.

'Christmas,' she cried.

The fireman looked surprised.

'That's her name,' Eve said, feeling tears coming. 'Thank you so, so much.'

'We gave her a little oxygen at the scene and then one of the crew took her to the vet. She's been recuperating but they rang to say she was ready to go home.'

'God, what do we owe for the vet bill?' Christmas was trying to climb out of the box and Eve held her in her hands.

'Nothing, they did it for Mr Priest.' He paused. 'How is he?'

'He's okay. They're trying to take him off the ventilator today,' Eve said as Christmas tried to climb up her shoulder.

The fireman nodded. 'That's a good sign. Tell him not to fight it, just to surrender and let his body do what it needs to do.'

As he spoke she noticed the scars on his neck that ran up one side of his head. He knew what Edward was going through. He understood at a personal level.

'Thank you,' she said. 'For saving him, and for saving Christmas.' She kissed the kitten's head.

He smiled and turned and walked back down the path.

Eve closed the door. 'Flora, someone just dropped something off for you,' she called up the stairs.

Flora came to the top of the stairs and looked down and screamed.

'It's Christmas,' she yelled and jumped down the stairs, missing three at a time to reach Eve's side.

Eve handed the kitten to her and watched as Flora wept into its fur while the kitten tried to pull her hair.

'How?' She looked at Eve.

'Your dad saved her,' she answered as Flora kissed Christmas's head.

'When you see Daddy today, can you tell him he saved Christmas?'

Eve nodded, trying to hold back the tears that threatened to burst. Everything was so fraught and terrible but this little kitten was the hope they needed right now.

'I absolutely will. Let me get a photo of you both to show him.' Flora stood proudly on the bottom stair and posed holding Christmas.

'That will cheer him up no end,' said Eve and she leaned forward and hugged Flora. 'I think you're the cat's pyjamas,' she said.

'What does that mean? Does Christmas need pyjamas?' Flora lifted the kitten up to assess the size needed.

'It means I think you're the best. There are lots of those sayings. You're the bee's knees, the fox's socks, the cat's whiskers. And I think you are all of them and more.'

Flora ran up the stairs calling for Myles when Donna came to see what the fuss was about.

'They saved Christmas. Edward had her. They gave the cat oxygen and she's been at the vet's.'

'My God,' said Donna.

'One good thing at least, for Flora anyway.'

'Has she talked about her mum to you yet?'

Eve shook her head. 'You?'

'No,' Donna said.

'She will when she's ready and I don't think that will be until Edward is better, whenever that is.'

'One day at a time,' said Donna. 'That's all you can do.'

'I know, you're right.' Eve thought about the words of the fireman. *Surrender*, he had advised.

She couldn't control anything other than her response to whatever was happening and everything that once seemed so important no longer mattered.

One day at a time, she reminded herself as she went to get ready to see Edward. Earlier in the week it had been one hour at a time but slowly, it was improving. The small wins like his blood levels coming back within an acceptable range, or slowly lowering the ventilator, or his body responding to the aggressive checks from the doctors or the gentle touch of Eve as she washed his face or held his hand.

Flora was sitting on the floor of the twins' room, as they got ready for school with Myles.

'Hil's on her way to see you,' she reminded her.

Flora looked up at Eve and smiled. 'Christmas is so happy to be with me again.'

Eve smiled and went to her room. *Me too, kid, me too*, she thought.

45

E ve walked into ICU and smiled at one of the nurses.
'How was his night?' she asked.

'Why don't you ask him yourself?' said the nurse with a smile.

'What?' Eve moved to the curtain and saw Edward lying in bed, propped up but looking more like himself without the tubes stuck to his face.

'Oh my God,' she said and started to cry.

Edward smiled weakly. 'Lovely Evie, come here, I've missed you,' he said, his voice hoarse and croaky from the damage and the medical intervention.

'I've been here every day,' she said, 'But you just ignored me,' she teased. 'So self-absorbed.'

Edward laughed and then coughed.

'Sorry, I need to stop being funny,' she said. 'But it's hard for me.'

He laughed and coughed again, and she sat next to him, leaning her elbows on his bed and touching his hands.

'You're here, you're alive, this is amazing.' She could feel the tears falling but didn't try to stop them. They felt like a relief after crying from sorrow for the past week.

'What happened?' he asked.

'The house, Cranberry, there was a fire,' she encouraged him to remember the bare minimum.

He was silent; she could see him trying to remember.

'The cat,' he said, looking at her for validation.

'Yes, Christmas the kitten, you saved her,' she said and moved his hair from his eyes.

He closed his eyes. 'That's good.'

The nurse came and adjusted his drip and looked at his blood pressure.

'He's tired,' she said to Eve. 'He needs to sleep.'

Eve nodded. 'Okay.'

The nurse opened the curtain and gestured to Eve to come to her.

'We haven't told him about his ex-wife yet; we need him to get rested and stronger. Any excessive stress could mean his lungs collapse and he will have to go back on the ventilator.'

'Okay, yes, absolutely.'

'I would suggest you focus on his future to get him stronger, something to look forward to before you unpack this incident with him.'

Eve went back to his bedside and sat quietly. She saw his hand reach for hers, patting the bed weakly for her hand.

'I'm here,' she said and she stared at his face.

'Evie,' he whispered.

'Yes, I'm here.'

'I love you.'

'I know.'

She smoothed the hairs on his arm.

'I love you too, Edward.'

'Call me, Ed.'

'If you insist.' She leaned forward and gently kissed each closed eye, his cheeks and nose and finally, a soft, lingering kiss on his lips.

'I insist,' he replied and fell into a deep sleep.

46

Every day Edward had to learn how to control his breath and speak slowly, so he didn't cough. He was walking but slowly and he was so tired, he wondered if he would ever have any energy again.

He went to physiotherapy; he did the exercises in his ward and now they were telling him he could go home. But to what home?

Hil had showed him some photos. The main building of Cranberry Cross was a shell. It had taken forty-eight hours for the fire brigade to put it out, but Hil had said it was still smoking from the tower.

And Amber. Beautiful, unwell Amber.

He wished he had done more but her illness was beyond him. And now his children were without a mother.

Hil had reminded him that she was never there from the start, but he had disagreed.

'The hope she would get better was always there for them,' he said.

'And so was so much worse,' Hil said. She was quiet for a moment but Edward had the feeling she wanted to say something.

'What is it, Hil?' he asked.

Hil looked away, and when she turned back to him, her face had changed.

'I grew up with a father like Amber. Charming, fantastical and a drunk. He didn't attend any of those fancy places to try and stop drinking but we did the best we could as a family. We had the village doctor and the policeman who would let him sleep it off at the station when he started at home.'

Edward watched her pull the memories from the past to the present, pain flashing across her face.

'There's nothing quite like waiting for your father to come home to find out if he's been drinking or not. The minute he opened the door and took off his shoes I could tell if we were in for a night or not. That uncertainty, that hope then despair changes a child. I am sad Amber died, but I also think there is another sort of pain watching her slowly kill herself in front of you. Flora will have very few memories and will slowly turn them into something that she will cope with. But Myles? That boy needs help, because if he doesn't get it, he will end up like his mother.'

'You can't say that.' Edward was shocked.

'I can because I saw it happen to my brother. He saw the most, he bore the worst of the abuse, probably more than Mum.'

Edward thought about how much Myles had seen, more than he should have, more than Edward himself.

'He needs help. I know the Pilkinses are kind and he has new friends in the boys and will be starting school with them, but this is more than just needing love. He needs to understand that none of this was his fault.'

She was right and Edward knew it. If he was honest with

himself, they all needed some support and tools to work through this trauma.

Sometimes when he lay in bed at night, he could smell the smoke, hear the sounds of Amber's laughter, his throat felt closed over and he had to call the nurse who told him he was having a panic attack and who sat with him and helped him breathe through it until he had stopped feeling sick.

Eve had arranged a place for him to stay while they worked out the next steps, a serviced apartment with a lift and a swimming pool, which the physiotherapist said would be good for his recovery.

Every time he mentioned work, Eve hushed him but he worried. He had made a deal with Henshaw and Carlson that relied on the sale of Cranberry Cross. Now it was a smoking pile of history and even with insurance it would be a stretch to make it work. He could have got a higher price from a cashed-up billionaire than what the building was insured for but he had to make it work somehow.

'Hey you.' He heard Eve come into his room.

'I have a friend with me,' she said as Tom came out from behind her.

'Ed, what a mess,' he said and he hugged his friend tightly.

'It's all going to be okay,' Tom said and he sat down next to Edward and pulled the small table towards him with Edward's untouched lunch still on top.

'Let me take this,' said Eve. 'And I'm going to get a coffee, so you two can work out the business stuff I know Ed's been worrying about.'

She swept in and took the tray, kissed Edward's head and then left the room.

'She's a keeper that one,' said Tom.

'I know, God how I know,' said Edward.

Having Tom in the room was comforting. There was something about the reliability of work, and the deadlines and commitments that made him feel secure.

Perhaps he had worked too hard in the past but right now, he needed to know his position so he could move forward.

'How are you recovering? Physically? I won't ask about the mental load because I'm sure that's a mess you haven't dealt with yet.'

Edward sighed. 'Okay, it's slow, lungs are a bit battered but I'm told they will recover, probably not to full capacity but not terrible. I probably won't be running the London Marathon anytime soon.'

'You've never run a marathon, have you?' Tom looked confused.

'Not physically but finishing a one-hundred-thousand-word novel feels like one,' he said.

'Fair enough.' Tom pulled a small notebook from his pocket.

'Shall I go through where you are and what I think are the options?'

Edward nodded. He was prepared for the worst outcome. He could become broke – he had seen plenty of authors lose their fortune through bad investments or poor deals.

But whatever Tom told him, he knew it would be smart and in Edward's best interests.

'I don't know how I can pay for my books now, since the house is gone. It's insured but not for what I think I could get in the market if it was still in one piece.'

'You didn't sign the papers,' said Tom with a little smile.

'What?' Edward tried to remember what happened in the meeting but everything felt like a blur and he only remembered talking to Zara about Eve in the lift.

'You left and I said I would sort the paperwork out. I was planning to email it to you on the following Monday and then this all happened.' He gestured to the hospital room.

Edward tried to understand. 'So that means they still own my books?'

'They do, which is fine, since Serena is gone. I mean let's not throw the baby out with the bathwater.'

'This goes against what I was hoping for,' he said. 'To start again, to make a point.'

Tom gave a small but not unkind laugh. 'I think you made your point, my friend, you nearly died. This will send your book sales through the roof. They're not going to let you go in a hurry.'

Tom leaned forward. 'But this is where it gets interesting. Serena has gone and she never sent us the signed contract. This is your leverage.'

'What do you mean?'

'Let them keep the other books and let's find you a new home for your detective.'

'Can I do that?'

'Of course you can. We can find her a lovely house who is smart and progressive and clever and who promotes women characters and cares about their authors.'

'Are there any?' Edward laughed. 'You're only as good as your last BookScan sales numbers.'

'Yes, there are, so stop being cynical. Jasper Harris is doing great work at the moment. You need to go somewhere smaller but boutique, who understands social media and how to promote at a grassroots level. Your existing readers will already follow you but you need to find new ones, younger ones.'

Edward thought for a moment. 'Jasper? He's great but I think I'm a bit commercial for him.'

'Your other books are but the detective book? No, that's right in his wheelhouse. Her fighting against the system and the oppression of a female in the police, the poverty in the area where she works, people not caring about her victims because they're not pretty white girls called Emma or Lucy.'

Edward was surprised. 'You've read it? I just forward things to you to keep on file. I didn't think you read them anymore.'

'I've read everything you've ever written, my friend, and I tell you, this book – if you can get it into a series – is what you were meant to write. Everything leading to this was practice.'

Edward felt his eyes sting with tears. 'It feels like that,' he said. 'Like I'm finally writing what I care about. Not the toffy, fake Indiana Jones guff.'

'Let me talk to Jasper. I'll keep it quiet and see what he says. They won't have the advances that Henshaw and Carlson gave you though.'

Edward shrugged. 'He should pay me what he thinks it's worth. This is a new genre for me and untested.'

'Let me and him thrash that out,' said Tom.

'I need to call my lawyers about the house,' Edward said. 'And I need to speak to Eve about the house stuff. I won't mention the books news to her yet; I don't want to talk shop with her about Jasper Harris until I know what's happening and if I can move there for the new series.'

Tom stood up. 'Good idea. Focus on her and the kids, and call me if you need anything at all, okay?'

'I will.'

Edward was exhausted once Tom was gone but he was grateful Eve had brought him all this way to talk.

'You finished? Has Tom gone?' he heard her say and he turned to see her in the doorway.

'Yes, he's off to do deals and make offers I can't understand.' He laughed.

Eve came and sat opposite him. The sunshine coming through the window promised more warmth than it delivered.

'I'm staying with Henshaw and Carlson,' he said.

She nodded but said nothing.

'I never signed the contract, and since the house is ruined, I can't sell it. I'll need to get better and write because I need the money.'

'Okay,' she said.

'But I don't want to talk shop, now. I just want to sit here with you in the sun.'

Eve handed him a coffee and they sipped in silence.

He wanted to ask what was in her head but knew better than to pry. Eve would tell him what she was thinking when she was ready and only when she was ready.

'I'm going to call Sanjeev,' he said after a while. 'I think that the kids and I will need some help to get through this. We can't just pretend it hasn't happened and I think the kids need really good support outside of us. You can't just get on with something like this. You have to understand it and the children need to know it's not their fault – any of it.'

Eve nodded. 'I think that's the smartest thing you've ever said.'

'God, it's not even that smart, just sensible, but perhaps you are teaching me to be more aware of this stuff.'

She smiled. 'Maybe, but I did grow up with very pragmatic parents.'

'I grew up with parents who never discussed emotional issues or emotions in general unless they were pleased with the weather. I told my mother I loved her once, she told me to not be vulgar. And that emotional outbursts were for people who had no self-control.'

Eve laughed. 'Sorry, it's not that it's funny but that it's just such terrible advice.'

Edward sighed and rolled his eyes. 'I know. Welcome to the dysfunctional home of the Priests.'

Eve reached out and lifted his hand to her mouth and kissed it.

'Lucky you're not there anymore and can create a new home that's emotionally kind and validating and supportive.'

'I can and I will with you, Eve, if you plan on staying with me, even though I am a wheezy, sad shell of a man. I'm too selfish to let you go, but you could do so much better than me.'

Eve laughed again. 'I don't want to do better. I want to be with you and the children.' She was silent for a moment. 'I'm sorry I left you like that. It was immature and unthinking.'

Edward shrugged. 'It was also a lot for you to see. Amber, the children's fear. It was so much and too soon.'

'Thank you for understanding,' she said to him.

'Thank you for coming back to me. But can I ask something?'

She nodded.

'Did you come back because you heard about the fire?'

She shook her head. 'I was on my way to you that day. I was on the train when Mum rang me to tell me. I was going to see you at their house when you came to get Flora. I wanted to talk to you then and explain and see if you would have me back.'

'Oh, Eve, I would have you back one thousand times. We will always be all right, even when we're not. You taught me that.'

Tears welled up in her eyes and in his and they kissed.

'I love you,' he said.

'I love you too.'

47

Eve looked up from the computer as Edward came into the living room of the rented apartment. Flora was sitting on the floor, colouring in, and Christmas the kitten was asleep in her little bed.

It had been a month since the fire and he was finally out of hospital.

'What are you working on?' he asked.

'Nothing, just sorting out some files,' she said and closed her computer.

'How was your shower?'

'Wet,' he said and he leaned down and kissed her.

He was doing well, all things considered, she thought, but they were living in an in-between state. Myles was still living at her parents' and since he was happy there, his psychologist had suggested he stayed there until Edward had found somewhere to live permanently.

'Would you like to come on an adventure?' he asked.

'Yes,' said Flora from the floor.

'Sure, where are we going?' Eve said.

'I will show you when we get there,' he said.

His strength was improving every day, and his

commitment to recovery was evident with his muscle tone and breathing better than it had ever been.

There was no doubt he would make a full recovery but Eve was feeling unsure about their relationship. They hadn't talked much about their future when so much of what was happening was present-focused.

Edward had organised a funeral for Amber, a small event with him, the children, her parents and Hilditch.

Eve didn't attend as she thought it wasn't appropriate but she had lit a candle for Amber's spirit and had sat for a while in silence to wish her soul safe travels to whatever was next. Not that Eve believed in life after death but everything was energy, she had told her mum.

'Life is too hard for some and they need to reset, I think, but what do I know?' Donna had said.

'You know a lot, more than most,' Eve had said to her mum as they shared a pot of tea afterwards.

But Edward wasn't talking about his writing, and she wasn't asking. He hadn't mentioned where he would be living, which she understood but she felt as though she was living between lives. She still had to pay her rent in London and she didn't have a job. She wouldn't ask Edward to support her in any way. She had always worked and would continue to, even if she was with him.

'Gather your things; we're heading off,' he said. 'We have to pick up Myles first though.'

Soon they were in the car and Myles and Jimmi were waiting at the front of her parents' when they arrived.

Edward was excited as he pulled up. 'Ah my trusted assistant is here,' he said.

Myles was laughing and had a smug look on his face as he bundled Jimmi into the car between him and Flora.

'Are you two planning something I don't know about?' Eve asked.

'Yep,' said Myles and Edward gave a pretend evil laugh.

'Myles has been helping me with this; his opinion is very considered and his aesthetic is flawless.'

'Gosh, this is exciting.' Eve turned to Flora who was patting Jimmi.

Edward drove through the city and then turned off and drove through a lovely village that Eve knew vaguely but hadn't spent much time in.

'This is sweet,' she said looking at the little white church in the centre of the village. There was a circular road that surrounded it and old gravestones dotted the green lawn. They went through the village, which was larger than Eve had thought, and then went past a small school with a pretty white picket fence that ran along the front. *Selwood Primary School*, read the sign.

Edward drove around the back of the school and then up a road and through an open set of iron gates with a *Private Property* sign.

There were bare trees lining the short driveway that soon opened onto a longer gravel drive with a beautiful Victorian house with a slate roof and some sort of vine that was growing up the side. There was an ornate wooden awning over the front door with little seats on the inside, and ornate windows with stained-glass panels by the front door, which was painted in a pale, duck-egg blue.

'What's this?' asked Eve as Edward stopped the car.

'This is the Beecroft Vicarage,' he said. He jumped from

the car and headed around to Eve's side to open the door for her and Flora. He did up Flora's coat and pulled her woollen hat on her head.

'It's still cold,' he said to her when he saw her about to protest.

Eve walked around the front of the house. 'Ed, what is this?'

'Myles? Would you like to do the honours?'

Myles stepped forward and Eve noticed his ear. 'You've had your ear pierced,' she exclaimed.

'Gabe did it for me. It's cool huh?'

Eve looked at the silver stud. 'It is. I hope you're twisting it daily.'

'I am and Donna gave me an antiseptic spray to use.'

Eve glanced at Edward who shrugged. 'I'm old, so I have no opinion.'

Eve laughed.

'Go on Myles,' encouraged Edward.

'We were talking in a therapy session about what to do now since our house burned down and Mom died.'

Eve felt Flora's hand slide into hers and she gave her hand a squeeze of reassurance.

Flora didn't talk about Amber to anyone but Hilditch, who had promised to keep everything confidential.

'And we talked about what I thought I wanted, because Mom's parents said I could go back to LA with them.'

Eve's heart was in her throat at the thought of losing Myles but she tried to remain impassive.

'And I thought, I don't want to go there; I want to be here. With your brothers.' He smiled at Eve.

'And the school is really cool; I have new friends. And

then I thought about Flora and she said she didn't want to leave here either.'

Eve felt her throat burning and her eyes stinging.

'And I looked at houses for sale. I thought about the right house for me and Flora and Edward.' He waited for a moment and he looked at Eve. 'And the house for you. Because we weren't a family until you came to Cranberry Cross. And even though the house was too big and the gardens were weird and spooky, it felt better when you were in it.'

Eve swallowed but her tears started to fall.

Edward stepped forward. 'Myles came and spoke to me and we started to look at houses and we would send each other ones we liked and one day, we sent each other this one at the same time.'

'So we want you both to have a look at it, because you're the most important people in Myles's and my life, and we want to be near your family, Eve. You and they are amazing. You all saved us to be honest.'

Eve gulped and looked at the house and then followed him inside, Flora still holding her hand.

'I know it's smaller than Cranberry Cross but I really don't want to be traipsing about to find you all. I miss you too much,' he said.

To Edward it might have seemed smaller but to Eve it was a generous and spacious home with beautiful high ceilings and honey-hued floorboards. It was empty but Eve could see there had been an extensive renovation done with a gorgeous kitchen including an Aga and flagstone floors.

She followed Myles and Edward around the house, while Jimmi followed Flora who ran ahead.

'There are bedrooms for everyone and two extras,' said Edward. 'In case anyone wants to stay, like Amber's parents or mine.'

Eve nodded, choked up at his generosity.

'And there are two smaller rooms downstairs,' he said, taking them down again.

He opened one door and walked inside the elegant room with bookshelves lining one wall. There was a fireplace and a window seat.

'This is a gorgeous study for you,' she said looking around. The window looked out over the green lawn, surrounded by a walled garden.

'Me? No, this is for you, my love,' he said and he walked to her side. 'I know you love your work and wherever you go next, maybe you can work from home and if you do, this has Eve's spirit all over it.'

She leaned her head on his shoulder.

'What about you?' she asked.

'Come,' he instructed and they walked through the foyer to the other side of the house and he opened an almost identical room but with more bookshelves.

'Matching studies,' he said. 'For all our important work. We can meet in the hallway for elevenses and kisses.'

Eve laughed as Myles and Flora wandered into the room.

'Come and look at the rest of it,' said Myles and they followed him out where he showed them the summerhouse they could use for the band and the pool for warmer days and a beautiful, simple, raised garden of growing vegetables.

'What do you think?' Edward asked Eve, his face hopeful, but she could tell he was nervous.

'I think it's wonderful,' she said slowly. 'But I wonder if

this is you. Cranberry Cross was so grand,' she said. 'This is so much more modest, simple.'

Edward looked around. 'I want modest and simple. I want a life that supports my writing. I don't want to worry about packs of gardeners and rooms that I can't fill and repairs that never end. I never really wanted the house. Amber did but now I need to see what helps me in my next phase. I can work here in peace with you, the children can go to school. We have support here for us and your family nearby is amazing.'

Eve nodded as she walked around.

'Could you live here?' he asked as she stood on the terrace overlooking the pool.

She nodded. 'I could.' She paused, thinking. 'Absolutely I could but publishing is in London. I don't know that I can find a job here and working really matters to me. I will always work – it's who I am.'

Edward nodded but she could see disappointment in his face.

'It's not like I have much pull in my career, Ed. I still have to turn up and earn my stripes.'

'I know,' he said.

She looked around at everything he was offering. She wanted it but she also wanted her own life. She couldn't live to support only his goals.

'I have applied for something,' she said. 'I can ask them if they would consider me working remotely and attending the office on occasion for important meetings and the like.'

Edward hugged her. 'Don't stress about it; we can work it out, I promise.'

'And what about you?' she asked him. 'The detective series, are you going to write another one?'

Edward shrugged. 'I had started one when you left Cranberry but it's lost now – my laptop was burned in the fire. It was a shame. Twenty thousand words and plotting for the next two books. I get tired just thinking about rewriting it.'

Eve pulled out her phone and tapped on the screen and then turned the phone to Edward.

'You goose, I hooked your laptop to the cloud, so everything is on there.' She pointed to the file. 'There it is.'

'Bloody hell, Eve, how do you keep saving me over and over again?' he cried and he hugged her.

'You are a luddite,' she said.

'I am but I'm willing to learn. I don't want you to think I don't want to do things so other people, namely you, will do them. I just don't think about that stuff when I'm writing.'

'I know, I never thought that about you,' she said.

She looked at her phone again and saw an email and clicked on it. 'I got the job,' she said without thinking. 'As an editor,' she added.

'You did? Of course you did,' said Edward kissing her. 'Amazing. What's the lucky company?'

Eve started to read the email aloud.

'Dear Eve, thank you for getting back to me. I am pleased to offer you a role as a new editor with us, where given your commercial understanding and exposure, you will be charged with the commercial fiction list for us. This is a new role and we are excited to announce we have recently signed a prominent author who is moving to us after undertaking writing in a new genre. We believe you will be the perfect fit to work with them as you are familiar with their work. They are not available right now for you to discuss the plans with, but once the announcement is made to the staff, then I will arrange a meeting for you both to meet.'

Eve looked at Edward and made a face. 'I wonder who it is? One of Serena's authors? Lots of people are moving from Henshaw now she's gone, Zara told me,' she went on.

'I understand you're in Leeds at the moment, which is fine for us. Most of the team work from home and come in as they need to. We aren't a meeting-heavy organisation and do most of it online, so please do not feel any pressure to be in London unless you wish to.'

'Oh, Eve, that's wonderful,' said Edward. 'How do you feel?'

Eve looked at the email again. 'I feel terrified and excited and relieved.'

'It's so wonderful,' Edward said, pacing the terrace.

'It is,' she said. 'God, what a relief. And he doesn't care about Serena. He told me he went to university with her and she used to pay smarter people to do her essays.'

Edward's face froze. 'Are you talking about Jasper Harris?'

She nodded. 'Yes, why? That's who the job is with.'

Edward started to laugh and cough simultaneously.

'Don't tell me he's bad. I mean I met him and he seemed lovely. And lots of people told me he was great,' she said. *Please don't let him be another Serena*, she thought.

Edward put his hands on her shoulders.

'I am about to tell you something and I need you to not react immediately. Okay?'

'I feel sick,' she said.

'Okay?' he pushed.

'Okay.' She threw her hands up at him. 'What?'

'When you brought Tom to the hospital, we talked about the deal and I hadn't signed the papers, so I have decided to leave the existing books with Henshaw and Carlson.'

'Right, I know,' she said, impatient with him.

'But the detective novel, Tom wanted to shop around. We wanted a new publisher – someone who would edit it properly, who would work with me closely and help me establish myself in commercial crime fiction but with difficult subject matter.'

'Oh no,' said Eve, unsure whether to laugh or cry.

'Tom said he was going to Jasper and I signed yesterday. That's why the offer's there for you, because they now have the author and they now need the editor.'

Eve couldn't speak for a moment. 'And you didn't know I was talking to him?'

He shook his head. 'He didn't mention you at all and I didn't mention you because I know this is so important to not use my reputation to boost your career in any way. Which I think is silly because I'm not that important really, but I also respect your feelings.'

'So you're going to Jasper Harris's house and so am I, and I think he's pairing us together without knowing any of this?' She gestured to the house, to the children, to each other.

'I think it's what the writers call fate,' he said.

'I think it's more serendipity,' she replied, putting her arms around his neck.

'Oh do you, Miss Pilkins, editor at large?'

'I do, Mr Priest, writer for hire.'

He kissed her as she heard Flora calling Jimmi from the garden below and Myles telling them he was going to go for a swim.

They both pulled apart.

'You're not going for a swim,' they both cried at him.

She looked back at Edward.

'You know, you will be a Priest living in the vicarage. That's a happy little accident,' she said.

'I won't be the only priest,' he said. 'Myles has agreed to let me adopt him.'

She couldn't believe how lovely this news was – better than anything else that had happened so far.

'That's so wonderful, really,' she said.

'And maybe one day, if you can see fit to marry an old Priest who lives in the vicarage and care for him in his dotage, you can become a Priest also.'

Eve smiled and kissed his nose. 'Is that a proposal?' she asked.

'Do I need to propose? Because I am fairly certain we are fated even if you don't see it, but I will get on bended knee if you wish, because I want you to be happy and I don't want to presume anything about you. I made that mistake once; I don't want to again.'

Eve looked around, and thought about what life was offering her and she shrugged.

'A girl still likes to be asked.'

Edward got down on one knee, pretending to groan as Flora and Myles came up the stairs and stood behind him.

'Eve Pilkins, you are the love of my life, you are the dot to my i's and the crosses on my t's,' he said and she laughed.

'But you are also the most caring, kind, loving person I know with an incredible temper and a power to bring me to my knees, as shown here.' He gestured.

'I know I am a selfish idiot who is too old for you and far too arrogant but I am working on myself every day to be the man you deserve. I promise to support you in everything you do, the way you support us all.'

Eve saw Myles wipe a tear and Flora nodding furiously.

'You have changed us, Eve, and nothing will ever be the same again, and nor do we want it to be. So I am asking, if you, Eve, will take me as your husband, and these children as your own?'

Eve nodded and fell to her knees and kissed him and pulled the children into a group hug.

'Yes, yes, yes. I love you all so much,' she said. 'I couldn't love anything more than the three of you. Thank you for wanting me to be in your family.'

Edward pulled away a little.

'You made us a family, Eve. Thank you.'

48

They were married at Beecroft Vicarage in the summer.

Eve wore an antique lace dress and a diamond hairclip in her bobbed hair. Edward wore a white and blue linen suit. Flora was a bridesmaid, with Christmas the cat on a white satin leash and Myles was the best man with Jimmi as ring bearer, the cushion attached to his collar, and the ring tied to it with some ribbon.

Hilditch officiated the ceremony, who revealed she was a celebrant after Edward said he needed someone to marry them.

'Is there no end to your skills, Hil? What can't you do?' he asked half joking.

'I'm not sure,' she had replied. 'I seem to be adept at most tasks I take on.'

The guest list was small but meaningful, with Zara and Anita and some other friends present. Jasper of course came with his delightful husband Armand who was an interior decorator – who had helped Eve and Edward create a beautiful family home – and their families, including Amber's parents who had become close to Edward, Eve, Flora and Myles.

The dinner was held in the garden with the pool covered over and a large marquee over the top.

They danced and drank and ate and danced and finished at six in the morning with Hilditch and Donna serving egg and bacon rolls to those who remained. All of Edward's friends came and Sanjeev gave a lovely speech about resilience and love and the importance of remembering the good times, and then he made a toast to Amber's memory.

Flora lay on her maternal grandmother's lap who stroked her hair and whispered stories about Amber when she was young to her, until the little girl drifted off in a peaceful haze of memories old and new.

Myles played a song on the guitar and Eve accompanied him, singing 'Songbird' by Fleetwood Mac, and there wasn't a dry eye when they finished.

It was as wonderful as they had hoped it would be and made better by the love and support in the room. Perhaps love can't fix everything but it certainly does make the road a little less bumpy, Eve often thought as she worked to build up her list of new authors and also edited Edward's new series.

The book was sold to a production company before it was even published and it debuted at number one on the best-seller list and is still there today. Another book was released and then the TV series was announced with Kristin Scott Thomas.

It was perfect.

It was two Christmases after their first at Cranberry Cross that Eve woke up feeling unwell.

She had made it to the bathroom just in time when Edward stood outside the door.

'Do you need me to call the doctor?' he asked.

'No, it's just a stomach bug,' she said but she sat on the toilet and wondered.

They weren't trying to get pregnant but they weren't trying not to. She counted back the days to her last cycle and realised.

A baby? She was thirty. That was far too young, she thought and then remembered her mother was only twenty-two when she had her. A baby – what would Edward say?

She opened the door and stood in front of him.

'I think I'm pregnant,' she said.

'Really? That's wonderful,' he said and then he checked, 'Is it wonderful?'

'I think so, maybe. I don't know, I've never been pregnant before.'

Eve was indeed pregnant and had a daughter called Agatha, because she loved Agatha Christie and because she liked the name. Aggie was her father's daughter, with a passion for throwing books at the fireplace if she didn't like them.

And Edward wondered often how he became so lucky and Eve wondered more often why she had stayed working for Serena for so long. But perhaps things are meant to be a certain way. You need to meet the dragons head on to get to the jewels you deserve. Or something like that, Eve thought. Zara could say it better. And then remembered what she had said to Zara once and she made a call.

'Hey, friend, what are you up to?'

'Not much. Working, slowly atrophying from the corporate life and toxic politics.'

Eve paused and then said, 'I don't know if you remember but ages ago, like two years or more, I made a joke about you writing a book for young women. Anyway, I was just wondering, is that something you might be interested in doing? I think the world needs a best friend like you.'

Zara laughed. 'I thought you'd never ask.'

'Come up for the weekend and we can plan and Ed can take care of Aggie?'

'Deal, I'm booking the train now.'

Eve put down her phone and looked out across the garden to where Flora and Hilditch were digging in the vegetable beds.

Hilditch had moved to Leeds with them and had started to help at the animal shelter with Donna.

Myles had a girlfriend who was also the lead singer in the band with the twins and they played any event that would have them. He was going to be a rock star he told Edward and Eve, and there was something about him, a charm and charisma, that certainly made him different. The band was slowly getting a following.

Donna and Sam retired and came to Beecroft to be with the children every week. Donna would have come daily if allowed. When Aggie was born, Donna cared for her when Eve went back to work and often when she came out of her study, there would be Aggie throwing food for the dog, Christmas the cat sitting on the kitchen table. Myles walking around playing his guitar without an amp and Flora dancing on the flagstones in a new pair of tap shoes.

It was a busy, sometimes chaotic life but what remained steady through it all was Edward at his desk, writing as the world at Beecroft Vicarage swirled around him. He had learned to write through the hardest time of his life, so writing in the best times was a cinch.

And neither Eve nor Edward would have wanted it any other way.

'This is what we wanted,' Eve reminded Edward when he looked as though he was about to lose it, and he would pause and look around and smile as Hilditch handed him a glass of wine.

He would kiss his wife and say aloud, 'Yes, this is what we wanted.'

Acknowledgements

Thank you to my editor, Martina Arzu for wise advice and support throughout the writing of this book. Thank you to my agent Tara Wynne for her continual cheerleading and smarts. And thanks to my husband David for the endless cups of tea and for keeping the home fire burning.

About the Author

K ATE FORSTER is a best-selling author of *Starting Over at Acorn Cottage, The Perfect Retreat, Finding Love at Mermaid Terrace* and many more books that she would want to read herself, so she wrote them. When not writing, Kate loves hanging out with family, friends, and her dogs. A dedicated houseplant lover, Kate also enjoys outdoor gardening and is the founder and moderator of one of largest online women's writing support groups on Facebook.